JUNIPER HILL

JUNIPER HILL

USA TODAY BESTSELLING AUTHOR

DEVNEY PERRY

Entangled Publishing, LLC
644 Shrewsbury Commons Ave., STE 181
Shrewsbury, PA 17361
rights@entangledpublishing.com

Amara is an imprint of Entangled Publishing, LLC.

Visit our website at www.entangledpublishing.com.

Edited by Elizabeth Nover
Cover art and design by Sarah Hansen at OkayCreations
Stock art by doodko and Nina Lishchuk/Shutterstock
Interior design by Britt Marczak

ISBN 978-1-64937-667-1

Manufactured in the United States of America
First Edition February 2024
10 9 8 7 6 5 4 3 2 1

an imprint of Entangled Publishing LLC

ALSO BY DEVNEY PERRY

CHAPTER 1

MEMPHIS

"Juniper Hill. Juniper Hill." I plucked the sticky note from the cupholder to double-check that I had the correct street name. *Juniper Hill.* "There. Is. No. Juniper. Hill."

My palm smacked on the steering wheel, adding a whack with each word. Frustration seeped from my pores as I desperately scanned the road for a street sign.

Drake screamed in his car seat, that wailing, heartbreaking, red-faced scream. How could a noise so loud come from such a small person?

"I'm sorry, baby. We're almost there." We had to be close, right? This miserable trip had to end.

Drake cried and cried, not giving a damn about my apology. He was only eight weeks old, and while this trip had been hard on me, for him it was probably akin to torture.

"I'm screwing everything up, aren't I?"

Maybe I should have waited and made this trip when he was older. Maybe I should have stayed in New York and dealt with the bullshit. Maybe I should have made a hundred different choices. A thousand.

After days in the car, I'd begun questioning my every decision, especially this one.

Escaping the city had seemed like the best option. But now...

Drake's scream said otherwise.

It seemed like a decade ago that I'd packed up my life—our life—and loaded it into my car. Once, I'd been a girl who'd grown up in a mansion. A girl who'd had a private jet at her disposal. The realization that the only possessions truly mine would fit into a Volvo sedan was...humbling.

But I'd made my choice. And it was too late to turn back now.

Thousands of miles and we'd finally made it to Quincy. The site of our fresh start. Or it would be if I could find Juniper Hill.

My ears were ringing. My heart was aching. "Shh. Baby. We're almost there."

Neither did he understand nor care. He was hungry and needed a diaper change. I'd planned to do it all when we arrived at our rental, but this was the third time I'd driven this stretch of road.

Lost. We were lost in Montana.

We'd come all this way and were lost. Maybe we'd been lost since the morning I'd driven out of the city. Maybe I'd been lost for years.

I swiped up my phone and checked the GPS. My new boss had warned me that this road wasn't on a map yet so she'd given me directions instead. Maybe I'd written them down wrong.

Drake's tiny voice cracked. The crying stopped for a split second so he could refill his lungs, then he just kept on wailing. Through the rearview and the mirror above his seat, his little face was scrunched and flushed and his fists balled.

"I'm sorry," I whispered as tears blurred my vision. They fell down my cheeks and I couldn't swipe them away fast enough.

Don't give up.

My own sob escaped, joining my son's, and I eased off the highway for the shoulder.

But God, I wanted to quit. How long could a person hold on to the end of their rope before their grip slipped? How long could a woman hold herself together before she cracked? Apparently, the answer was from New York to Montana. We were probably only a mile from our final destination and the walls were beginning to crumble.

A sob mixed with a hiccup and the tears flowed until my tires were stopped, the car was in park and I was hugging the steering wheel, wishing it could hug me back.

Don't give up.

If it was only me, I would have given up months ago. But Drake was counting on me to endure. He'd survive this, right? He'd never know that we'd spent a miserable few days in the car. He'd never know that for the first two months of his life, I'd cried nearly every day. He'd never know that today, the day when we'd started what I hoped would be a happy life, had actually been the fifth-worst day of his mother's life.

Don't give up.

I squeezed my eyes shut, giving in to the sobs for a minute. I blindly felt along the door, hitting the button to roll down the windows. Maybe some clean air would chase away the stink of too many days in the car.

"I'm sorry, Drake," I murmured as he continued to cry. As we both cried. "I'm sorry."

A better mother would probably get out of the car. A better mother would hold her son, feed him and change him. But then I'd have to load him into his car seat again and he'd cry, like he had for the first hour of our trip this morning.

Maybe he'd be better off with a different mother. A mother who wouldn't have made him travel across the country.

He deserved a better mother. And a better father.

We had that in common.

"Miss?"

I gasped, nearly jumping out of my seat belt as a woman's voice cut through the noise.

"Sorry." The officer, a pretty woman with dark hair, held up her hands.

"Oh my God." I slapped a hand to my heart as the other shoved a lock of hair from my face. In the rearview, I spotted the familiar blue and red lights of a police car. *Shit*. The last thing I needed was a ticket.

"I'm sorry, Officer. I can move my car."

"It's all right." She leaned in, peeking inside my car. "Is everything okay?"

I wiped furiously at my face. *Stop crying. Stop crying.* "Just a bad day. Actually, a really bad day. Maybe the fifth-worst day of my life. Sixth. No, fifth. We've been in the car for days and my son won't stop crying. He's hungry. I'm hungry. We need a nap and a shower, but I'm lost. I've been driving around for thirty minutes trying to find this place where we're supposed to be staying."

Now I was rambling to a cop. *Fantastic*.

The rambling was something I'd done as a kid whenever my nanny had busted me doing something wrong. I didn't like to be in trouble and my go-to response was to talk my way through it.

Dad had always called it making excuses. But no matter how often he'd scolded me, the rambling had become a habit. A bad habit I'd correct later in life on a day that didn't rank in the top ten worst days.

"Where are you going?" the woman asked, glancing at Drake, who was still yelling.

He didn't care that we'd been pulled over. He was too busy telling her that I was a horrible mother.

I scrambled to find the sticky note I'd dropped, showing it to her through the open window. "Juniper Hill."

"Juniper Hill?" Her forehead furrowed and she blinked, reading the sticky note twice.

My stomach dropped. Was that bad? Was it in a sketchy neighborhood or something?

When I'd tried to find a rental in Quincy, the pickings had been slim. The only options had been three- or four-bedroom homes, and not only did I not need so much space, they'd been outside of my budget. Considering this was the first time in my life I'd had a budget, I was determined to stick to it.

So I'd called Eloise Eden, the woman who'd hired me to work at her hotel, and told her that I wouldn't be able to move to Quincy after all.

When she'd promised to find me an apartment, I'd thought maybe a guardian angel had been looking out for me. Except maybe this studio apartment on Juniper Hill was really a shanty in the mountains and I'd be shacked up next to meth dealers and criminals.

Whatever. Today, I'd take the crackheads and murderers if it meant spending twenty-four hours not in this car.

"Yes. Do you know where it is?" I tossed a hand toward the windshield. "My directions led me right here. But there isn't a road marked Juniper Hill. Or any road marked, period."

"Montana country roads rarely are marked. But I can show you."

"Really?" My voice sounded so small as another wave of tears crashed open the dam.

It had been a while since anyone had helped me. The little gestures stood out when they were rare. In the past month, the only people who'd offered me help had been Quincy residents. Eloise. And now this beautiful stranger.

"Of course." She held out a hand. "I'm Winslow."

"Memphis." I sniffled and shook her hand, blinking too fast as I tried to stop the tears. It was useless. I was exactly the train wreck I appeared to be.

"Welcome to Quincy, Memphis."

I breathed and damn those tears just kept on falling. "Thank you."

She gave me a sad smile, then hurried back to her car.

"We'll be okay, baby." There was a sliver of hope in my voice as I scrubbed at my face.

Drake continued to cry as we eased off the road and followed Winslow down to a cluster of trees. Between them was a narrow dirt road.

I'd passed this road. Three times. Except it wasn't a real road. Certainly not a residential street. She slowed, her brake lights glowing red, and turned down the lane. Dust flew from beneath her tires as she followed the trail, driving farther and farther away from the highway.

My wheels found every bump and every hole but the bouncing seemed to help because Drake's wailing simmered to a whimper as I followed a bend in the road toward a hill that rose above the tree line. Its face was covered in dark evergreen shrubs.

"Juniper Hill."

Wow. I was an idiot. Had I stopped and looked at my surroundings, I probably would have figured this out.

Tomorrow. Tomorrow, I'd pay attention to Montana. But not today.

The road went on for another mile, following the same line of trees, until finally we rounded one last corner, and there, in a meadow of golden grasses, was a stunning home.

No mountain shanty. No questionable neighbors. Whoever owned this property had plucked it straight out of a home decor magazine.

The house was a single story, stretched long and wide with the hill as its backdrop. The black siding was broken up by enormous sheets of crystal-clear glass. Where a normal house would have walls, this place had windows. Through them I could see the open kitchen and living room. On the far end, a bedroom with a white-covered bed.

The sight of its pillows made me yawn.

Detached from the house was a wide, three-stall garage with a staircase that ran to a door on a second story. Eloise had said she'd found me a loft.

That had to be it. Our temporary home.

Winslow parked in the circular gravel driveway. I eased in behind her, then hurried out of my seat to rescue my son. With Drake unstrapped, I lifted him to my shoulder, hugging him for a long moment. "We made it. Finally."

"He was just sick of his car seat." Winslow walked over with a kind smile. "I have a two-month-old. Sometimes he loves the car. Most times, not so much."

"Drake's two months too. And he's been a trooper," I breathed. Now that he'd finally stopped crying, I could breathe. "This has been a long trip."

"From New York?" she asked, glancing at my license plates.

"Yep."

"That *is* a long trip."

I hoped it had been worth it. Because there was no way I was going back. Forward steps only, from now on. The city was a memory.

"I'm the chief of police," she said. "You know Eloise Eden, right?"

"Um...yes?" Had I told her that?

"Full disclosure. Memphis is a unique name and Eloise is my sister-in-law."

"Ah." *Damn it to the moon and back*. This was my new boss's sister-in-law, and I'd just made an epically horrible first impression. "Er...what are the chances?"

"In Quincy? Pretty good," she said. "You'll be working at the inn?"

I nodded. "Yes. As a housekeeper."

Before Winslow could say anything else, the front door to the house opened and a pretty brunette rushed outside, smiling and waving.

Eloise. Her blue eyes sparkled, the same color as the cloudless September sky.

"Memphis!" She rushed my way. "You made it."

"I did," I breathed, shifting Drake to extend my hand.

Whatever makeup I'd put on two days ago at our hotel in Minnesota had worn off from fatigue and tears. My blond hair was in a sloppy ponytail and my white tee was stained orange at the hem from an energy drink that had exploded on me this morning. I looked nothing like the version of Memphis Ward who'd done a virtual interview with Eloise weeks ago. But this was me. There was no hiding reality.

I was a mess.

Eloise moved right in to my space, ignoring my offered hand to pull me in for a hug.

I tensed. "Sorry, I smell."

"Not at all." She laughed. "You met Winn?"

I nodded. "She was kind enough to help me when I got lost."

"Oh no." Eloise's smile dropped. "Were my directions bad?"

"No." I waved it off. "I've just never driven on a dirt road. I didn't expect it."

Up until this trip, I hadn't driven much at all. Yes, I'd had a car in New York, but I'd also had a driver. Thankfully, I'd spent enough time behind the wheel going to and from the Hamptons to feel comfortable making this journey.

"Can we help you get unpacked?" Winslow asked, pointing toward the loft.

"Oh, that's okay. I can manage."

"We'll help." Eloise squeezed the trunk's release button.

The duffel bags and suitcases I'd shoved inside practically jumped out. Yes, all of my belongings fit into my Volvo. But that didn't mean it hadn't been a chore to stuff them inside.

She hefted a backpack over her shoulder, then lifted out a suitcase.

"Really, I can do this." My face flamed red at the sight of my new boss hauling out my things. The bag she carried had my underwear and tampons.

But Eloise ignored me, marching to the garage's steel staircase.

"Trust me on this one." Winslow walked to the trunk. "The sooner you just go along with Eloise, the easier your life will be. She's persistent."

Like how she'd refused to listen when I'd had to decline the job offer. She'd ordered me to get to Montana, promising we'd have a home once we arrived.

"I'm learning this." I giggled. It was the first laugh I'd had in...well, in a long time.

I held Drake closer, breathing in his baby smell. Standing there, with my feet on the ground, I let myself breathe again. For one heartbeat. Then two. I let the soles of my shoes be warmed by the rocks. I let my heart sink out of my throat and return to my chest.

We made it.

Quincy might not be our forever home. But forevers were for dreamers. And I'd stopped dreaming the day I'd started ranking my worst days. There'd been so many, it had been the only way to keep moving forward. To know that none had been as awful as the first-worst day. To know that if I'd survived that one, I could endure the second and the third and the fourth.

Today marked the fifth.

It had started at a gas station in North Dakota. I'd pulled over last night to get some sleep. Twenty minutes, that's all I'd wanted. Then I'd planned to get back on the road. Drake had been zonked and I hadn't wanted to wake him up by hauling him into a seedy hotel.

Napping in the car had been a reckless decision. I'd thought I was safe beneath the parking lot's bright lights. My eyes hadn't been closed for more than five minutes when a truck driver had knocked on my window, licking his lips.

I'd sped away and, hopefully, run over his toes.

My heart had hammered for the next hour, but once the adrenaline had worn off, soul-deep exhaustion had burrowed under my skin. I'd been afraid of falling asleep at the wheel so I'd pulled over on the interstate to hop out and jog in place under the stars. I'd stretched for all of thirty seconds before a bug had flown under my shirt and left two bites along my ribs.

The sting had kept me awake for the next hour.

At dawn, I'd found another turnoff to stop and change Drake. When I'd lifted him out of his seat, he'd spit up all over my shirt, forcing me to give myself a baby-wipe bath. Any normal day, it wouldn't have been a big deal. But it had been one more straw and my back was close to breaking.

During our last gas station stop, he'd started crying. With the exception of a few short naps, he hadn't really stopped.

Hours of that wail and I was fried. I was weary. I was scared. I was nervous.

My emotions were battling each other, fighting to take first place. Fighting to be the one that pushed me over the edge.

But we'd made it. Somehow, we'd made it.

"Let's go check out our new spot." I kissed Drake as he squirmed—he had to be hungry—then shifted him to the cradle of my arm. With one hand, I hefted out the next duffel in the stack, but I'd forgotten how heavy it was. The nylon strap slipped from my fingers, the bag plopping to the ground. "Ugh."

"I'll get it." A deep, rugged voice sounded from behind me, then came the crunch of boots on gravel.

I stood, ready to smile and introduce myself, but the second I spotted the man walking my way, my brain scrambled.

Tall. Broad. Tattooed. *Gorgeous.*

Why had I kept driving last night? Why hadn't I stopped at a hotel with a shower?

I was in no place to crush on a guy. The new Memphis—mom Memphis—was too busy getting formula stains out of her shirts to preen for men. But the old Memphis—single, rich and always up for an orgasm or two Memphis—really, *really* liked sexy, bearded men.

He bent and picked up the duffel before grabbing the largest suitcase from the trunk. His biceps strained the sleeves of his gray T-shirt as he carried them both toward the garage. Narrow hips. Sinewed forearms. Long legs covered in faded jeans.

Who was he? Did he live here? Did it matter?

Drake whined and that sound snuffed the laser beam that had been my gaze on this guy's sculpted ass.

What the hell was wrong with me? *Sleep.* I needed sleep.

Before anyone could catch me staring, I dropped my chin and rushed after him, pausing long enough to snag the diaper bag from the backseat.

The metal on the stairs gave a low hum with each step. The man had almost made it to the landing when Eloise popped out.

"Good, you're helping." She smiled at him, then waved us all inside. "Knox Eden, meet Memphis Ward. Memphis, this is my brother Knox. This is his house."

Knox set down the bags and jerked up his chin. "Hi."

"Hi. This is Drake. Thanks for renting us your apartment."

"I'm sure another spot will open up in town." He shot Eloise a glare. "Soon."

The tension rolling through the loft was thicker than traffic on East Thirty-Fourth from FDR Drive to Fifth Avenue.

Winslow studied the honey-colored floors while Eloise narrowed her gaze at her brother.

Meanwhile Knox did nothing to disguise the irritation on his face.

"Is, um…is this place not for rent?" It would be on par for my day to arrive somewhere I was unwelcome.

"No, it's not," he said as Eloise said, "Yes, it is."

"I don't want to cause any trouble." My stomach churned. "Maybe we should find another place."

Eloise crossed her arms over her chest, raising her eyebrows as she waited for her brother to speak. She was too pretty to be intimidating, yet I wouldn't want to be on the receiving end of that look.

"Fine," Knox grumbled. "Stay as long as you need."

"Are you sure?" Because it sounded a lot like he was lying. I'd heard my fair share of lies as a New York socialite.

"Yeah. I'll get the rest of your bags." Knox breezed past me, the scent of sage and soap filling my nose.

"Sorry." Eloise put her hands on her cheeks. "Okay, I need to be honest. When you called and said there weren't any apartments around town, I did some checking too. And you're right. Nothing is available in your price range."

I groaned. So she'd pawned me off on her unwilling brother. I was a charity case.

Old Memphis would have refused charity.

Mom Memphis didn't have that luxury.

"I don't want to intrude."

"You're not," Eloise said. "He could have told me no."

Why did I get the feeling it was hard for people to tell her no? Or that she rarely accepted it as an answer? After all, that was how I'd driven out here.

After an hour-long Zoom interview, I'd fallen in love with the idea of working for Eloise and I hadn't even seen the hotel premises. She'd smiled and laughed through our conversation. She'd asked about Drake and complimented my résumé.

I'd taken this job not because I aspired to clean rooms, but simply because she was the *anti-Father*. There was nothing cold, ruthless or cunning about Eloise. My father would hate her.

"Are you sure about this?" I asked.

"Absolutely. Knox just isn't used to having people out here. But it will be fine. He'll adjust."

Was that why he'd built a home full of glass? Out here, he didn't need the privacy of walls. The location gave him seclusion. And I was intruding.

We didn't have a lease agreement. As soon as a vacancy in town came open, I doubted Knox would mind losing my rent check.

He came striding up the staircase, the thud from his boots reverberating through the loft. His frame filled the doorway as he walked inside carrying another three bags.

"I can get the rest," I said as he set them on the floor. "And I'll be quiet. You won't even know we're here."

Drake chose that moment to let out a screech before nuzzling toward my breast.

Knox's mouth pursed in a thin line before he retreated

down the stairs.

"Can we help you get unpacked?" Winslow asked. "I'd much rather stay here than head back out on patrol and write speeding tickets."

"No, that's okay. I can handle it. There isn't much." Just my entire life in bags. "Thank you for rescuing me today."

"Anytime."

"Are we still on for an orientation tomorrow?" I asked Eloise.

"Sure. But if you want a day or two to settle in before work—"

"No." I shook my head. "I'd like to jump right in."

Dive headfirst into this new life. Drake was starting at his daycare tomorrow and though I hated leaving him for the day, that was the life of a single mother.

The daycare cost would swallow thirty-one percent of my income. Quincy had a low cost of living compared to larger Montana towns, and renting this loft at only three hundred dollars a month would allow me to build a cushion, but unpaid weekdays were not an option. Not yet.

Life would have been easier, financially, in New York. But it wouldn't have been a life. It would have been a prison sentence.

"Okay." Eloise clapped. "Then I'll see you tomorrow. Come in whenever you're ready."

"Thank you." I held out my hand once more because shaking her hand was important. It was one of the few lessons my father had taught me that I didn't loathe.

"I'm so glad you're here."

"Me too."

Winslow and Eloise waved as they walked out the door. Another whimper from Drake sent me flying into action, digging out a bottle from the diaper bag before we settled on the couch. While he chugged, I surveyed my new temporary home.

The white walls were pitched with the roofline and a thick wooden beam the color of the floors ran the length of the space. Three dormer windows had been cut into the side facing the house, giving me a view of Juniper Hill and the indigo mountains beyond. Alcoves and half walls created different compartments in the floorplan.

Across from the couch and behind a short partition was a bed covered in a patchwork quilt. The kitchen was on one side of the loft, next to the door, while the bathroom was at its opposite. The space was just large enough for a shower stall, sink and toilet.

"You'll have to have baths in the sink," I told Drake, taking the empty bottle from his mouth.

He stared up at me with his beautiful brown eyes.

"I love you." I hadn't told him that enough on this drive. We hadn't had enough moments like this, just the two of us together. "What do you think about this?"

Drake blinked.

"I like it too."

I burped him, then dug out a baby blanket, settling him on the floor while I rushed to bring in the last couple of loads and unpack.

Hours later, my clothes were refolded and put away in the one and only dresser. The drawers built into the bedframe I used for Drake's outfits. The small closet was stuffed by the time I hung a few coats and sweaters, then stowed the large suitcases stuffed with smaller suitcases stuffed with bags and backpacks.

I'd bought two sandwiches at the last gas station I'd

stopped at, thinking there wouldn't be time to make a grocery store run, so I ate my dry ham and swiss, chasing it down with some water, and went about giving Drake his first kitchen-sink bath.

He fell asleep in my arms before I placed him in his portable crib. I summoned enough energy to shower and wash my hair, then crashed within seconds of my head hitting the pillow.

But my son wasn't much for letting me rest these days and just after eleven he woke up hungry and fussy. One bottle, one clean diaper and one hour later, he showed no signs of sleep.

"Oh, baby. Please." I paced the length of the loft, walking past the open windows, hoping the clean, cool air would settle him down.

Except Drake was not having it. He cried and cried, like he did most nights, squirming because he just was not comfortable.

So I walked and walked, bouncing and swaying with every step.

A light from Knox's house flipped on as I passed a window. A flash of skin caught my eye and stopped my feet.

"Whoa."

Knox was shirtless, wearing only a pair of black boxer briefs. They molded to his strong thighs. The waistband clung to the V at his hips.

My neighbor, my landlord, wasn't just muscled, he was cut. He was a symphony of rippled muscle that sang in perfect harmony with his handsome face.

Pure temptation, poised at the window of a woman who could not afford to stray from her path.

But what was the harm in a look?

I hovered beside the window's frame, staying out of sight, and stole another glance as he raised a towel to dry the ends of his dark hair.

"Not everything about today was bad, was it?" I asked Drake as Knox strode out of his bedroom. "At least we've got a great view."

CHAPTER 2

KNOX

There was no place I'd rather be than standing in my kitchen, a knife in hand, with the scents of fresh herbs and baked bread swirling in the air.

Eloise swept through the swinging door that connected the kitchen to the restaurant. "And right through here is the kitchen."

Correction. There was no place I'd rather be than standing in my kitchen *alone*.

"Isn't it awesome?" she asked over her shoulder.

Memphis stepped out from behind Eloise, and I did a double take. Her blond hair was straight and hanging in sleek panels over her shoulders. The bright lights brought out the caramel flecks in her brown eyes. Her cheeks were rosy and her soft lips painted a pale pink.

Well...fuck.

I was in trouble.

It was the same woman I'd met yesterday, but she was a far cry from the frazzled, exhausted person who'd moved into the loft. Memphis was...striking. I'd thought the same yesterday, even with blue circles beneath her eyes. But today her beauty was distracting. Trouble.

I had no time for trouble.

Especially when it came to my new *tenant*.

My knife worked through a batch of cilantro, my hand moving faster as I focused on the task at hand and ignored this intrusion.

"If the fridge in the break room is ever full, you can keep your lunch in here," Eloise said, gesturing to the walk-in.

Wait. What? The knife dropped from my palm, nearly hitting a finger. No one kept their lunch in here. Not even my waitstaff. Granted, they rarely had to bring meals because I'd typically cook them a meal. Still...that walk-in was off-limits.

Eloise knew it was off-limits. Except my wonderfully annoying sister seemed intent on forcing Memphis into every aspect of my life. Wasn't my home enough? Now my kitchen?

"Okay." Memphis nodded, scanning the room, looking everywhere but at where I stood at the stainless-steel prep table in the center of the space.

She inspected the gas range along one wall, then the industrial dishwasher at her back. On the walls were shelves filled with clean ceramic plates and coffee mugs. She studied the tiled floor, the rows of spices and racks crammed with hanging pots and pans.

"Here's the ice machine." Eloise walked to the cooler, lifting the lid. "Help yourself."

"All right." Memphis's voice was no more than a murmur as she tucked a lock of hair behind an ear. She'd promised yesterday to be quiet. I guess she intended to keep that vow at the hotel too.

I glanced at Eloise, then jerked my chin to the door. The tour was over. This was a kitchen. Just a commercial kitchen with bright lights and shiny appliances. And I was busy. This was my time alone to breathe and think.

But did Eloise take the hint and leave?

Of course not. She took up space against my table and leaned. Why the fuck was she leaning?

I clamped my teeth together and picked up my knife, gripping the handle until my knuckles were white. Normally I'd tell Eloise to scram, but I was making nice at the moment. Very nice.

This *niceness* was the reason I'd agreed to let Memphis crash in the loft above my garage. My sister had asked for a favor, and at the moment, I was granting them all. Soon enough, we'd have a difficult conversation. One I'd been dreading and avoiding. One that would change our relationship.

Until then, I'd let her invade my kitchen and allow her newest employee to stay at my home.

"So that's the hotel," Eloise told Memphis.

"It's beautiful," Memphis said. "Truly."

Eloise circled the room with a finger. "Knox renovated the kitchen and restaurant last winter. That's when my parents annexed the building next door for events."

"Ah." Memphis nodded, still looking anywhere but at me.

The crunch of cilantro beneath my knife filled the silence.

My parents owned the actual hotel, The Eloise Inn, but the restaurant and kitchen were mine. The building itself we'd incorporated as a separate entity, the shares split equally between us.

Originally, this space had been a smaller industrial kitchen attached to a basic ballroom. They'd rented out the space for weddings and events, but when I'd moved home from San Francisco years ago, I'd filled the room with tables. It had worked as a restaurant for a while, but it had lacked style and flow. When I'd told Mom and Dad that I wanted to convert it to an actual restaurant, they'd jumped at the chance to expand the hotel's footprint and grab the building next door.

According to our projections, the annex would pay for itself within the next five years. My renovations would pay for themselves in three assuming the traffic at the restaurant didn't die off. Considering I had the only upscale restaurant in town, I'd happily cornered that market.

"Would you mind if I stepped out for a minute?" Memphis asked Eloise. "I'd like to just call and check in with Drake's daycare. Make sure he's doing all right."

"Sure." Eloise stood straight, escorting her to the door and finally leaving me in peace.

I put the cilantro aside and went to the walk-in to grab a handful of tomatoes. Then I shoved the sleeves of my white chef's coat, not yet stained, up my forearms before I resumed chopping.

Could I run this hotel? Did I even want to? Change was on the horizon. There were decisions to make, and I dreaded them all.

Beyond the renovations, a lot had changed here in the past year. Mostly, my parents' attitude. Besides our family's ranch, The Eloise Inn had been their most time-consuming business venture. Their desire to keep a finger on the hotel's pulse was dwindling. Fast.

Now that Dad had retired from running the ranch and handed control to my older brother Griffin, Mom and Dad seemed in a hurry to offload the rest of their business ventures to us kids.

That, and Dad had gotten spooked. As Uncle Briggs's dementia progressed, Dad had all but convinced himself that he'd be next. *While his mind was fresh*, he wanted his estate settled.

Griffin had always loved the Eden ranch. The land was a part of his soul. Maybe that was why the rest of us hadn't taken an interest in the cattle business. Because Griffin was the oldest and had claimed that passion first. Or maybe that passion was just a part of his blood. Our family had ranched for generations and he'd inherited a joy for it beyond anything the rest of us could comprehend.

Mom always said that Dad gave his love of the ranch to Griffin while she'd passed her love of cooking to my sister Lyla and me.

My dream had always been to run a restaurant. Lyla's too, though she preferred something small, and owning Eden Coffee fit her perfectly.

Talia hadn't taken an interest in any of the family businesses so she'd used her inheritance of brains to attend medical school.

Mateo was still young. At twenty-three, he hadn't yet decided what he wanted to do. He worked on the ranch for Griffin. He pulled a few shifts every week for Eloise, covering when she was short staffed at the front desk—which was often.

Eloise loved The Eloise Inn and working as the hotel's manager.

My sister was the pulse of this hotel. She loved it like I loved cooking. Like Griffin loved ranching. But my parents hadn't approached her about taking over.

Instead, they'd come to me.

Their reasons were solid. I was thirty years old. Eloise was twenty-five. I had more experience with business management and more dollars in my bank account to fall back on. And though Eloise loved this hotel, she had a soft and gentle heart.

It was the reason Mom and Dad had just come out of a nasty lawsuit.

Her tender heart was also the reason she'd hired Memphis.

That, and desperation.

Our proximity to Glacier National Park brought people from across the world to Quincy. Tourists flocked to this area of Montana. Given that The Eloise was our town's best hotel, during the summer months, we were booked solid.

Turnover in the housekeeping department was constant and we'd recently lost two employees to desk jobs. Their vacancies had been open for six weeks.

Eloise had taken to cleaning rooms. So had Mateo. So had Mom. With the holiday rush fast approaching, we couldn't afford to be understaffed. When Memphis had applied and agreed to move to Quincy, Eloise had been ecstatic.

Not only was Memphis an able human body—a sexy, lithe body at that—but she was also so overqualified for a housekeeping job that, at first, Eloise had thought her application a joke. After their virtual interview, Eloise had said it was really a dream come true.

I'd been happy for my sister because solid hires were hard to find. That happiness had lasted a whole week until Eloise had shown up at my doorstep and begged me to let Memphis live in the loft.

I favored a solitary life. I preferred to go home to an empty house. I liked peace and quiet.

There'd be none of that with Memphis and her baby in the loft. That kid had cried for hours last night, so loud I'd heard it all the way from the garage.

There was a reason I'd built my house on Juniper Hill and not on a plot on the ranch. Distance. My family could visit and if they needed to spend the night because they drank too much, well…they could crash in the loft. No pavement. No traffic. No neighbors.

My sanctuary.

Until now.

"It's temporary," I told myself for the thousandth time.

The swinging door that led to the restaurant flew open and Eloise waltzed in once more, a wide smile on her face.

I glanced past her shoulder, looking for Memphis, but Eloise was alone. "What's up?"

"What are you making?" She hovered over my shoulder.

"Pico de gallo." I didn't have a huge menu, but it was enough to give the locals and hotel guests some variety. Each weekend, the dinner menu featured a special entrée. But for the most part, breakfast and lunch were consistent.

"Yum. Will you make Memphis a plate of tacos?"

The knife in my hand froze. "What?"

"Or whatever else you have on hand. I noticed that she didn't bring anything with her this morning."

The clock on the wall showed it was ten thirty. My two

waitresses were in the dining room, rolling silverware into cloth napkins and refilling salt and pepper shakers. Mondays weren't typically busy, but they weren't quiet either.

There was no such thing as quiet these days.

Apparently not even at my own home or kitchen.

"I don't make the other housekeepers lunch."

"Knox, please. She just got here. I doubt she's even had a chance to get to the grocery store."

"Then let her leave early. You don't need her cleaning today."

"No, but we have paperwork to do. And orientation videos. I get the impression that she'd like the hours. Daycare is expensive. Please?"

I sighed. *Please*. Eloise wielded that single word the way a warrior would a sword. And I was being *nice*. "Fine."

"Thank you." She plucked a tomato cube from the cutting board and popped it into her mouth.

"What's her story?"

"What do you mean?"

"That baby is the same age as Hudson." Our nephew was two months old, and Winslow, though she pulled a shift here and there, was still on maternity leave. "Isn't that young to have a kid in daycare full-time?"

"She's a single working mother, Knox. Not everyone has the luxury of maternity leave."

"I get that but...what's the story with the kid's father? Why'd she move all the way to Montana from New York?" And why had she taken that drive alone? That wasn't a safe trip, especially with an infant. She should have had help. How did an educated, gorgeous woman end up traveling across the country alone with a baby and what seemed like every one of her possessions stuffed into a Volvo?

"I don't know because it's none of my business. If Memphis wants to talk about it, she will." Eloise narrowed her gaze. "Why are you asking? I'm usually the curious one. Not you."

"She's living at my house."

"Afraid she's going to murder you in your sleep?" Eloise teased, stealing another tomato.

"I'd like to know who's on my property."

"My new employee, whose personal life is her own. And a mother new to Quincy. Which is why you're going to make her lunch. Because I'm guessing she hasn't had anyone make her a meal in weeks. Fast food doesn't count."

I frowned and stalked through the kitchen, swiping up a mixing bowl, an onion and a lime.

Once again, Eloise was getting attached to an employee. After the lawsuit, both Mom and Dad had warned her to keep professional boundaries. But where Memphis was concerned, Eloise had already crossed them.

So had I, the day I'd agreed to let a strange woman and her child move onto my property.

Eloise checked the clock. "I'll be at the front desk for the rest of the day. Memphis is going to work on paperwork in the staff lounge and then go through orientation videos. What time should I send her here for lunch?"

"Eleven." Memphis could eat with the rest of us before the lunch rush hit. "You need to find out more about her story."

"If you're so curious, you ask her when she comes in to eat." Eloise smiled her victorious smile and disappeared.

Damn. I loved my sister, but along with that big heart, she was naive. Other than her four years away for college, she'd only lived in Quincy. This community loved her. She didn't realize just how devious and horrible people could be.

Memphis hadn't done anything worrisome. Yet. But I didn't like how little we all knew about her story. There were too many unanswered questions.

I shoved the worries aside, focusing on the prep I'd been doing since five this morning. My days started early, working before we opened the restaurant for hotel guests at seven. After making a handful of omelets and scrambles this morning, I'd been gearing up for tonight's meals. My sous chef, Roxanne, would be cooking dinner tonight so I could have an evening off.

The minutes passed too quickly and when the door opened, I glanced at the clock to see it was exactly eleven.

"Hi." Memphis gave me a whisper of a smile.

With an actual smile, she'd be more than trouble. She'd be a hurricane leaving devastation in her wake.

"Um…Eloise said something about coming in for lunch."

"Yeah." I nodded to the opposite side of the table where I kept a few stools. "Have a seat."

"I don't need anything. Really. I'm sure you're busy, and I don't want to intrude."

Before I could respond, Eloise breezed through the door with my line cook, Skip, right behind her. "You're not intruding."

"Hey, Knox." Skip glanced at Memphis, his footsteps stuttering as he did his own double take.

Memphis's beauty turned heads twice.

"We're making lunch." I pointed for Skip to put on an apron.

Introductions could wait. At the moment, I just wanted to make this meal and send Eloise and Memphis on their way so I could concentrate without Memphis's chocolate-brown eyes tracking my every move.

But did Skip get an apron off the row of hooks? No. Because apparently no one was listening to me today.

"I'm Skip." He held out his hand.

"Memphis."

"Beautiful name for a beautiful lady. What can I make you for lunch?" He held her hand for a moment too long with a stupid grin on his face.

"Tacos," I snapped, rounding the table to get a package of tortillas. "We're having tacos. Or we would be if you'd let go of her hand and get to work."

"Ignore him." Skip laughed but released her hand and went to pull an apron over his head. Finally. He tied his graying hair out of his face before going to the sink to wash his hands. The entire time he worked the soap into a lather, he stared at Memphis.

"Skip," I barked.

"What?" He smirked, knowing exactly what he was doing.

Skip had worked in my kitchen since I'd moved home five years ago. This was the first time I'd ever wanted to fire him.

"So Knox owns the restaurant," Eloise said, getting both her and Memphis a glass of water. "My parents own the hotel. There might be times when we ask you to help run room service deliveries, just depending on how busy we are. It's sort of an all-hands-on-deck approach around here."

"I'm happy to help with whatever is needed. Do you also run a bar service? Or just have the in-room fridges?" Memphis asked.

"What's a bar service?" Eloise asked.

"Oh, it's a newer trend," she said. "Most upscale hotels in the major cities offer a bar service, like Bloody Mary carts delivered to individual rooms or an on-call service to the hotel's bar."

Eloise's face lit up.

Shit. "No bar service." I squashed that brainchild before it grew legs. "We don't have a full bar here. All I serve are beer and wine. Both are included on the room service menu, which is different than the restaurant's menu."

"Got it." Memphis took a sip of her water, her gaze darting to my hands as I began plating.

Skip made short work of grilling the shrimp I'd had in a quick marinade.

Memphis's eyes widened as he placed six on her plate, like this was the first real meal she'd had in a while. "So, um...how does Chief Eden fit into your family?"

"She's married to our oldest brother, Griffin," Eloise explained. "There are six of us. How about you? Any brothers or sisters?"

"One sister. One brother."

"Maybe they'll come out to visit. We give employees a ten-percent discount."

Memphis shook her head, her gaze dropping to the table. "We're not, um...close."

That explained why her sister or brother hadn't come to Montana with her. My siblings drove me bat-shit crazy, but I couldn't imagine life without them. But what about her parents? Memphis didn't offer anything else, and Eloise, who I could normally count on to be nosy as hell, didn't ask.

My hands moved automatically to assemble two plates, and when they were ready, I slid them across the table.

"Thank you." Memphis inched the plate closer, carefully

folding a taco before taking a bite.

Some chefs didn't like watching people eat their food. They feared the raw reaction. Not me. I loved watching that first bite. In my early days at culinary school, I'd learned from expressions, both good and bad.

Except I should have looked away.

Memphis moaned. A smile tugged at the corner of her lips.

Any other person and I'd give myself a pat on the back and take it as a job well done.

With Memphis, my heart thumped and a surge of blood raced to my groin. Watching her eat was erotic. Only one other woman had had the same impact. And she'd fucked me over ruthlessly.

Trouble. Goddamn trouble. I needed Memphis out of my kitchen and, before long, out of my loft.

"This is amazing," she said.

"It's just tacos," I grumbled, focusing on the other plates. I didn't want her compliments. I'd rather she hate the food.

"Knox is the best," Eloise said, taking her own bite.

"It's been a long time since anyone has cooked for me." Memphis scooped a spoonful of my fresh pico, readying her next bite. "Unless you count Ronald McDonald."

Eloise's mouth was too full for her to speak but that didn't matter. *I told you so* was written all over her face. Her phone rang and she plucked it up from the table, muffling a groan as she swallowed. "I've got to take this. Come find me when you're done," she told Memphis before picking up her plate and scurrying out of the room.

The doorbell at the alley door buzzed. Our food supplier came every Monday. Bless him for being three hours early. It was the perfect excuse to escape this kitchen, but before I could make a move, Skip shut off the flat top and untied his apron. "I'll get it. You eat."

"Thanks," I said through gritted teeth.

I didn't take my plate to the stool beside Memphis. I inhaled a taco while standing beside the prep table. The sound of our chewing mixed with Skip's muted voice as he chatted with the delivery driver.

Then a phone rang.

Memphis put her food down and dug her phone from her pocket. She frowned at the screen, then silenced the call. Not two seconds later, it rang again. She declined it too. "Sorry."

"Do you need to get that?"

"No, it's fine." Except the strain on her face said it wasn't fine. And she didn't touch her food again. What the hell? "Thank you for lunch. It was delicious."

I waved her off when she stood to clear her plate. "Just leave it."

"Oh, okay." She wiped her hands on her gray slacks. Her black sweater hung on her shoulders, like it had once fit but now was too loose. Then she was gone, rushing out of the kitchen with her phone clutched in her grip.

Skip came down the hallway with a box, setting it on the table. The delivery guy followed with a dolly.

I signed for the order, then began putting my produce away in the walk-in.

"So who was that?" Skip asked. "New front desk clerk?"

"Housekeeper."

He grinned. "She's a looker. You interested?"

"No," I lied, picking up an apple to run my thumb across the taut, waxy skin. "Once the lunch rush is over, let's make an apple pie or two for the dinner dessert menu."

In another life, another world, I'd chase a woman like Memphis. But I'd spent the last five years in reality.

She was a hotel employee. My temporary tenant. Nothing more.

Memphis Ward was none of my damn business.

CHAPTER 3

MEMPHIS

The numbers on the microwave's clock taunted me as I paced the length of the loft. With every turn, the green glow caught my eye and earned a sigh of despair.

Three nineteen.

Drake had been crying since one.

I'd been crying since two.

"Baby." A tear dripped down my cheek. "I don't know what to do for you."

He wailed, his face red and his nose scrunched. He looked as miserable as I felt.

I'd fed him a bottle. I'd changed his diaper. I'd swaddled him. I'd unswaddled him. I'd rocked him in my arms. I'd propped him against a shoulder.

Nothing had worked. Nothing I was doing would make him stop crying.

Nothing I was doing was…right.

Did all new mothers feel this helpless?

"Shh. Shh. Shh." I walked toward an open window, needing some fresh air. "It's okay. It will be okay."

Before I'd left New York, his pediatrician had told me that colic typically peaked at six weeks old, then began to decline. But Drake's seemed to be getting worse.

His legs stiffened. His eyes were squeezed shut. He squirmed, like the last person on earth he wanted to be stuck with was me.

"It's okay," I whispered as my chin quivered. This would pass. Eventually, this would pass. He'd never know how he'd tormented me as an infant. He'd never know that I was hovering above rock bottom. He'd never know that being a mother was so damn hard.

He'd simply know that I loved him.

"I love you, baby." I kissed his forehead and closed my eyes.

God, I was tired. I'd stopped nursing because he'd been so fussy. Maybe that had been a mistake. The expensive, sensitive-tummy formula that was supposed to help only drained my bank account.

My feet hurt. My arms hurt. My back hurt.

My heart hurt.

Maybe I was in over my head. Maybe this move had been a horrible idea. But the alternative…

There hadn't been an alternative. And since I'd been here less than a week, I wasn't ready to call this a mistake. Not yet.

Don't give up.

"One more day, right? We'll make it one more day, then rest this weekend."

Tomorrow—or today—I'd be splurging on a triple-shot latte before going to the hotel. Caffeine would get me through my Friday. And this weekend, we'd recharge.

I only had to survive one more day.

My first four days at The Eloise Inn had flown by. Monday, I'd spent doing paperwork and orientation. Tuesday, I'd jumped into cleaning. After three days of scrubbing, dusting, vacuuming and making beds, every muscle in my body ached. Muscles I hadn't even known existed were screaming.

But it had been a good week. Granted, the bar for good days wasn't all that high, but we'd made it to Thursday—or Friday—and that was a win.

Drake had been an *angel* at daycare. Every evening when I'd picked him up, I'd braced for news of an expulsion. But Drake seemed to save these fits for the night. For the dark hours when the only person around to hear him cry was me.

Drying the last of my tears, I stepped away from the window and resumed pacing. His crying didn't seem as loud when I was moving.

"Shh." I bounced him softly, cradling him in one arm as my other hand rubbed his belly. Maybe it was gas. I'd tried the drops before I'd put him in his crib at eight. *Should I give him more?*

Motherhood, I'd learned in the past two months, was nothing more than a ritual of second-guessing yourself.

I yawned, dragging in a long breath. The energy to cry was waning. I'd let my son carry that torch for the rest of the night.

"Want to try your binky again?" I asked, walking to the kitchen counter where I'd left it earlier. I'd tried it around two thirty. He'd spit it out.

"Here, baby." I ran the plastic across his mouth, hoping he'd take it. He sucked on it for a second, and for that second, the loft was so quiet I could actually hear my own thoughts. Then the binky went sailing to the floor and if babies could talk, he would have told me to shove that plastic nipple imposter up my ass.

His cries had this staccato rhythm with a hitch each time he needed to breathe.

"Oh, baby." My eyes flooded. Apparently, my tears hadn't vanished after all. "What am I doing wrong?"

A pounding shook the door, cutting through Drake's noise.

I yelped. *Shit.* The light from outside was brighter. I'd been so focused on the baby I hadn't noticed when Knox's bedroom light had turned on. I swiped at my face, doing my best to dry it with just one hand, then I rushed to the door, seeing Knox through the small, square window in its face.

Oh, he did not look happy.

I flipped the deadbolt and whipped the door open. "I'm sorry. I'm so sorry. I opened the windows for some air because it was stuffy and didn't even think you might hear him."

Knox's dark hair was disheveled. The sleeves of his gray T-shirt had been cut off, revealing his sculpted arms. In the moonlight, the black ink of tattoos blended almost invisibly with his tanned skin. The sweatpants he wore hung low on his narrow waist, draping to his bare feet.

He'd crossed the gravel driveway without shoes.

I gulped. Either he had really tough feet or he was really pissed. Given the tension in his jaw, probably the latter.

"Sorry." I glanced down at Drake, willing him to stop. *Please stop. Five minutes. Then you can scream until dawn.*

Just stop for five minutes.

"Is he sick?" Knox fisted his hands on his hips.

"He has colic."

Knox's broad chest rose as he drew in a long breath. He ran a hand over his stubbled jaw before crossing his arms over his chest. God, he had a lot of muscles. The scowl on his face only added to his appeal.

Old Memphis always wanted to come out and play dirty when Knox was around. She wanted to tug at the long strands of hair that curled at his nape.

Please stop. That one was for me, not Drake. There'd be time to fantasize about Knox later, like when Drake was eighteen and headed off to college. I'd lock this mental image away for a time when my kid wasn't screaming and I hadn't been crying. When I'd slept for more than two hours in a row.

"Does he always cry?" Knox asked.

"Yes." The truth was as depressing as it would have been to lie. "I'll shut my windows."

Knox dropped his gaze to my son and the expression of pain that crossed his face made me want to climb in my car and drive far, far away.

"I'm sorry," I whispered.

To Knox. To Drake.

Another depressing truth. That apology was all I had to give.

Knox didn't say another word as he descended the stairs, then crossed the space between the garage and the house, wincing at a few steps on the gravel, before disappearing into his house.

Apartment hunting just got bumped up the to-do list.

"Damn." I stepped onto the landing, letting the cool air

soothe the flush of my face. "Baby, we need to get this under control. We can't get kicked out. Not yet."

Drake let out another cry and then, like he could sense my desperation, sucked in a hitched breath and closed his mouth.

I froze, letting the night air slip past us into the apartment. I held my breath and counted seconds, wondering how long it would last.

Drake squirmed and let out a whimper, but then his eyes drifted shut.

Sleep. Please, sleep.

His chest shook with the aftershocks of such a massive fit. The hitches racked his tiny body, but he snuggled deeper into my arms and gave up the fight.

"Thank you." I tipped my head to the stars. Each was a jewel scattered on black silk coated in diamond dust. There were so many out here, more than I'd ever seen in my life. "Wow."

The light in Knox's bedroom turned off.

Was this karma's doing, putting me next door to a man so fine? Was this her test to see if I truly had changed?

A year ago, I would have batted my eyelashes and donned my sexiest dress with six-inch heels. I would have flirted and teased until he paid me the attention I craved. Then, when I'd tired of the game, I would have worn my ruby-red lipstick and left streaks over his entire body.

That lipstick tube was somewhere in New York, in a box with my sexiest dresses and six-inch heels. Maybe my parents had tossed that box in the trash. Maybe one of their assistants had stowed it in a storage room where it would collect dust for years.

None of it mattered.

I had no need for lipstick, not here.

And I suspected that Knox wasn't your typical man. He probably would have laughed at an attempt to turn him into my personal toy. I liked that about him.

A yawn forced my eyes away from the heavens and I retreated inside. Rather than risk laying Drake in his crib and waking him up, I took him to my bed, blocking him in with some pillows. Then I curled up at his side with my hand on his belly.

There'd only be one man in my bed.

My little man.

When my alarm rang at six, I jolted awake, groggier than I had been in years. Drake was still asleep, so I left him on the bed and hurried through a shower. We had no coffee pot in the loft, probably because any of Knox's guests would simply walk to his gigantic kitchen for a morning cup.

If I had enough cash after rent and daycare and gas and food and formula and diapers and a few new outfits for Drake because he was growing out of his others, I'd buy a maker with my first paycheck. Or I'd just drink the free coffee at the hotel because I already knew there wouldn't be money.

That word had changed in two short months. Once, money had been a concept. An afterthought. Now, it was a luxury lost.

I'd traded it for my son.

Drake woke as I swapped out his pajamas for clothes and I yawned so many times as I got him ready for daycare that my jaw hurt. Not even the bright morning sun could chase away the brain fog as I stepped outside and rushed to my car.

Knox's truck was gone already. At first, I'd assumed he parked in the garage, but I'd since learned he parked outside, closer to the house.

"Ooo-ooh," Drake cooed as his car seat clicked into the base.

"Friday, baby. Let's make it through our Friday, okay?"

Daycare drop-off was painful, like it had been painful every morning this week. I hated leaving Drake with another person. I hated missing his happy hours. But it wasn't like I could clean hotel rooms with a baby strapped to my chest.

There was no choice. The money I'd saved from my job in New York was nearly gone. Most, I'd used to buy the Volvo. The rest was stashed in case of an emergency.

So Drake would go to daycare.

While I carved out a life for us with my own two hands, sweat and tears.

Main Street was my favorite part of this little town. It was the heart and hub of Quincy. Retail shops, restaurants and offices crowded the blocks. The Eloise stood proud as the tallest building in sight.

I glanced longingly at Eden Coffee as I drove by. Eloise had told me that her older sister Lyla owned it. Lattes had once been a staple of my diet. And though I had a twenty in my purse and had planned to splurge, I couldn't bring myself to stop.

Not when the coffee at the hotel was free.

Twenty dollars was over an hour's worth of work.

I parked in the alley behind The Eloise, grabbing my purse and the small plastic container that held my peanut butter sandwich. No jelly. It, like the latte, was an indulgence that must wait. The best meal I'd eaten in weeks had been Knox's tacos. Why was it so sexy that a man could cook? No man I'd ever dated had cooked me a meal.

Knox's truck was in the space closest to the employee

entrance. Had he been able to sleep last night? Or had he escaped to the restaurant after we'd woken him up?

"I'm so getting evicted." But thanks to my dad, it wouldn't be the first time.

A chime jingled in my pocket. One glance at the screen and I silenced the noise. Any time I seemed to think about New York, my phone would ring.

Thirty-seven. That made thirty-seven calls in a week. Asshole.

I hurried inside, finding Eloise in the staff room, filling a coffee mug.

"Good morning," I said as I stowed my things in a locker. Hopefully I'd covered up the dark circles beneath my eyes with the last of my concealer.

"Morning." She smiled. Eloise always had a smile.

I'd learned yesterday that we were both twenty-five. Her twenty-five seemed much lighter than my own. I envied that. I envied her smile. Had she been anyone but Eloise, I probably would have hated her for it. But Eloise was impossible not to love.

Shoving my lunch in the fridge, I went to the time clock and punched my card. Old fashioned, like the hotel. For my first hourly job, I liked the *thunk* of the machine as it stamped. Then I rushed to the cupboard for a mug, filling it to the brim from the pot. The first sip was too hot but that didn't stop me from blowing across the top, then taking another drink, scalding tongue and all.

"This might save my life."

Eloise laughed. "Long night?"

"Drake was up for a couple of hours." I cringed. "We woke up Knox."

"Ah. That's why he came in so early. The night clerk said

he showed around four. Usually he's not in until five."

"Oh no." I closed my eyes. "I'm sorry. I promise I'll get on finding a new place."

"You're fine." Eloise waved it off. "Besides, there isn't another place, and I need you."

It was nice to hear someone say they needed me. I hadn't heard that in, well...in a long time. "Thank you, Eloise."

"What for?"

"For taking a chance on me. And for giving me such a good schedule."

Eloise had given me the weekday shift. I was here to clean as guests checked out of their rooms, from eight until five, Monday through Friday. The weekend shift paid more, but without daycare, it wasn't an option.

"I'm glad you're here," she said. "I hope you're enjoying it."

"I am." Cleaning rooms was honest work. I hadn't realized how much my heart had needed something true and real. And part of me loved it simply because I imagined my family cringing at the thought of me in yellow rubber gloves.

Hotels had paid for my entire life—first in New York, now in Montana. It was fitting. The years I'd spent in five-star hotels—and some online tutorials—had been my education for cleaning.

"I love this hotel." Another truth. The Eloise Inn was charming and quaint and inviting. Exactly the atmosphere that many hotels strived to create and few achieved.

"So do I," she said.

"Okay, well, I'd better get to it." I raised my mug in salute.

"I'll be here all day if you need anything." She walked out of the break room with me, heading toward the lobby while I rounded the corner for the laundry room, where we kept the cleaning carts and the list of rooms ready to be tackled.

The other dayshift housekeeper must not have arrived yet because both cleaning carts were pushed against the wall. I chose the one I'd been using all week, then grabbed a master key card from the hook on the wall. With my coffee in one hand, I steered the cart with the other toward the staff elevator.

The Eloise Inn was four stories with the largest on the top floor. I rode to the top where a couple had vacated the biggest corner room. I worked tirelessly for two hours to get that room and another two ready for the next guests, yawning the entire time.

By the time my first fifteen-minute break rolled around at ten, I was dead on my feet. The black coffee wasn't cutting it.

A couple passed me as they walked down the hallway, each carrying to-go cups from Eden Coffee, and my stomach growled.

One latte. I'd go without jelly and fruit for the week in exchange for a single latte.

I rushed to get my wallet from my locker, then I hurried out the lobby's front doors. Three doors down and across the street, the cute green building beckoned.

The scent of coffee beans, sugar and pastries greeted me before I even reached the entrance to Eden Coffee. My stomach growled louder. I hadn't had breakfast this morning, so I dug into my wallet, searching for enough change to afford a muffin or a scone.

Hell, I'd clean the coffee shop's bathrooms for a cinnamon roll or slice of banana bread.

Seven quarters, three dimes, and six nickels later, I was digging for another quarter when I rounded the corner to step inside the doorway. My gaze lifted just before I crashed into a very solid, very broad chest.

My coins went flying.

So did the man's coffee.

"Oh my God, I'm so sorry." My gaze traveled up, up, up to a pair of familiar, stunning blue eyes. Angry blue eyes.

Knox's bearded jaw was clenched again, that frown fixed on his supple lips. In one hand he held his own coffee. In the other, his phone. Neither of us had been paying attention.

Neither of us was running on much sleep.

His gray T-shirt had a brown blob over his sternum. He shifted his coffee cup to the other hand, shaking the droplets off his knuckles. "You're everywhere, aren't you?"

"I promise, I'm not trying to bother you."

"Try harder."

I flinched.

He moved past me and disappeared without another word.

Yep, I was getting evicted.

Which meant I couldn't afford that latte after all. *Damn*.

CHAPTER 4

KNOX

Try harder.

It was a dick thing to say. I blamed lack of sleep for my short temper.

"Morning, Knox." A loan officer from the bank waved as he walked my way, slowing like he wanted to stop and chat.

"Hey." I raised my cup and kept on going toward the hotel. Given my mood, it would be better to stay in the kitchen today and avoid conversation.

The fall air was crisp and clean. Normally I'd take a few minutes to breathe it in, slow my pace, but at the moment, all I could focus on was the coffee on my damn shirt.

Downtown Quincy was quiet this morning. Kids were in school. The shops and restaurants on Main were open, but the bustle from summer was mostly over. People were enjoying the September lull and recovering from their months spent pandering to tourists. This was the time when locals took vacations.

I'd planned one. A vacation at home. Finish a few projects in the yard before winter. Find out if I still remembered how to turn on the television or read a book. But with Memphis there...

Vacation was canceled, effective immediately. I didn't trust myself around her. Not with those pretty brown eyes flecked with honey and brimming with secrets.

I sipped the last of my Americano as I walked, hoping the half cup remaining would fuel me through the morning. Instead of heading through the hotel's front doors, I ducked around the corner, following the length of the brick building to the alley and the service entrance to the restaurant.

The key was tight in the lock, something I'd fix on my canceled vacation. The door slammed shut behind me as I stalked toward my small office off the kitchen.

My desk was clear except for the staff schedule I'd been putting together this morning. Bills had been paid. Payroll information was off to my bookkeeper. One benefit of being here before dawn was that for the first time in months, my office work was done before breakfast instead of after the dinner rush.

I tossed my coffee cup in the trash, then went to the closet in the corner, reaching behind my head to yank off my shirt. With it shoved into a backpack, I tugged on the spare shirt I kept here in case of spills.

Try harder.

The shame on Memphis's face was punishment for my sharp words. What the hell was my problem? She lived in the loft. I'd agreed to let her move in. It was time to stop grumbling and deal.

"Damn it." I owed her an apology.

The Friday lunch hour would be busy with plenty of locals here to enjoy the end of their week. I was covering all meals today, which meant I wouldn't get home until after dark. My window to track down Memphis was now. So I strode out of the office and left the kitchen, weaving through the restaurant.

"Hey, April."

"Hey." She smiled from her seat at one of the round tops, where she was cleaning check folders. "I'm almost done with this. Then what would you like me to do?"

"Would you mind checking the ketchup bottles in the walk-in?"

"Not at all." April had only been waitressing here for a few months, taking the job after she and her husband had moved to Quincy. He was a truck driver and gone more often than not, which meant April was always up for an additional shift because home was a lonely place.

"I'll be back in a few. If Skip comes in before then, would you tell him to start on the list I left on the table?"

"Sure thing."

"Thanks." My footsteps thudded in the empty room.

The restaurant was my favorite like this, when it was quiet and still. Soon there'd be people at the tables, conversation mixing with the clink of silverware on plates. But seeing the tables set and ready for customers was about the only time I could really appreciate what this space had become. Later, when it was busy, I'd be too focused on the food.

For most of the building's life, this had been a ballroom with gaudy wallpaper, worn carpet tiles and no intimacy. Now it was utterly different, save the tall ceilings.

Knuckles.

The vibe was as moody and smooth as the food. I'd carved pockets out of the large space, shrinking the number of tables. Along the back wall, I'd built a room for the waitstaff to fill water and soda. Beside it was a cooler for wine and beer. There were no available liquor licenses in Quincy, but I'd left space to add a bar one day should one open up.

The tables were a rich walnut. A row of caramel-leather booths hugged one wall. A black grid separated a corner for large dining parties. One of the original, exterior brick walls that had been hidden beneath sheetrock had been exposed. The hanging pendant lights and sconces cast a golden glow onto the tables. The windows along the far wall let in light during the day and added to the mood at night.

This was my dream realized. And part of why I loved it so much was because I could push through the glass doors and walk into the hotel lobby.

As a kid, I'd spent a lot of hours here with Mom. While Dad had been busy running the ranch, Mom had taken charge of the hotel. How many coloring books had I filled sitting beneath her feet at the lobby's mahogany reception counter? How many toy cars had I sent flying across the floor? How many Lego sets had I built on the fireplace's stone ledge?

This was the scene of my youth. Griffin had preferred to ride shotgun with Dad on the ranch. I'd tagged along with Mom. When I'd moved home after finishing culinary school and working for years in San Francisco, it hadn't even been a question of where I'd wanted to start a restaurant.

Mom and Dad had been renovating and updating the hotel for the past five years. Knuckles was the last major project for a while. Eloise had some ideas of her own, but those would have to wait.

At least they would if I took over.

She was talking to a guest at the reception counter. I turned the opposite direction and headed for the laundry room. One of the washing machines was churning while two dryers hummed as the sheets inside tumbled. There was a cleaning cart outside the break room so I moved to the doorway, finding Memphis at the coffee pot.

Her shoulders were slumped forward as she filled a ceramic mug. The phone in her pocket rang and she dug it out, checking the screen. Then as she'd done in my kitchen, she silenced it and shoved it away.

"Thirty-nine," she mumbled.

Thirty-nine what? Who was calling her? And why didn't she answer?

Those questions were not my business. And not why I was here.

"Memphis."

She gasped and jumped, the pot in her hand shaking. "Oh, hi."

"Sorry to startle you."

"It's okay." She stared at my clean T-shirt. "Sorry about your other shirt."

"It's fine." I eyed the mug. "You didn't get a coffee from the shop?"

"No, I, um…just changed my mind. This coffee is good."

That was a damn lie. It was bitter and boring, hence why I went to Lyla's each morning for espresso.

When we'd collided, I'd been focused on my cup, wishing I had put a lid on it. Wishing I hadn't been texting Talia. I'd sent her a note this morning asking if it was normal for a two-month-old baby to cry so fucking much. She'd replied with yes and an eye-roll emoji.

Memphis's head must have been down too. And there'd been the distinct sound of coins clattering on cement.

She'd been digging for change. That was why she hadn't seen me walk through the door. She'd planned to pay for a coffee with loose change. Change that I'd knocked out of her hand.

Maybe she hadn't collected it after I'd left her on the sidewalk. Or maybe she hadn't had enough.

"Why didn't you get a coffee?"

"I changed my mind." She tipped her mug to her lips. From beyond the rim, she sent me a glare. It was subtle, but fire sparked in those brown eyes. If she let that flame blaze, she'd level me to the ground and leave nothing behind but ash.

"If you'll excuse me, I'm trying not to be everywhere." Then she breezed past me into the hall.

Yeah, I'd deserved it. And worse.

The cleaning cart rattled as she steered it away, then the elevator doors dinged as they closed.

"Why can't I say no to my sister?" I muttered before returning to the kitchen, where Skip whistled as he diced a pile of red potatoes.

"Morning," he said.

"Morning." I swiped a clean white coat from the hook and buttoned it up, shoving the sleeves up my forearms. I was about to reach for a knife when I hung my head.

I'd gone to apologize to Memphis.

I hadn't actually apologized. *Fuck.*

This plan to keep my distance wasn't going to work if it took two trips to deliver every message.

I pinched the bridge of my nose.

"Headache, Knox?" Skip asked.

"Yeah." Her name was Memphis Ward.

She had smooth skin, flawless beneath the moonlight. She had dark circles under her eyes that bothered the hell out of me. She had a men's black T-shirt that she wore in place of pajamas, and as often as I'd replayed last night, I couldn't remember if she'd had a pair of shorts on underneath or just panties.

Maybe if we could just coexist, her going one direction while I went the other, we'd survive this short-term lease. With some space, I could banish all thoughts of her toned legs and pink lips.

"I forgot something," I told Skip, then made my way to the lobby.

Eloise was at the reception counter, perched on a tall chair as she clicked away at the computer screen. The guests she'd been talking to earlier were now sitting on the couch in front of the unlit fireplace. When my sister saw me coming, she smiled. "Hey. What's up?"

"I'm looking for Memphis. I saw her head upstairs. Do you know what floor she's on?"

"The second, I think. Why?"

"Nothing." I waved it off. "Just wanted to talk to her about something."

"How's it going with her at your place?"

"Fine," I lied, then before she could ask more questions, I strode toward the staircase, preferring it over the elevators.

When I reached the second floor, I glanced down both sides of the hallway, spotting the cleaning cart to my left. My tennis shoes sank into the plush hallway carpet as I walked toward the room. The smell of lemon furniture polish and glass cleaner wafted from the open doorway.

I paused beside the cart. Her coffee mug was propped between a stack of clean washcloths and paper towels. The black liquid still steamed. When I looked into the room, my mouth went dry. My cock twitched.

Memphis was bent over the bed, stretching a fitted sheet to the mattress. Her tight jeans clung to the slight curves of her hips. They molded to the perfect shape of her ass. Her blond hair swung over her shoulder as she worked.

Fuck me. Why her? Why had Eloise put a woman like Memphis on my property? Why couldn't she have found me a fifty-seven-year-old retiree named Barb who taught swimming lessons at the community center?

It had been a while since I'd been attracted to a woman. Why Memphis? She was as complicated as duck pâté en croûte. Yet I couldn't look away.

Her phone chimed again and she stood, digging it from her pocket. She huffed at the screen and, like she'd done in the break room, hit decline.

"Forty."

Forty calls? Memphis's nostrils flared as she tucked the phone away and stared blankly at the unmade bed.

What the hell was her story? Curiosity had me hooked. Why was she here? Was it the kid's dad who'd been calling nonstop?

None of my damn business. *Too much drama.* And I'd sworn off drama after Gianna.

I cleared my throat, stepping past the cleaning cart like I hadn't been watching or listening. "Hey."

"Oh, um…hey." Memphis's eyes widened as she brushed a stray lock of hair off her forehead. Then she crossed her arms over her chest, her gaze sparking with that same fire.

She was short, her gaze hitting me midchest. Or maybe I was just tall. I'd never gone for short women. But the urge to pick her up, haul her to eye level and kiss that delicious mouth hit so hard I had to force myself not to move.

"Did you need something?" she asked.

"Came to apologize. About what I said outside Lyla's. I'm sorry."

Her shoulders fell. "I'm sorry we woke you up last night. I should have left the window closed but it was stuffy."

"Don't worry about it."

In truth, it hadn't been the kid's crying that had woken me up. It had been a pair of headlights. By the time I'd shoved out of bed and blinked the sleep of fog away, I'd only caught the glow of taillights down the road.

I'd chosen Juniper Hill because it got no traffic. But every now and then, someone would take a wrong turn. Or high school kids would think they'd stumbled on a deserted road where they could park and go at it in the backseat only to come up on my house.

After the car, that's when I'd heard the kid. Once I'd heard his cry, I couldn't not hear it. It had carried through the night, bringing with it memories I'd tried for years to forget.

"Well…I'm still sorry," Memphis said.

"Do you always apologize this much?" I teased. I thought maybe it would earn me a smile. Instead, she looked like she was about to cry.

"I guess I'm making up for the apologies I should have made but didn't."

"Why do you say that?"

"Never mind." She waved it off with a flick of her delicate wrist. "Thank you for your apology."

I nodded, turning to leave, but stopped myself. "Don't worry about the window. Leave it open at night if that helps."

"Okay."

Without another word, while I could still stop myself from asking more questions, I ducked out of the room and returned to my kitchen.

. . .

It was after midnight by the time I made it home. The sky was dark. So was the loft. I slipped inside, stripped out of my clothes and rushed through a shower.

It was warm in the house, too warm, so I cracked a window before flopping on the bed. With a sheet tugged over my bare legs, I was seconds away from sleep when a piercing wail split the air.

A light turned on above the garage. It only seemed to make that baby scream louder.

That tiny cry was like a dagger to my heart.

It was the sound of a dream lost. The sound of a family gone.

I rolled out of bed and slammed the window closed. Then I snagged my pillow, carrying it to the other side of the house. Where I slept on the couch.

CHAPTER 5

MEMPHIS

The microwave in the break room dinged. With my fork between my lips, I carried the steaming container to the round table in the corner. Lunch wasn't fancy—none of my meals were fancy these days—but my mouth watered as I stirred the yellow noodles before blowing on a bite. I had the fork raised to my lips when a large body filled the doorframe.

"What is that?" Knox asked.

I set my utensil down and glanced at myself. "What?"

"What are you eating?"

"Macaroni and cheese." *Duh*. I bit back the smart-ass remark and didn't point out that most chefs were familiar with the concept of mac 'n' cheese. I was treading lightly where Knox was concerned. Well...where everyone was concerned but especially him.

It had been nearly a week since our coffee collision,

and I'd only seen him in passing. Until I had a replacement rental lined up, I was giving Knox a very wide berth.

Apartment hunting had been unsuccessful at best. Every Thursday when the local newspaper came out, I scoured the classifieds for a listing, but nothing new was available. I'd called the real estate office in town, hoping they might have a lead, but the woman I'd spoken to had no information and she'd warned me that rentals in my price range grew even scarcer through winter.

Eviction was not an option. Avoiding Knox would be the key to staying in his loft until spring.

I'd spent the past weekend resting and playing with Drake. We'd braved the grocery store for some essentials and then I'd taken him to a local park for a walk beneath the colorful fall trees. I'd walked into my Monday morning shift with more energy than I'd had in weeks. But today was Thursday and Drake had been up last night for three hours.

Knox needed to leave me alone so I could scarf these simple carbohydrates in the hopes they'd give me a boost to finish the day.

He had a pen and notepad in one hand. Sometime in the last week, he'd trimmed his beard, shaping it to the chiseled contours of his jaw. The sleeves of his chef's coat were pushed up his forearms like he always seemed to do, and even though it was a fairly shapeless garment, it molded to his biceps and broad shoulders.

My heart did its little Knox-induced trill. No matter how many times I saw him, he stole my breath away. Even when he was glowering at my food.

"What kind of macaroni and cheese?" he asked.

Was that a trick question? "Um...the regular kind you buy at the grocery store?"

Eloise appeared behind Knox's shoulder, pushing past him into the room. "Hey. What's going on?"

Knox tossed a hand in my direction. "I came in to inventory the coffee supply. She's eating macaroni and cheese."

Eloise's gaze, the same striking color as her brother's, darted to my lunch. She cringed. "Oh. Is, um…is that the blue box kind?"

"Yes."

She scrunched up her nose, then turned and disappeared down the hallway.

"What's wrong with the blue box kind?" It was the cheapest. And I was using my dollars wisely.

One day, I'd move out of Knox's loft. One day, I'd like to have my own home. One day, I'd like to have a garden and a fenced yard where Drake could have a puppy.

One day.

If I was going to make it to that one day, it would require sacrifices like blue box mac 'n' cheese and ramen noodles.

Knox walked over, straight into my space, and I tilted up my chin to keep his face in view. He frowned and swiped up my plastic container, walking it to the garbage can in the corner. One tap on the side and my noodles went plopping to the bottom of the black liner.

"Hey." I shot out of my chair. "That was my lunch."

And I couldn't afford to walk down Main to a restaurant for a replacement. *Damn him.* I bit the inside of my cheek to keep my mouth shut.

Don't call him an asshole. Don't call him an asshole.

"We have a rule in this building," he said, going to the break room's cupboard where we kept the coffee. He opened the door, surveyed the contents, then scribbled something on his notepad. "No blue box mac 'n' cheese."

"Well, I didn't know that rule. Next time, tell me the rules and I'll be sure to follow them. But don't throw my lunch away. I'm *hungry*." On cue, my stomach growled.

"Come on," he ordered and strode from the room.

I sighed, my shoulders slumping, and trudged behind him with my fork still in hand.

Knox didn't so much as spare me a glance as he led the way to Knuckles.

It was still early, only eleven fifteen, but already half of the tables were full. Two waitresses moved around the room, delivering menus and glasses of water.

Knox strode past the *Please Seat Yourself* sign, following the main aisle through the room.

I hadn't been in here with the lights on. When Eloise had brought me through on my first day of work for the tour, it had been dark and quiet. Even now with the pendants glowing and light streaming through the exterior wall's windows, the room held a dim edge.

The style fit Knox. Modern and moody and masculine. Exposed brick. Deep wall color. Rich wood tones. Cognac leather booths. It was exactly the style my father loved for his hotel restaurants.

All that was missing from a Ward Hotel eatery was the dress code. Dad required men wear a jacket and tie. He also required his housekeepers and desk clerks wear uniforms. I was happy that Knuckles and The Eloise were so laid-back, that my jeans and tees and tennis shoes were standard housekeeping attire.

People waved when they spotted Knox. He nodded and waved back but didn't slow his pace. He breezed past them, and in his wake, faces turned my way.

I ducked my chin and kept my eyes on the floor, not wanting to be noticed.

Old Memphis—the naive, spoiled girl—would have strutted through a room like this. She would have reveled in the attention. She would have accentuated every step with the click of a stiletto heel that cost thousands of dollars. She would have had diamonds in her ears and gold on her wrists. She would have sat at the best seat in the restaurant, ordered the most expensive meal and picked at her food, letting most of it be thrown in the trash.

How many housekeepers had I walked past in my lifetime? I'd never acknowledged a single one. Or the maids who'd worked on my parents' estate. If a housekeeper had walked by, Old Memphis would have turned up her nose.

Old Memphis was dead. I'd killed that version of myself. I'd stabbed her to death with the shards of a broken heart.

Good riddance. Old Memphis, though not all bad, had been a brat. Soft and silly. She wouldn't have survived the past year. She would have caved and given into her family's demands. She wouldn't have been the mother that Drake needed.

My son would not be spoiled. I would teach him how to work hard. How to fight for a life on his own terms. When he walked past a housekeeper in a hotel, he'd pause to say thank you.

Maybe I'd lost my shine, but I was a better person without it.

Knox pushed through the swinging door to the kitchen, holding it for me to follow him inside.

The scent of bacon and onions and buttered bread filled my nose, making my hunger claw. The stainless steel table in the center of the room was crowded with mixing bowls.

The smaller ones had sauces, the larger salads. Five cutting boards were placed in between. One had an array of sliced vegetables, lettuce and pickles and tomatoes, all ready for sandwich and burger toppings. Another had a beef brisket, sliced thin.

"Did you bring me here to torture me?" I asked.

Knox chuckled, not quite a laugh but more a rumble from deep in his chest. He went to the side of the table where Eloise and I had sat on my first day, taking out a stool. "Have a seat."

"Hey, Memphis." Skip glanced over his shoulder from where he stood at the flat top, caramelizing some onions.

"Hi." I waved and sat down.

"Want some lunch?" he asked.

"I've got it." Knox held up a hand and walked to a shelf teeming with pots and pans. He took down a pot and filled it with water. Then he set it over a flame with a dash of salt before disappearing to the walk-in, returning with four different blocks of cheese. He chopped and grated until the water boiled, then he dumped in a box of dried pasta.

Knox moved through the kitchen with command and grace. It was like watching a dance.

A movement at my side stole my attention. Skip slid a plate and napkin in front of me, then winked. *Busted.* I hadn't so much been staring at Knox as caught under a spell.

I blushed. "Thanks."

"Want a new fork?" He nodded to the one still in my fist.

"This one is fine." I set it on the plate.

Skip returned to his tasks, tearing off a ticket that rolled from a small black printer against the wall. He read it, then attached it to a clip that hung beside a warming rack. The bulbs glowed orange against the silver metal shelf.

My gaze drifted to Knox as he plated salads on three white plates. His hands plucked exactly the right amount of lettuce from a mixing bowl. His forearms flexed as he sprinkled the greens with shredded carrots and croutons from a roasting pan. Then he added sliced cherry tomatoes and drizzled on a purple vinaigrette.

Those blue eyes stayed focused, never once drifting my way. If he felt me staring, he didn't glance up.

And once more, I became entranced with his every move. His steps. His hands. His face. His hair was long enough to curl at the nape of his neck. My mother would have called it shaggy, though I'd argue it was sexy. I'd seen what was beneath that coat my first night in the loft. I knew what those curls looked like dripping wet.

A low pulse bloomed in my core. There was always a rush where Knox was concerned but this was a curl, like thread wrapping around a spool, winding tighter and tighter with every turn.

Knox was more tempting than any meal.

More dangerous than the knife in his grasp.

The swinging door flew open and a pretty woman with brown hair hurried inside. A black apron was tied around her waist. Her white long-sleeved button-down was perfectly starched. "Hey, Knox. We're out of chardonnay in the wine cooler. Do we have more stashed away?"

"There's more in the cellar," he answered, returning to the cutting board, this time with a red chili pepper. What would have taken me minutes to chop, he diced in seconds, the pieces precise and delicate. "I forgot to grab it this morning. Give the front desk a call. Eloise or someone else can bring some up for us."

"I can go get it," I offered.

The woman looked to me and smiled. "You're Memphis, right? One of the housekeepers? I'm April."

"Hi." I waved. "Nice to meet you."

"Here." Knox dug a set of keys from his pocket. "The wine cellar is two doors down from the break room. Would you mind?"

"Not at all." I took the keys and hurried from the kitchen.

I couldn't, wouldn't, let myself get distracted by a handsome man. Not again. My heart couldn't handle another break.

Not that Knox was in any way interested. In truth, I wasn't all that interesting. I'd given up worrying about my appeal the day Drake's life had stirred in my belly.

Hurrying to the cellar, I unlocked the door and stepped inside, scanning the dimly lit shelves. The temperature was cooler in here and goose bumps broke across my bare arms.

I'd been hot all morning. Usually when I cleaned a room, it was right after the guest had showered, and it made the rooms muggy.

I scanned the wine labels, some I recognized. My fingers drifted along the sleek neck of a cabernet from a winery I'd visited in Napa years ago. It was a bottle I could no longer afford.

One day.

I moved to the shelves of white wine, loading up on a variety, then hauled them out of the cellar, locking up behind me. In the short time I'd been gone, the number of restaurant patrons seemed to have doubled. Without Knox snagging attention, fewer noticed me as I rushed back to the kitchen, depositing the wine bottles on the prep table.

"Thanks." Knox nodded to my plate. "Lunch."

A steaming bowl of macaroni and cheese sat beside the

plate Skip had brought over. On it was the same salad Knox had made for an order.

I took my chair, knowing I would never eat it all, but picked up my fork and dove into the mac 'n' cheese first. Rich, creamy flavors exploded on my tongue. A moan escaped my throat. The chili peppers gave the sauce a kick. The cheese was gooey and tangy and complex.

Knox stood on the opposite side of the table, and when I met his gaze, there was nothing but utter satisfaction on his face.

"This is really good."

"I know." He arched an eyebrow. "No more blue box."

"I bought a ten-pack."

"Ditch it. I always keep the ingredients on hand if you want some."

"Thank you." A smile tugged at the corner of my mouth as I dove for another bite. I wouldn't bother him to cook for me. I'd just save my cheap pasta and powdered cheese for dinners alone at home.

By the time he came home most nights, he'd never know otherwise.

I'd paid too much attention to his schedule this week, mostly in hopes of staying out of his way. But also for a rare glimpse. The thrill that came with Knox was addicting. Only a foolish woman wouldn't appreciate such a good-looking man, and I was trying very hard not to be a foolish woman.

Knox went back to cooking as I ate with abandon. He tore off an order slip from the printer, and it joined the lineup of others. While Skip manned the flat top, Knox arranged plates, then dropped a basket of shoe-string-cut potatoes in a fryer.

"Why Quincy?" His question was spoken as he sliced a ciabatta roll. He was so intent on the bread that it took me a moment to realize his question was for me.

"I wanted a small town. A safe place to raise Drake. I was thinking California. An influencer I follow on Instagram was raving about these small towns up and down the coast. But they were too expensive." As much as I would have loved to live beside the ocean, there was no way I'd be able to afford it.

"You're from New York?"

"I am. I was tired of the city."

He pulled the fries, then smeared the ciabatta with an aioli, balancing what seemed like ten orders at once.

When I was in the kitchen, I had to concentrate only on the food, cooking one thing at a time. He'd probably grimace if he knew that preparing my blue-box macaroni had taken me just as long as it had taken him to make it from scratch.

"So how'd you land on Montana?" he asked. .

"That same blogger did an interview with this baker in LA. She, the baker, said her favorite place to vacation was Quincy. That she and her husband spent a Christmas here and fell in love with the town. So I looked it up."

The pictures of downtown had charmed me instantly. School ratings and the cost of living had sealed the deal.

Knox gave a dry laugh as he shook his head. "Cleo."

"Cleo. Yes, that was the baker's name. You know her?"

"She invaded my kitchen on her vacation here that Christmas. I've never seen anyone make so much food in a few hours. We've kept in touch. I actually just sent her some recipes a few weeks ago. Including that one." He pointed toward my plate. "Small world."

"That it is."

Though I hoped, for my sake and Drake's, there was a bit that remained big. That over the miles between Montana and New York, I'd be able to put some distance between the future and the past.

Montana had an appeal for many reasons. This intimate, friendly community was one. Another was the lack of Ward Hotels in the entire state.

My grandfather had started the first Ward Hotel in his twenties. Over his lifetime, he'd grown his enterprise into a chain of boutique hotels before passing the business to my father. Under Dad's rule, the company had quadrupled in the past thirty years. Nearly every major metropolitan area in the country had a Ward Hotel, and he'd recently begun expanding into Europe.

But there were none in Montana. Not a single one.

"I read Cleo's interview, then saw the application for a housekeeping position and applied," I said.

"And now you're here." Knox stopped plating and braced his hands on the table, locking his gaze with mine. Questions swam in his eyes.

Questions I wasn't going to answer.

"Now I'm here and had better get back to work." I stood from the table. "Thank you for lunch. It was delicious."

"See ya, Memphis," Skip called over his shoulder.

"Bye." I headed for the door, glancing back one last time.

Knox's gaze was waiting. His expression was almost unreadable. Almost. Suspicion was written across his handsome features. And restraint. Probably because he wanted my story.

But that confession was mine and mine alone.

I was halfway through the restaurant when my phone

rang in my pocket. I dug it out, checking to make sure it wasn't the daycare. It wasn't. So I hit decline and stowed it away.

Sixty-three.

At this rate, it would be one hundred before the end of September.

Maybe by then, the calls would stop.

CHAPTER 6

KNOX

"Thanks for dinner." Griffin clapped me on the shoulder as we stood on the front porch of his house.

"Welcome."

The macaroni and cheese I'd made Memphis last week had given me a craving, so I'd made a huge batch today with plenty to spare. Before coming to see Griff and Winn with a pan for dinner, I'd dropped one off at Mom and Dad's place too.

"Nice night." Griffin drew in a long breath. The scent of leaves and rain and cooler temperatures was in the air.

"Sure is." I leaned against one of the wooden beams, glancing out across the land as I took a sip from my beer.

Surrounded by trees with the mountains in the distance, Griffin's place was the reason I'd built my own. I'd wanted my own haven away from the bustle of town. Our styles were entirely different. Griff preferred a traditional look with an abundance of wood, while I favored the sleek, modern lines of glass.

Though our houses were different, the setting was the same.

Rugged mountain countryside. Evergreens with the year-round scent of pine. Sunshine and blue sky. *Home*.

A cry came from inside the house and Griffin straightened, turning toward the front door as Winn came outside with my two-month-old nephew, Hudson, fussing in her arms.

"Tag, you're it." She handed her son to his father. "He wants me during the day but only Griff at night."

My brother nodded at his son. "We've got lots to talk about at night, don't we, cowboy? And sometimes you just need a new set of arms."

Hudson's fussing ceased as my brother walked the length of the porch.

My heart twisted at the sight.

I loved Hudson. But his birth had triggered memories I'd done my best to forget these past five years. Memories that weren't as buried as I'd once thought.

Griffin hadn't known Gianna, nor had any of my siblings. Mom and Dad had met her once on a vacation to San Francisco, but that had been before Jadon. My family knew what had happened, but it was something I'd refused to discuss after I'd moved home.

No one knew how hard it was to be around a baby.

"Dinner was amazing." Winn gave me a sleepy smile. "Exactly what I was craving."

"Anytime." I winked as she pressed a hand to her belly.

It was early in her second pregnancy, but I suspected

before too long they'd all come to the restaurant more frequently. While she'd been pregnant with Hudson, I'd taken it as my personal challenge to feed my sister-in-law's cravings.

"How are things at the restaurant?" she asked, sinking into one of the porch's rocking chairs.

"Good. Busy." Roxanne was running the show tonight. Wednesdays were typically slow this time of year, so when she'd told me to stop hovering and head home after lunch, I'd actually listened.

Griffin kept pacing with Hudson, murmuring words to his son that I couldn't make out.

"It's his voice." Winn followed my gaze. "I think because it's deeper. This time of night, Griff's voice is about the only thing that will put him to sleep."

"Makes sense." It wasn't always easy to see Griffin with his son, but that wasn't something I'd admit to them. To anyone.

"You feeling okay?" I asked Winn.

"Just a little tired. But I think that will be the norm for a few years."

Griffin strode our way. "Maybe by the time we have this next one, Hudson will sleep through the night."

"That's the dream." Winn crossed her fingers. "How's it going with Memphis?"

"All right. I don't see her much." And that had been by design. There was a reason that I hadn't taken much time off lately. That I hovered at Knuckles. There was a reason that on my rare night away from the restaurant, I'd escaped to the comfort of my brother's home and not my own.

Griffin and I had a bond formed from youthful years of hiding mischief and suffering the consequences when our parents inevitably caught us causing trouble. He'd been my best friend since birth. We knew each other better than most, which was probably why he hadn't asked about Memphis. He could sense I didn't want to talk about her.

What would I say? I was attracted to her. Every time she walked into the room, my heart stopped and my dick twitched. If that had been the end of the story, if it had been just a woman passing through town, I would have chased her that first night.

But she wasn't a tourist here today, gone tomorrow. There was no escaping her, at work or at home. Then there was the kid.

Seeing Drake was harder than seeing Hudson. I wasn't sure why but every time he cried, it cut right through my chest. Maybe it was because Memphis was dealing with it alone. She bore the brunt of his screams. She carried the weight on her slender shoulders.

But it wasn't my business. It wasn't my place to interfere.

I'd had enough dramatics for a lifetime and Memphis had drama written all over her pretty face.

It had taken me five years to build a life in Quincy. I'd walked away from San Francisco a broken man. I'd come home to recover. To start again. To return to a place where I'd had good days in the hope of finding them again.

Five years and I was there. I loved my job. I loved my family. I loved my life.

Unchanged.

As soon as Memphis was gone from the loft, it would be easier to put her out of my head.

I drained the last swallow of my beer as Hudson's eyelids began to droop. "I'd better get home. Let you guys get him to bed."

"Thanks, Knox." Winn yawned.

"Have a good night." I walked over, bent to kiss her cheek, then shook my brother's free hand. I ruffled the dark hair on my nephew's head and touched his button nose. "Give your parents some rest, kid."

Hudson had a tiny hand over Griff's heart.

Damn, that stung. As Hudson grew, it had dulled, but not disappeared. I let it spread through my chest, then jogged down the porch steps for my truck.

My drive home was through a maze of gravel roads. The highway was more of a direct route to home, but taking the back roads gave me time to roll down the windows and simply think.

When I'd stopped at Mom and Dad's earlier, they'd asked me if I'd made my decision about the hotel. Uncle Briggs had had a rough week. He'd gone out for a hike without telling anyone, and though he'd probably been lucid at first, he'd had an episode and gotten lost.

Lost on the land where he'd lived his entire life.

Thankfully, Dad had found him just before dark. Briggs had tripped and twisted his ankle. So after a trip to the ER—Talia had been the doctor on call—they'd gotten Briggs home. But the scare had spurred Dad's urgency to get my answer.

An answer I didn't have to give.

Part of me wanted to agree, simply because it would make them happy. I had the best parents in the world. They let us fail when we needed to fail. They gave us a hand when it was clear we couldn't get back up on our own two feet. They loved us unconditionally. They'd given us every advantage possible.

But if I said yes to the hotel, it wouldn't be for me. It

would be for them.

Did I want The Eloise? I didn't want it to go to someone outside of the family. But me? Maybe. I just wasn't sure. Not yet.

I reached my turnout and rolled toward Juniper Hill, disappearing through the trees to my secluded corner of the world. As the house came into view, my eyes went to the loft. Even hidden behind walls and doors and windows, Memphis drew my attention. She had since the day she'd arrived.

Her Volvo was parked beside the stairs, and that car was as much of a mystery as my tenant. It was a newer model and Volvos weren't exactly inexpensive. So why was she surviving on cheap meals and spare change?

Not my business.

I'd flown to Gianna's rescue all those years ago when I should have minded my own fucking business. Lesson learned.

Parking in the space closest to my door, I headed inside. Before winter, I'd have to figure out a different parking situation so both of our rigs weren't left outside in the snow, but for now, leaving my truck outside meant one more way to keep my distance.

The house was quiet. The scent of macaroni and cheese lingered in the kitchen. I walked to the fridge, getting another beer, then retreated to the living room to watch TV until dark.

The abundance of windows meant that when the sun began to set below the crest of Juniper Hill, I caught it from all angles. Pink and orange and blue light cascaded over the walls, fading with every minute until the silver glow of moonlight took its place.

It should have been relaxing. The number one trending

movie on Netflix should have kept my attention. This was supposed to be my sanctuary, yet since the day Memphis had moved in, she'd held a constant chain to my thoughts. A distraction.

Was she cooking dinner? Was she sleeping? Was the place big enough for her? Was she searching for another apartment? Did I want her to find another apartment?

Yes. She had to leave. We couldn't do this forever, right? I needed my home back. Yet the idea of her in town, on her own, made me uneasy.

She wasn't my responsibility. She was a grown woman, an adult, capable of living alone. She was twenty-five, the same age as Eloise. Close to the same age as Lyla and Talia, who were twenty-seven. Did I feel the need to keep my sisters close? No. So why Memphis? And where the hell were her parents? What had happened with those siblings she'd mentioned?

I stared at the TV, realizing I'd watched almost the entire thriller and hadn't a damn clue what it was about. "Christ."

Restlessness rattled beneath my skin. I shoved off the couch, went to my bedroom for a pair of workout shorts, then disappeared to the gym I'd set up in my basement.

After an hour spent alternating between the treadmill and the heavy bag, I climbed the stairs, drenched in sweat. Thankfully, the workout had served its purpose and my pent-up energy had burned out, so I headed to the shower.

Sleep had been scarce over the past few weeks. The last solid eight-hour stretch had been before Memphis had moved in. Drake had a set of lungs, and though I should just sleep with the windows closed, every night, I got too hot and had slept with them cracked for as long as I could remember.

Wearing only a pair of boxer briefs, I climbed into bed,

killing the light on the nightstand. My head hit the pillow, and as a gentle breeze swept through the room, exhaustion won out.

But like it had for weeks, my sleep was broken by the wail of a baby boy.

I jolted awake and scrubbed a hand over my face before glancing at the clock beside my bedside lamp. *Two fourteen.*

He'd slept longer than normal. This past week he'd woken me up around one. Or maybe he'd been up for an hour and I'd just been too tired to notice.

I buried my face in the pillow, willing sleep to come again. But as the crying continued, echoing through the dark night, I knew I'd be awake until he stopped.

"Fuck."

That kid was determined, I'd give him that. As I lay on my back, staring at the moonlit ceiling, he cried and cried.

If it was loud here, how loud was it in that loft? I hadn't slept, but neither had Memphis. Though she tried daily, no amount of makeup could hide the dark circles under her eyes.

The image of Griffin holding Hudson popped into my mind. Then another baby, another set of arms from years past. A scene I didn't let myself remember.

Drake's cries built, one upon the next upon the next, louder and louder, minute after minute, night after night, until it was like he was screaming for me. Enough was enough. I couldn't lie here and do nothing.

I flung the sheet off my legs and swung out of bed, stopping at the walk-in closet for a T-shirt. Then I headed for the door, pausing to step into a pair of flip-flops so I didn't shred the soles of my feet on the gravel.

The night air was cool against the bare skin of my arms

and legs as I crossed the driveway. I took the stairs two at a time, moving before I second-guessed my decision, and knocked.

A light flipped on, illuminating the glass window in the door.

Memphis's face was in the glass next, her brown eyes wide and swimming with tears. She looked beautiful. She always looked beautiful. Except tonight she looked to be hanging on by her last thread.

She wiped at her cheeks before flipping the lock. "I'm so—"

"Don't apologize." I stepped inside and kicked off my shoes, then held out my arms, waving with one. "Hand him over."

"W-what?" She shied away, putting a shoulder between me and her baby.

"I'm not going to hurt him. I just want to help." Maybe what that kid needed was another pair of arms. Another voice.

She blinked. "Huh?"

"Listen, if he sleeps, I sleep, you sleep. Can we just...try something other than this? Let me walk him around for a while. Probably won't matter but at the very least, you can take a breather."

Memphis's shoulders fell and she glanced down at her crying son. "He doesn't know you."

"There's only one way to fix that."

She hesitated another moment, but when Drake let out another wail and kicked his tiny feet, she shifted my way.

The handoff was awkward. Her arms seemed reluctant to let him go, but finally, when I had him cradled in the crook of an elbow, she inched away. Her shoulders remained stiff as she wrapped her arms around her middle and barely gave me enough room to breathe.

"I won't drop him," I promised.

She nodded.

I stepped past her, walking the length of the loft. My bare feet sank into the plush carpet, and it wasn't until I'd made it across the room that I finally took a good look at the kid in my arms.

Christ, this was a bad idea. A really fucking bad idea. What the hell had I been thinking? He kept crying, because yeah, he didn't know me. And it was too similar. It was too hard.

The only thing that kept me from bolting was his hair.

He had his mother's blond hair.

Not black, like Jadon's. Blond.

This was not the same child. This was not the same situation.

I swallowed hard, past the ache, and walked toward the door. "Drake."

Blond, baby Drake. It was a great name. He was a solid kid. That was different too. Drake seemed strong. Like Hudson, he had a good weight. And Memphis had been hefting him around on her own every night.

"All right, boss," I told Drake. "We need to tone this down."

His chest shook as his breath hitched between a cry.

"I need sleep. So do you. So does your mom. How about we quit the night shift?" I set out for the opposite end of the room again, passing Memphis, who still hadn't moved. I hit the wall and turned, going to the door again. All while Drake cried.

"You're okay." I bounced him as I walked, patting his

diapered butt. He was in a pair of footed pajamas, the blue print fabric full of puppies. "When I was a kid, I had a dog. Her name was Scout."

I kept walking, slow and measured strides, to the door, then the window. "She was brown with floppy ears and a stubby tail. Her favorite thing in the summer was to run through the yard sprinklers. And in the winter, she'd jump in the biggest snowbanks, burying herself so far down we weren't sure she'd make it out."

Memphis finally unstuck her feet and walked to the couch, perching on an arm. She was in a thin black night shirt with sleeves that draped to her elbows and a neckline that scooped low. The hem ended at her thighs, riding up as she sat.

She wasn't tall, but damn she had some legs. I tore my eyes away from the taut, smooth skin and shifted Drake so he was propped up on a shoulder. Then I patted his back, my hand so long that the base of my palm was at the top of his diaper and my fingertips brushing the soft strands of hair at his nape.

It took one more trip to the door and back before the crying changed to whimpers. Then it vanished, swept away through an open window.

The quiet was deafening.

Memphis gasped. "It usually takes me hours."

"My brother Griffin has a kid this age."

"He's married to Winslow, right?"

I nodded. "Yeah. I was over there tonight and Hudson was not about his mom. But Griffin took him and it settled him down. Probably just a different voice."

Memphis dropped her chin, her blond hair falling around her face. But it couldn't hide the tear that dripped to her lap.

"Do you need me to carry you around too? Pat your back? Tell you about my childhood pets?" I teased.

She looked up and smiled, wiping her face dry. "I'm just really tired."

Drake let out a squawk but didn't start wailing again.

"I can take him," she said.

"Go lie down. I'll walk him until he's asleep."

"You don't—"

"Have to do that." I finished her sentence. "But I'm going to. Go. Rest."

She stood and trudged to the bed, sliding beneath the covers. Then she clung to a pillow, holding it close to her chest. "How did you become a chef?"

"That's not sleeping."

"Tell me anyway."

I walked to the wall and hit the light switch, bathing the loft in darkness. "My mom is a fantastic cook. When I was growing up, my dad was always so busy on the ranch. He'd take Griff with him a lot but I was too young, so I'd stay home with Mom and my twin sisters when they were babies. She'd cart us to the hotel with her during the day, and then in the evenings, she'd put them in swings or a play area and set me on the counter to help make dinner."

My earliest memory was from when I was around five, the summer before I'd started kindergarten. Mom had been pregnant with Eloise. The twins had been little and were always chasing me around. Griff had been learning to ride and I'd felt left out.

Mom had been busy with something so I'd told her I'd make dinner. She must have thought I was kidding because she'd agreed.

It wasn't so much the plates of chips and crackers that I

remembered, it was the shock on her face when she'd come into the kitchen from wrangling the twins and found me sitting on the counter, attempting peanut butter and jelly sandwiches.

"I had other interests. Sports. Horses. I spent my summers working on the ranch beside Griffin and Dad. But I always gravitated back to the kitchen. When I finished high school, I knew college wasn't for me, so I enrolled in culinary school. Learned a lot. Worked at some amazing restaurants until it was time to come home."

Memphis hummed, a dreamy, sleepy sound.

And her son was totally out on my chest.

It was probably safe to put him down, retreat to my own bed, but I kept walking. Just in case.

"Why is it named Knuckles? The restaurant?" Memphis's voice was no more than a whisper, muffled by the pillow.

"It was my nickname in culinary school. My first week I tried to impress an instructor. Got cocky. I was grating some carrots and not paying attention. Slipped and grated my knuckles instead."

"Ouch," she hissed.

"Had a bunch of cuts and made a fool of myself." A few scars still remained on my hand.

"And earned yourself a nickname."

"When we did the restaurant remodel, I sat down with the architect and he asked me about a name for a sign. Knuckles popped into my head and that was it." I drifted off my path and carried Drake to the crib in the corner, bending low to set him down.

His arms instantly rose above his head. His lips parted. His eyelashes formed half-moons above his smooth cheeks. He was...precious.

My hand came to my chest, rubbing at the sting. Then I stood and glanced to the bed.

Memphis was asleep, her lips parted too. A man could lose himself in that sort of beauty.

Before I did something stupid, like stand there and stare at her until dawn, I eased out of the loft, turning the lock on the door behind me before heading to my own bed.

Sleep should have come easy. It was quiet. Dark. Except every time I closed my eyes, the image of Memphis would pop into my head. The blond hair sweeping across her cheek. The part of her lips. The soft swell of her breasts beneath that night shirt.

Maybe her kid's crying hadn't been keeping me from sleep.

Maybe it was the woman herself, haunting my dreams.

CHAPTER 7

MEMPHIS

The thud of footsteps climbing the loft's staircase and the soft knock that followed were becoming my favorite sounds. He might only come up to hold Drake, but every time Knox showed at my door in the middle of the night, it was like a warm hug.

It had been a long time since I'd been hugged.

He came right inside, toeing off his shoes before stealing a crying Drake from my arms. A flash of pain crossed his face, like he'd gotten a papercut. Maybe it was just my imagination, but I swore I saw it each time he held Drake. It was gone in an instant as Knox set out on his regular path across the room.

"What's the problem tonight, boss?" That smooth, deep voice was as comforting to me as it was my son.

"Sorry we woke you up."

He turned at the wall and frowned. Knox, I'd learned, wasn't a fan of my apologies.

I made them regardless.

"Rest, Memphis." He nodded toward the bed, but I went to the couch, wrapping a blanket around my shoulders.

In the past month, I'd spent twelve nights on this couch, watching as the most handsome man I'd ever laid eyes on carried my son. Twelve nights, and my crush on Knox Eden was as strong as the coffee I made each morning in my new maker.

The weather had shifted and October's cold night temperatures meant there was no need to leave the window open. How Knox heard Drake cry from his house, I wasn't sure, but I hadn't mustered the nerve to ask. Whatever, however, he knew, I was simply grateful for the reprieve.

And for a little time alone with a man almost too good to be true.

"Was he like this last night?" Knox asked.

"No. He only cried for a bottle but after I fed him, he went right back to sleep."

"Progress. Just keep growing and we'll get through this." Knox put Drake on his broad shoulder, exactly where my son preferred to be.

Maybe it was because Knox had such a big shoulder to sleep on. Maybe it was his smell or his voice or the easy cadence of his swagger. My son preferred Knox's chest to mine.

My son was no fool.

I was as enchanted as my baby.

Knox was wearing gray sweats tonight that pooled at his feet. He had on a white sleeveless T-shirt, his tattoos on display.

"What do your tattoos mean?" I asked.

It had been on the tip of my tongue for weeks. My curiosity about Knox was as insatiable as it was dangerous. The more I learned, the harder I crushed.

"The eagle is my favorite bird." He nodded to his left side and the feathered wings curled around his biceps. The face of the fierce creature was as haunting as it was beautiful.

Knox passed the couch, shifting to show me his right side. The blue-white nightlights I'd added to the loft illuminated the black lines and circles on his skin. "These are planets. I have one on my shoulder blade that's an outline of Mars. Not that I'm into astronomy. They represent our horses. Dad bought eight horses years ago and Eloise named them all after the planets. Mars is mine."

"Do you go riding often?"

"Not as much as I'd like. I keep him at the ranch so he can have company. I try to take him out once a month or so."

My horse's name had been Lady. She'd pranced around like one too. My sister and I had both taken riding lessons as kids because at the time, it had been the popular extracurricular activity for New York socialites. Then one of Mom's friends had called the activity *antiquated*, refusing to send her own daughters. A week later, my parents had sold Lady and I'd been forced to endure piano lessons instead.

"You ever ride before?" he asked.

"Not for a long time."

He didn't offer to take me out on Mars. I wouldn't have accepted.

This, these dark nights, were all I'd let myself have of Knox.

Drake was making progress and before long, these visits would stop. We'd return to being his temporary tenants. I'd be his coworker, rarely crossing his path. And someday, I'd move on. When that day came, I needed my heart intact. My whole heart.

Drake's crying began to ebb, shifting from a broken string of screams to a whine between hitched breaths.

"There we go," Knox murmured, his hand splayed on the baby's back. The broad shoulder, the hum of our conversation, worked like a charm on Drake every time.

"Shouldn't it be me who makes him stop crying?" The admission slipped from my lips before I could stop it. Guilt and shame clouded my voice. It should be me, shouldn't it? Drake was mine.

"You are." Knox paused in front of me, towering over me with my tiny son in his massive arms. "You let me in the door, didn't you?"

"Yeah." Maybe motherhood wasn't always being the person your child leaned on, but finding the person they needed when you weren't enough. For Drake's sake, for him to get some rest, I'd set aside my pride and let Knox step in to help.

The woman who actually earned his strong arms for real hugs would be a lucky, lucky girl. I snuggled deeper into my blanket, curling my legs beneath me as I followed Knox's every step.

Exhaustion was a constant companion to my waking moments. The only reason I was able to keep my eyes open was because the picture of Knox and Drake was one I didn't want to miss. It was the reason I chose the couch over snuggling into bed.

Watching them together was a dream. A fantasy of a different life had I made better choices.

Drake had stopped crying and was moments away from

sleep. This interlude was nearly over. For my son's sake, I was grateful. For mine...

It would be difficult to close the door behind Knox when he left.

A yawn stretched my lips and I waved it off. "Sorry."

"Now you're apologizing for yawning?" He shot me a grin as he passed the couch.

"My father once scolded me for yawning during a meeting. I apologized then and haven't stopped since."

It was the first time I'd mentioned my father aloud. For over a month, I'd kept my past locked away. I'd dodged questions about my family and the reasons why I'd moved across the country. Sleep deprivation had caused my walls to drop.

Or maybe it was just Knox. He shared freely. He made me want to do the same.

"Seriously?" he asked.

I shrugged.

"You don't talk about your family."

"I don't talk about much."

"This is true." The corner of his mouth turned up. "Where are your parents?"

I sighed, sinking deeper into the couch. "I figured you'd ask eventually. But I haven't figured out how to answer that question yet."

"It's a simple question, Memphis."

"Then the simple answer is New York."

"What's the complicated answer?"

"The truth makes my family seem...ugly." As frustrated as I was with them, I didn't want strangers to think they were bad people. They were who they were. Distant. Self-absorbed. Proud. They were the product of their surroundings and extreme, selfish wealth.

Once, I hadn't been all that different. Maybe they were ugly. But their awful actions had been the catalyst to my change. Because of them, I would be a better person. Despite them.

Knox walked to the door, pausing beside his discarded tennis shoes. "Better let me be the judge."

I glanced to the clock on the microwave. "This isn't really a conversation for two oh seven in the morning."

He crossed the room, taking a seat on the opposite end of the couch with my son asleep on his chest. "Are they less ugly during the day?"

"No," I whispered. "My father never held Drake. You're the only man to ever carry him in your arms."

A crease formed between his eyebrows. "Did he…"

"Die? No. He's very much alive. My parents, my dad in particular, doesn't approve of my choices. He sets the tone for our family, and when I refused to do things his way, he disowned me. My mother, my sister and my brother followed suit. Though it doesn't really matter because I disowned them too."

Knox studied my face. "What do you mean, they disowned you?"

"I worked for my dad. He fired me. I was living in one of their Manhattan townhouses. Drake was four weeks old when his attorney served me my thirty-day eviction notice. My grandparents set up trust funds for each of their grandchildren but required my father be the conservator until we turned thirty. I went in to take out some money so I could move and Dad denied the bank from granting me any withdrawals. He left me with nothing but the money I had in my own bank account and my final paycheck."

"Are you fucking serious? Why?"

"He wants to know who Drake's father is. I refuse to tell him. I refuse to tell anyone." There was a hidden warning in my tone, that if Knox asked, I'd deny him an answer. "Dad didn't like being told that it was none of his business. But there's a reason why no one knows who Drake's father is. I plan to keep it that way."

Knox leaned forward, his hold on Drake tightening. "Is there something I need to know?"

"No. He's gone from my life."

"Are you sure?"

"Quite." I had a signed document to prove it. "My dad thought he'd call my bluff. That if he made my life hard enough, I'd tell him everything he wanted to know. That he could continue to pull my strings and I'd dance as one of his little puppets. I'm twenty-five, not sixteen. My decisions are my own. My secrets are my own."

Knox leaned into the couch, shaking his head. "You're right. I'm not really liking your family at the moment."

"My father isn't used to being told no. He owns a hotel conglomerate. And he runs his family as heavy-handedly as he does his business."

"A hotel?" Knox's eyebrows arched. "Which one?"

"Ward Hotels."

"No shit?" He huffed a laugh. "After culinary school, I worked in San Francisco. The restaurant was in a Ward Hotel."

I blinked. "Really?"

"Small world."

"That it is." And I knew exactly which restaurant he was talking about too.

I'd been to San Francisco numerous times, always staying

at the hotel. Had Knox been the one to cook my meals? It wouldn't surprise me. It had been a favorite place to eat.

"I'm named after Dad's favorite hotel in Memphis. My sister is named Raleigh. My brother is Houston."

Knox studied my profile. "Ward Hotels is not a small company."

"No, it is not."

It was a privately owned multimillion-dollar business. The real estate holdings alone were worth a fortune.

And I'd traded my thirty-million-dollar trust fund for a fourteen-dollar-per-hour housekeeping job.

Maybe it had been a reckless decision driven by betrayal. We didn't have much in Quincy.

But we were free.

"You're cleaning toilets," Knox said.

I raised my chin. "There's nothing wrong with cleaning toilets."

"No, there isn't." He gave me a small nod. "What did you do before you came here? You worked for Ward?"

"I was a marketing executive for the company. My brother is being groomed to take over for my father, but my sister and I grew up knowing we'd always have jobs with the company. We were expected to work there. I started the day after I graduated from college."

"Where did you go to school?"

"I have a degree in sociology from Princeton. Not exactly useful, but it was interesting."

Knox was silent for a long moment, then he laughed. "Princeton. Why did you choose to work at The Eloise? Why not find something that paid more?"

"Hotels are what I've always known." And though I probably could have found a cushy resort and worked my way into a general manager position, Dad had required his executives, including his daughters, to sign a ten-year noncompete.

"It seemed like the easy choice," I said. "Not that the work is easy. It's the hardest job I've ever had. But with so many other changes, I wanted the familiarity of a hotel. Even if I've never cleaned a room in my life."

He blinked. "Seriously? You've never cleaned before this?"

"I had a maid," I admitted. "I watched a lot of videos on YouTube before I started."

"Well...according to Eloise, you're doing a hell of a job."

"Thank you." I was glad it was dark so he wouldn't see me blush. "I won't be a housekeeper forever, but I was never given the chance to choose my own path. When I'm ready, I'll find something that pays more. That leans on my education. There aren't a ton of opportunities in a small town, but I'll keep my eye out. For now, I like where I'm at."

"You could have picked any other town."

I shook my head. "I chose Quincy."

This town was mine.

It was hard to explain how I'd become so attached to this place in such a short time. But every time I drove down Main, it felt more and more like home. Every time I went to the grocery store and my favorite cashier—Maxine— complimented me on having such an adorable baby, I felt my heart settle. Every time I walked into The Eloise, I felt like I belonged.

"My parents would hate it here." I smiled.

"Part of its appeal?"

"At first." I dropped my gaze to my lap. "I know how all of this sounds. It's part of the reason why I haven't told anyone. Poor little rich girl gives up her fortune, moves to Montana, and lives paycheck to paycheck all because she was sick and tired of her father ordering her around."

Saying it aloud made me cringe.

"I didn't turn my life upside down to spite anyone. I did it for Drake. Because I believe in my heart of hearts, this is a better life. Even if it's hard. Even if we're alone." We'd been alone since the beginning.

"Would they have made your life miserable in New York?" Knox asked.

"They would have controlled it. They would have ripped the decisions out of my hands, especially when it came to Drake." He would have had a nanny and been shipped away to boarding school at age ten. "I don't want to live by someone else's rule simply because he pulls the strings with my money."

"I can appreciate that. So what happens when you turn thirty? When he's not in charge of your trust fund?"

"I don't know," I admitted. "I'm not going to hold out hope that the money will be there. I expect my father to find a way to take it himself. Probably buy another hotel in another city."

"Can he do that? Is it legal?"

I lifted a shoulder. "I always have the option to fight. To hire an attorney and go after it. In a few years, maybe I'll feel differently, but at the moment, I don't want any part of it. I had enough money saved up to buy my car. Once I get ahead, I'll see what my options are for buying a house. Right now, it's more important for me to count on myself than anyone else. My family was supposed to be there for me, but on the first-worst day of my life, they let me down. So I've let them go."

His forehead furrowed. "You keep track of your worst days?"

"It's silly, but yes."

"What was the first?"

I gave him a sad smile. "The day I had Drake. It was also the first-best day of my life."

"I get why it was the best day." He splayed his fingers across Drake's back. For whatever reason, he didn't seem ready to put the baby in his crib. Knox simply held him, ensuring that my son slept. "Why was it the first-worst day too?"

"Because I was alone. My brother and father are cut from the same cloth so I hadn't expected much from them, but I thought my mom would at least show at the hospital for the birth of her first grandchild. Maybe my sister. But they all ignored my calls and didn't respond to my texts. I was in labor for seventeen hours."

The crying. The pain. The exhaustion.

That was the day Old Memphis had died. Because she'd realized that the life she'd lived was so shallow that not a single person had come to simply hold her hand. No family. No friends.

"The epidural didn't work," I said. "The doctors finally told me that I had to have an emergency C-section. I woke up a day later after almost dying from a postpartum hemorrhage."

"Fuck," Knox muttered.

"Drake was healthy. That was all that mattered. We camped in the hospital for a couple of weeks, and when they sent us home, I was already planning an exit from the city. When Dad called to tell me that I had to move out, I simply escalated my departure date."

Thankfully, he hadn't fired me until after Drake was born. Or maybe I'd quit. Considering I'd resigned and he'd fired me during the same phone conversation while I'd been in a hospital bed, I wasn't exactly sure how Human Resources had processed that one. All I cared about was that my insurance had still been active, so it had covered my medical bills.

Dad must have thought that after Drake was born, I'd change my mind. That I'd bend to his iron will. Maybe had he shown up at the hospital, I would have.

"I chose Quincy. I applied at the inn. I bought the Volvo, and after Eloise offered me a job, I started searching for rentals here. When I couldn't find one after a week of looking...well, here I am."

"Here you are." There was something in his voice. A fondness where irritation had once been.

Knox and I sat on the couch, eyes locked through the dark.

Now he had my story, or most of it. Some pieces were mine and mine alone. One day, they might be Drake's but that was a worry for the future.

There were pieces to my tale I loathed. Parts of the story where I'd failed. But mostly, I was beginning to feel...proud.

Coming to Quincy had been the right decision.

"You'd better get some sleep." Knox stood from the couch in one fluid movement, taking Drake to his crib. Knox laid him down, brushing the hair away from his forehead, then stood and walked to the door where I waited to see him out.

"Thank you." Like I always apologized when he knocked, I thanked him before he left.

Knox bent to pull on his shoes, then he stood tall and

nodded, reaching for the door's handle. But he paused before stepping outside and into the night. He turned to me, a tower at over six feet tall. In my bare feet, I was only five four.

"You're not alone. Not anymore."

I opened my mouth but no words came out. He was hugging me again, holding me so tight with those invisible arms that I couldn't speak.

Knox lifted his hand to my cheek and tucked an errant lock of hair behind my ear. Just one brush of his fingertips and every nerve ending in my body sparked. My breath hitched.

"Good night, Memphis." Then he was gone, closing the door behind him as he retreated to his house.

A smile ghosted my lips. "Good night, Knox."

CHAPTER 8

KNOX

A bird chirped outside and my gaze snapped to the windows for the hundredth time in an hour. The driveway was empty, just like it had been three minutes ago.

"Gah." I dragged a hand through my hair and swiped the last T-shirt from the pile of clean clothes on my bed, taking it to the closet for a hanger. Then I carted the empty basket to the laundry room and headed for the kitchen.

The dishes were done. The fridge stocked. The entire house clean.

For the first time in months, I'd taken an entire day off. Not a huge feat. The actual accomplishment had been not going into Knuckles on my day off. The restaurant had a tether on my mind and most vacation days, I'd stop to check in. *Mothering*, according to Skip.

But today, I hadn't left my home. I hadn't even called

to see how things were going. Mondays were a quiet day so I doubted there'd be a mad rush, especially at the end of October. Still, my fingers itched to dial the phone simply for the distraction. Simply to take my mind off the clock.

It was six. Shouldn't Memphis be home by now? I wasn't actually sure what time she came home—I was always at the restaurant—but her shift ended at five. Where was she?

Five days had passed since she'd told me about her family. Five days and five nights without Memphis. The restaurant had been busy over the weekend with a rush of hunters staying at the hotel. Our paths hadn't crossed. And each night when I'd come home after dark, the lights had been off in the loft. Drake hadn't woken me up.

With or without his crying, I'd be going over tonight.

I just...damn it, I missed her. I missed the sweet scent of her perfume. I missed her soft whisper. I missed the way she'd duck her chin to hide a blush.

I'd find an excuse to visit, even if it was just to stay hello. To let her know that the story she'd shared about her parents hadn't scared me away. No wonder she'd escaped to Montana.

What she'd gone through, alone, was unthinkable.

My family was nothing but supportive—borderline overbearing, but only because they cared. Not in a million years would Mom and Dad treat their daughters the way Memphis had been treated. Not in a million years would they not have held their grandchild.

Fuck, but she was strong. I respected the hell out of her for walking away. From the money. From the legacy. From the control. I admired her for putting her son's life first.

Risky as it was, I had to see her. And hopefully I'd manage to keep from kissing her.

Because damn, did I want to kiss her. Like I'd almost kissed her the other night.

Six eleven. Why didn't I know her schedule? What if she needed help? Who would she call? Did she even have my number?

The tap of my fingers on the granite counters filled the quiet house. I'd thought I'd miss this. The quiet. The solitude. But I'd had this anxious knot in my gut all day, the place too still. Too empty. Where was she?

Housework hadn't helped settle the nerves. Neither had cleaning out the garage. All three stalls were now clean, giving both Memphis and me plenty of space to park once the snow arrived. I hadn't planned on cooking today. I had plenty of leftovers to pick at.

But I needed an outlet, anything to get my mind off the empty driveway, so I stalked to the pantry and took out a bag of semolina flour.

It shouldn't have taken long to make pasta dough and roll it out. Except every thirty seconds I glanced down the lane, hoping to see a gray Volvo heading my direction. The only thing beyond the glass was a chilly fall day.

The grasses in the meadows had faded from green to gold. The ponderosa pines were dusted with frost. The mountains in the distance were capped white.

Fall was my favorite season, and other than a small influx of hunters to the area, there were more familiar faces than not on Main these days. We'd be slow at the hotel until the holidays. This was the time to catch up on some rest.

But today had been anything but relaxing, and if I was going to feel this way on a day off, well...I'd *mother* Skip until Christmas.

With the pasta cut and ready, I found a pot and set it to

boil. Then I pulled a bundle of baby spinach and mushrooms from the fridge. I was digging for cream to make a simple sauce when, outside, gravel crunched beneath tires.

The smart thing to do would be stay right here, my face buried in my refrigerator, but I slammed it shut and strode for the front door.

Memphis was unlocking Drake's car seat when I stepped outside. She stood tall, hefting his carrier over an arm, and when she glanced over the Volvo's roof, my heart dropped. Her face was splotchy. Her eyes were rimmed in red like she'd cried the entire drive here. And Drake was screaming.

It reminded me of her first day in Quincy. I hadn't liked seeing it then. I sure as fuck didn't like seeing it now.

"What's wrong?" I crossed the driveway, moving right into her space and taking the handle of the car seat.

"Nothing." She waved it off and sniffled. "Just a Monday."

"Memphis," I warned.

"I'm fine." She reached into the car and pulled out Drake's diaper bag before shutting the door and moving to the trunk, lifting it open. Another tear, one that she hadn't been able to dry, dripped down her cheek.

I didn't like to see Drake cry. But Memphis? It was like getting the wind knocked out of me.

"Hey." I went to her side and fit my hand to her elbow. "What happened, honey?"

"I just..." Her shoulders sagged. "I had a bad day."

Had something happened at the hotel? Was it about her family? Or Drake's father? There were a hundred unanswered questions when it came to Memphis and her past, but Drake was crying and now wasn't the time to dig.

So I reached past her for the package of diapers in the trunk, then strode for the door.

"Where are you going?" she called to my back as I walked toward my place, not hers.

"Taking these inside."

"You're going the wrong way."

"Come on." I kept walking straight for my house, where the scent of floor cleaner and laundry soap clung to the air.

As I made my way to the kitchen with the baby, the door closed behind me. I set the diapers on the island along with Drake's seat, unbuckling him as Memphis's footsteps sounded over my shoulder.

"This bad day. Did it rank in your top five?"

She came up beside me, watching as I lifted Drake from his seat. "No."

"Good."

Before I could settle Drake on my shoulder, she stole her son from my hands, cradling him in her arms. Then she breathed, a breath so deep and long it was like she'd been underwater for five minutes and was finally breaking through the surface.

She closed her eyes and peppered Drake's forehead with kisses. His fussing stopped almost immediately.

How could she not see how much she settled him? Yeah, maybe they struggled at one in the morning. But that kid needed her like she needed him. Those two were destined to be together.

Watching them was like intruding on a ritual, a moment that they had each day, coming home and finding peace together.

I gave them a minute, heading to the fridge to uncork a bottle of pinot grigio and pour two glasses.

"You're busy," she said. "We won't interrupt your night."

I carried over her glass of wine. "Stay for dinner."

"What are you making?" She hovered at the corner of the island, surveying the pasta and vegetables on the cutting board.

"Dinner." I smirked. "You'll find out if you stay."

She rolled her eyes, a smile toying at the corner of her pretty mouth. But she took the wine and her shoulders began their slow creep away from her ears. "Thank you."

"Make yourself at home."

With Drake on her hip, she glanced around the space. "You weren't at the restaurant today."

"You noticed?"

She shrugged. "I usually park beside your truck."

That, or she looked for me. Maybe as often as I looked for her.

I went to the cutting board and began chopping the spinach while she rifled through the diaper bag and took out a bottle with powdered formula in the bottom.

She eased past me for the sink, filling the bottle with water before shaking it up. Then she walked to the living room, taking a seat on the couch to feed Drake.

I dropped the pasta into the boiling water, then picked up her wineglass, taking it to her in the living room.

"You have a beautiful home." There was a sadness in her expression as she spoke.

"What's that look for?" I perched on the edge of the coffee table, my knees just inches from hers.

It was too close.

It wasn't close enough.

Whatever lines I'd intended to keep between us were melting away.

"I don't know what's wrong with me today." She looked down at Drake. "He's almost four months old. How did that happen? How did he grow so fast?"

"I've been told that's what kids do."

She gave me a sad smile. "Do you think he loves me?"

"Look at him and you'll get your answer."

Because that little boy was staring at his mother like she'd hung the moon and stars. He chugged his bottle, resting in her arms without a care in the world.

She closed her eyes and nodded. Then she straightened, shaking off the sadness. "This is not your typical Montana-style home. Not that I've been to many. But it's different than anything I've seen driving through town. It's very modern."

"If you're looking for traditional country homes, you'll have to visit my parents' place. Or Griff and Winn's."

"This suits you. The clean lines. The windows. The moody atmosphere."

"Are you saying I'm moody?"

She smiled wider, the biggest victory in my day. "Look in the mirror and you'll get your answer."

"Well played, Ms. Ward." I chuckled and stood, returning to the kitchen.

Memphis finished feeding Drake, then carried him to the island, watching as I worked. "Why did you choose this style of design?"

"When I was living in San Francisco, I was in this cramped, two-bedroom apartment with three total windows. They all faced the brick building across the alley. Drove me nuts not being able to look outside and see farther than twenty feet."

No trees. No grass. Not even the sky. For a Montana guy who'd grown up on a sprawling ranch, that apartment might as well have been a prison cell.

"When I moved home, I knew I wanted to live in the country, but I was selective about the property. My parents and Griffin suggested a part of the ranch, but I wanted to be closer to town. When the winter roads are shit, they don't have to leave but I have to drive into town each day. I took my time, waiting for the right property to come on the market. While I waited, I lived in the caretaker's apartment at the hotel."

"Oh, I didn't know there was a caretaker's apartment."

"Apartment is a generous term," I said. "It was smaller than your loft. But it's gone now. It was beside the kitchen, and when we remodeled, I took the wall out to use that space for the walk-in and my office."

"Ah." She nodded. "I'm guessing there were no windows in that apartment."

"Not one. I was so tired of artificial light that when I bought this land and hired my architect, I told him that I wanted enough windows that I could see outside from every inch of the house. Even the bathrooms."

Her eyes scanned the walls. "Now I have to see these bathrooms."

I chuckled and pointed down the hallway. "There's two down that way. And then one in my suite. Go ahead. I'll finish this up while you check it out."

She smiled and went off exploring, taking Drake with her.

I watched her disappear, my gaze raking down her slender shoulders to the soft sway of her hips. Her jeans clung to the curve of her ass and those lean, long legs. The tendrils of her hair swished against her waist.

Damn that hair. So often at work, she had it up in a ponytail. When I went to the loft, it was usually in a messy bun. It was longer than I'd realized. And all I wanted was to wrap those blond waves around my fist while I took her mouth. I wanted that hair spread on my pillow and threaded between my fingers.

My cock swelled. "Focus," I muttered.

I finished with the pasta, making the sauce and adding the vegetables. Then I served us each a bowl, topping it with fresh parmesan and Italian parsley. I was refilling her wine glass as she passed the kitchen, heading toward my bedroom.

With napkins and forks out, I set up Drake's car seat on the table so he could sit and watch us eat.

"Do you ever worry that someone will walk into your backyard and catch you in the shower?" Memphis asked as she returned to the room.

The living room, kitchen and dining room were all connected in an open concept. It meant that from the kitchen, I could still participate in conversations when I had people over.

"Nah. No one comes out here. I did have a deer check me out this summer."

She giggled, another win, and put Drake in his seat. Then she took the chair closest to him and placed the napkin on her lap. "Thank you for this. For making me dinner and making me smile."

"That's two thank-yous since you've walked through the door." She opened her mouth but I held up a hand to stop her. "Don't apologize."

"Okay." A laugh sparkled in those chocolate-brown eyes, the caramel flecks dancing. That laugh shot straight to my groin.

"Dig in." I swallowed hard and picked up my fork, but it froze midair as she twirled a bite of pasta and lifted it to her mouth. When her head lolled to one side as she chewed and she closed her eyes, a look of sheer pleasure crossed her face.

A look I wanted to see while I was buried inside her tight heat.

She didn't even realize her beauty, did she? Memphis was a sweet temptation and a sinful craving.

Drake kicked in his chair, letting out a happy squeal. I dropped my gaze to my bowl, focusing on the meal instead of his mother.

"This is delicious," she said.

"It's fairly simple."

"Maybe for you."

"Do you cook much?" I asked.

She shook her head. "No. My parents had a chef growing up. And I ate out a lot in the city."

"Want me to teach you how to cook?"

"Maybe." Another smile. Another victory.

Drake made another string of noises, keeping us both entertained as we ate.

"I guess he didn't have much of a nap at daycare today." Memphis pinched his shoe-covered foot. "Maybe he'll actually sleep all night."

"Maybe." I hated that I hoped he didn't.

"I wanted to tell you that I think I found a new rental."

The fork dropped from my hand, clattering into my empty bowl. "What? Where?"

When Eloise had asked me to give Memphis the loft, she'd said Memphis would likely be out by winter. Well, winter was just around the corner, and the idea of her moving made my stomach twist.

It was too soon, right? She'd just moved here. They were

just getting settled into a routine. What was the goddamn rush?

"It's not far from the hotel, actually." She rattled off the address and my heart climbed down from my throat.

"You can't live there."

Her forehead furrowed. "Why not?"

"Because I know which place you're talking about. A light-blue duplex, right?"

"Yeah."

"I almost moved in there when I came back to Quincy. It has a pretty high turnover because it's right by Willie's."

"What's Willie's?"

"A bar and the local hangout. It'll be loud."

"Oh." She frowned. "I was just there and it was quiet."

"It's a Monday. Drive by on Friday or Saturday night."

"Dang." She sighed. "Well, I promise I'm looking."

"Don't worry about it. You can stay here as long as you need."

In the weeks she'd been here, I'd grown attached to her car in the driveway. I'd gotten used to looking for her light in the mornings. And I liked knowing she was asleep, close by, when I came home each night.

"This was a temporary arrangement," she said.

"Do you want to leave?" I held my breath, waiting for the answer.

"No."

Thank fuck. "Stay. You don't need to move out."

"Are you sure?"

I shrugged. "It will be a lot easier to teach you how to cook if you're my neighbor."

She smiled again and stood, collecting our empty dishes. "I'll clean up."

"You've been cleaning all day."

"I don't mind." She moved around the kitchen easily.

I stared unabashedly.

I didn't like having people in my kitchen. Even Mom and Lyla knew not to intrude when they came over. For Memphis, I'd make an exception.

"I'd better get Drake home and in the bath," she said as she hung a dish towel on the oven's handle.

"I'll carry him up."

She didn't argue as I hoisted Drake with one arm, using my free hand to take the car seat while Memphis hauled her purse and the diapers to the loft. When her things were put away and Drake was lying on a blanket, she walked me to the door. "Thanks again for dinner."

"Welcome." The lock of hair, the same one I'd tucked behind her ear the other night, fell across her forehead.

My fingertips smoothed it away, earning a hitch in her breath. Her gaze dropped to my mouth.

I inched closer, until the curve of her pert breasts brushed against my T-shirt.

She rose up on her toes, her hand lifting to my pec. Her palm pressed into my hard nipple.

I was leaning down, ready to take that mouth and make it mine, when Drake cooed.

My entire body tensed before I took a step away. *Damn.* The pretty pink blush on Memphis's cheeks matched the color of her lips. "I gotta go."

"Yeah." She shied away. "I'd, um…better get him ready for bed."

"Night." I forced myself out the door and to my house for a cold shower. Then I spent the rest of the night reading—or staring at the same page for hours because my concentration was shit, thanks to that almost kiss.

God, I wanted her. It had been a long time since I'd craved a woman. Her body. Her mind. Her time. I wanted it all.

Except...Drake.

The kid changed everything.

Darkness crept through the house as I crawled into bed, wishing for the first time that I wasn't beneath this roof alone.

My parents and siblings used to drop by more often. But that was before Hudson was born, and now we all seemed to congregate at Griff and Winn's place so that he was close to his crib.

Memphis and Drake had brought life to my home. Laughter and noise that I hadn't even realized I'd wanted.

I hated giving cooking lessons. It was my own personal brand of torture. But for the chance to have Memphis here, just a little while longer, I'd endure.

Memphis. Her name was on my mind as I drifted off to sleep.

Memphis. I never had found out why she'd been crying when she'd come home.

And the next morning, when she came down the loft's stairs with a bright smile, I decided not to ask.

CHAPTER 9

MEMPHIS

Drake cried the minute I lifted him out of Jill's arms. "Come on, baby. Time to go home."

Every day it seemed harder and harder to pick him up from daycare. She seemed more reluctant to let him go. And he was fussier to be swept away.

"It's okay, Drakey." Jill smoothed out his hair. "You have to go with your mom now. But I'll see you tomorrow."

The way she said *your mom* grated on my nerves. Like I was an intruder here, not his parent. I forced a tight smile, practically ripping him out of her reach. "Thanks, Jill."

Drake kept crying, staring at her like she should save him.

"Have a fun night." Her smile looked forced and tight too.

Jill was probably in her mid-twenties. Her brown hair

was cut into a bob and she had these cute black-framed glasses. When we'd met, I'd thought it was great that she was so young. Her aunt owned the daycare center and she'd been working here for years. I'd actually thought maybe we could be friends.

Now, I wanted to spend the least amount of time with her as possible.

"Bye." I picked up the diaper bag and carried Drake to his car seat, shoving aside the Halloween costume she'd put on him to get the straps over his shoulders. The harness was too tight because this wasn't the costume I'd put him in this morning.

Apparently my homemade lamb outfit hadn't been good enough.

When I'd arrived five minutes ago, I'd found Drake in a pumpkin suit, complete with a green hat.

Jill had bought it herself, just for him. The other three babies in the nursery didn't have special costumes, but Drake was her favorite and she made no qualms about showing it daily.

I doubted he'd been put down since I'd dropped him off this morning. Jill carried him constantly, so at home, when I would lay him on a play mat or put him in a bouncer just so I could go to the bathroom or try and fix a meal or change my clothes, he'd scream his tiny head off.

I'd asked her this morning to make sure he had some floor mat playtime. She'd laughed and teased that he was just too cute to let go.

Tears welled in my eyes as he cried, his voice bouncing down the hallway. The daycare center was a house the owner had converted for childcare. There were four rooms, each for different age groups.

I'd hoped that Drake could stay here, advancing to the various rooms as he got older, but I couldn't keep doing this. I couldn't show up here every day, leave him with a heavy heart, then pick him up and cry on the way home because he wanted Jill, not me.

It was an entirely selfish reaction. I'd been chastising myself for weeks.

He was happy here. That's why he cried. She spoiled him because she loved him. That wasn't a bad thing, was it? Why did I feel this awful?

A week ago, the night Knox had made me pasta, I'd almost answered the phone when it had rung. I'd almost caved. Yesterday had been the same. The most recent call marked 126 total. I'd declined them all. But damn, it was tempting.

I could go back to New York and live off someone else's money. I could be a stay-at-home mom until Drake went to kindergarten. No more cleaning hotel rooms. No more eating Cup Noodles. No more budget.

No more freedom.

Don't give up.

The snow was falling in a polka-dot curtain as I hurried Drake to the car. It had started snowing around noon, and the weather showed no signs of changing.

"So much for trick-or-treating." I'd have to settle for a stop at the hotel, where Eloise had a bowl of candy. Then we'd go home.

I just wanted to be home.

With Drake's seat latched, I slid behind the wheel and brushed away the unshed tears. Then I squared my shoulders and drove to The Eloise, parking beside Knox's truck in the alley.

I ducked my head as I walked inside so the flakes wouldn't fly in my face. The blanket I'd put over Drake kept him dry until I made it to the break room, where I went about changing my son into his actual Halloween costume.

The pumpkin suit was stuffed in the trash.

It would be easier if Jill didn't like Drake. So much easier. What kind of mother wanted her son's caregiver to dislike him? A jealous one.

"Why am I such a mess?"

Drake stared at me but didn't give me an answer. He'd stopped crying on the drive over.

I had to get over this issue with Jill. This had to end.

She bugged me. God, she bugged me. It was her attitude toward me that rubbed raw. But I didn't have a lot of options.

There weren't other daycare centers with infant openings. I'd called every single one last week. And it wasn't like I could talk to the owner. What would I even say? Tell your niece to stop loving my child so much?

Jill spoiled him. So what? I could not. That was my sad reality. I couldn't afford an expensive costume or to stay home with him all day, carting him around on a hip. Somehow, I had to get rid of this gnawing envy and just let her favor my son.

And I'd settle for the moments that were mine. Like tonight.

I tugged the hat I'd made over Drake's hair and blew a raspberry on his neck, earning a smile. "I'm not so bad, am I?"

He kicked his legs, squirming to be picked up.

I lifted him into my arms and kissed his soft cheek. "You're a cuter lamb than you are a pumpkin."

I'd taken a white onesie and glued cotton balls all over it, then done the same with a white cap. Then I'd pulled the onesie over a long-sleeved black shirt and matching pants. With a pair of black felt ears, he was a little fluffy lamb.

The majority of the trick-or-treating would happen in the local neighborhoods tonight, but Eloise had made sure that any kids who stopped by here wouldn't leave empty-handed. She'd splurged on king-sized Reese's Cups, Butterfingers and Twix.

I expected the leftovers would be in the break room tomorrow morning. Hopefully I could snag a Snickers for breakfast.

With his car seat stowed in the corner of the room, I carried Drake to the lobby, where a cluster of people were gathered around the candy bowl.

"Memphis." Eloise waved me over to the huddle. She was wearing a black witch's hat and held the broomstick she'd been toting all day.

"Hey, Memphis." Winslow stood beside a handsome man who looked a lot like Knox—which was why I thought he was handsome.

"Hi, Winn." I'd seen her a few times at the hotel when she'd come down with her grandfather for lunch. As the chief of police, she usually wore her badge and gun. Tonight, a baby boy about Drake's age, dressed as a lion, was propped on her hip instead.

"I'm Griffin Eden." His blue eyes crinkled at the sides as he held out his hand. Though he had the same height and build as his brother, Griffin lacked the tattoos and bearded jaw. "Nice to meet you."

"You too."

Griffin was one of the last Eden siblings I had yet to meet.

Lyla visited the hotel often, usually bringing along a tray of her pastries from Eden Coffee. Mateo, the youngest, worked as a front desk clerk. The days when he was around I'd walk through the lobby and usually see at least one woman flirting with him at the counter. It was always a different girl.

Now the only sibling I had yet to meet was Lyla's twin, Talia. She was a doctor at the hospital and I'd meet her at Drake's four-month checkup next week. When I'd called to make my appointment, they'd told me I'd be seeing Dr. Eden.

In my short time in town, I'd learned that the Edens were practically famous. An Eden had founded Quincy and their family had lived here for generations. Their ranch was one of the largest in the state and they had their fair share of businesses in the area, in addition to the hotel.

Apparently the Edens were a big deal in Quincy.

In New York, a family of prestige would have flaunted it. The Wards certainly did. But every Eden I'd met seemed so humble. So real. Like Knox.

It was a thrill, meeting his family. Knowing the people who loved him most. Maybe that was because Oliver had hidden his life from me. Because I'd been his dirty little secret.

I wasn't sure what was happening with Knox. He'd almost kissed me the other night. I would have let him. My better judgment screamed at me to keep our relationship platonic. Stay on this side of the line, where he was just a friend.

"Hey." The deep rumble of his voice sent a rush of

shivers down my spine.

Hell. This was the problem with that line. Every time he was around, I wanted to cross it.

I turned to watch Knox cross the lobby. He'd shed his chef's coat and was in a long-sleeved thermal, the sleeves pushed up his sinewed forearms.

My heart did its expected skip.

He glanced my way as he walked but otherwise, his focus was on his brother. "You guys here for dinner?"

Griffin held out a hand to shake with Knox. "No, we're heading to Mom and Dad's so they can see Hudson's costume. But we thought we'd raid the candy dish here first."

"Raid away." Eloise handed Winn four candy bars. "Two for Hudson. And two for the baby."

"Thanks." Winn splayed her hand over her flat belly. "This one loves the sugar."

"Maybe that means you're having a girl." Eloise smiled.

Winn's belly was flat, not yet showing. Just the idea of adding another baby to the mix would have sent my head spinning. But she had help. She had a husband.

I had a Knox. Sort of. For now. Whatever that meant.

"We're going to head out," Griffin said. "Get to the ranch before the roads get worse. See ya later."

The phone rang from the other side of the lobby as Griffin escorted his family out the glass doors.

"Will you man the candy dish for me?" Eloise asked and before I could figure out if she was asking me or Knox, she ran away, broom in hand, to the reception counter.

"All decked out, huh, boss?" Knox raised a hand to touch Drake's nose, but pulled it back at the last minute. The flash of anguish was there and gone before I could blink.

"I made it. It's not perfect but..."

He met my gaze and it was like those blue eyes could see my every insecurity, my every doubt. "What are your plans? Trick-or-treating?"

"No, it's too cold. Eloise told me how much candy she bought and was worried no one would come."

"Are you heading home? Or can you stick around for a while?"

Home was the right choice, but all that waited for me in the loft was laundry and his hated blue-box macaroni and cheese. "Um…stick?"

"Good. Come on."

"What about the candy dish?"

Knox grabbed a handful of bars, grinned and nodded for me to follow.

I fought a smile and walked with him through the lobby, waving at Eloise as she waved back, hanging up the phone to return to her post by the door.

"It's so quiet in here," I said as we walked through Knuckles. All but one table was empty.

"First snow. Halloween." Knox pointed to a booth. "Take a seat. Be right back."

"Okay." I picked the table in the farthest corner in case Drake got fussy. Then I set him on my lap, bouncing him lightly and handing him a spoon to grasp in his chubby fist.

It was strange to sit at a table like I was an actual guest. With the exception of fast food drive-thrus on the trip to Montana, I hadn't been out to eat since New York.

Knox's menu had the perfect blend of lighter fare and heavy entrées. None of it was in my budget. Not even the McDonald's dollar menu was in my budget. But that didn't matter because Knox had been regularly dropping off meals.

He'd worked every night the past week so there'd been no cooking lessons or visits to his home. But each night, after dark, when Drake was sleeping and I was curled in bed, rereading one of the e-books I'd bought in my former life, Knox had stopped over on his way home.

The visits had been wordless. I'd see the flash of his headlights. I'd feel the vibration of the garage door open and close. I'd hear the thud of his footsteps on the steps.

Up, then down the staircase without a knock in between before he disappeared into his house.

The first night, I'd rushed to the door, wrapped in a blanket. He'd already been halfway across the driveway. One glance over his shoulder, then he'd nodded at the to-go container at my feet.

The first night, he'd brought chicken chili. The second, a stew with fresh bread. The list went on. Those meals gave me something to look forward to. Something warm and comforting to greet me at home.

The swinging door to the kitchen opened and he strode out with two plates, each loaded with what looked like pulled pork sandwiches. He set them down, one on my side, one on his, then slid into the booth.

"You looked hungry." He popped a french fry in his mouth.

"You don't have to feed me."

He shrugged. "I tweaked my barbeque sauce recipe. Give me your honest opinion and we'll call it square."

My stomach growled, and I shifted Drake to pick up the sandwich. The first bite was…incredible. I closed my eyes, savoring the smoky sweetness, and let out a moan. "Wow."

Knox's gaze was locked on my lips. His jaw was clenched.

"Sorry," I whispered.

"You're apologizing for eating?"

No, I'd apologized for the moan. I had ears. I knew how it had sounded. The last thing we needed was more sexual tension.

"Don't," he ordered, shaking his head. "How was your day?"

"Good." Up until daycare pickup, it had been fine. "There weren't many rooms to clean today and the other housekeeper wanted to head home early so it was just me."

"It'll probably be quiet for a couple more weeks until Thanksgiving. I bet you could take a few days off if you wanted."

"That's okay." I needed the hours. "I've been thinking about something."

"Yeah?"

"Last week, you said I could stay. I'd like to until spring, if that's okay." The idea of moving in the winter was daunting. Not that my apartment hunt had yielded any other possibilities.

"Like I said, stay as long as you need."

Need, not want. I hadn't realized it until just now, but he'd said need last week too. Not want. Need.

There was a difference. One that caused a stiffness to creep into my shoulders.

I set my sandwich down and sat a little taller. "Then I'd like to pay more rent."

Knox chuckled.

"It's not a joke."

"I know it wasn't a joke. But it's unnecessary."

"Your place is two hundred dollars cheaper a month than any other place I looked at."

A crease formed between his eyebrows. "I thought you

just looked at the one next to Willie's."

"I called a few more."

Now it was his turn to put his sandwich down. "When?"

"Ever since I moved in. The loft was only supposed to be a temporary spot."

"But you don't need to move."

There was that word again. *Need*. "Then let me pay more rent. Let me make it fair."

"No. It's fair already."

"That's ridiculous."

Knox scowled. "You wasting money is ridiculous. Save it. Spend it on a Halloween costume or whatever."

I flinched and stared at Drake. Three of the cotton balls I'd glued onto his hat were coming apart. Maybe that was why Jill had bought a costume. Because she'd had no faith that I could make one on my own.

Because she was better.

"Why won't you let me pay more?" I asked, my voice weak.

"Because you don't—"

"Need to?" I finished for him. The slime of shame crept across my skin, and a realization with it. Is that how this family saw me? As a charity case?

It would make sense. It made sense why Eloise had given me the best shifts. How she'd set me up with an apartment. Why Knox made sure to keep me fed.

"Memphis, I don't need the rent money."

"It's not about you needing the money." I met his gaze and the pity in his eyes was crippling. "It's about me being able to pay it."

"But you don't need to, honey."

Honey. This was the second time he'd called me honey. I'd missed the undertone the first time, but at the moment, it felt like an endearment he'd give a child. Someone less.

Me. I was less.

"The sauce is delicious." I pried the spoon from Drake's fist, then slid out of the booth. "Excuse me."

"Memphis."

I didn't stop moving as he stood too. But he didn't follow as I hurried from the restaurant straight to the break room to collect Drake's things. Then we were out the door, rushing through the storm to my car.

There were no tears as I drove through town to the highway, navigating that familiar path to Juniper Hill. I was too stunned to cry. Whatever confidence I'd built here in Quincy melted, like the snowflakes that hit my windshield.

How had I not seen this? How could I be so blind? The Edens were a wealthy and well-known family. Wealthy and well-known families didn't associate with people like me unless they were trying to save them. Save the poor people.

How many galas had I attended where that had been the unspoken cause?

I was the poor, helpless woman who'd come to Quincy with her belongings in the trunk of a car. I was the woman who couldn't afford decent meals, so I got the leftovers. I was the girl who'd never cleaned a room before her first day as a housekeeper.

Eloise had given me compliment after compliment since I'd started working at the hotel. But she swept through every room after I was done. Every single one. She always had one or two pairs of white slippers in her hand, a complimentary gift for the guests. Except I could have added the slippers myself.

Had she fixed my mistakes? Had she sent in another housekeeper to clean what I'd missed?

My stomach was in knots by the time I parked in the garage at home. I took Drake inside and fed him a bottle before peeling off his silly costume. More cotton balls came loose and by the time I had him naked for his bath, it all sat in a sad heap on the floor.

I'd hoped to save that costume, to put it in a bin with his baby shoes and hospital bracelet. Instead, when Drake was dressed in his pajamas and in his bouncer, I balled it up and tossed it in the trash. It was garbage. It hurt so badly that I pressed a hand to my chest, rubbing at the ache.

The phone rang from where I'd left it on the kitchen counter. I froze, staring at it from a distance. The name was unreadable from where I stood but I knew who it was.

Let it ring.

But I moved closer, staring at that green button.

This could all stop. The hard work. The tears. The pain. All I had to do was answer that call. All I had to do was hit that green button.

No more rent checks. No more time clocks. No more toilet-bowl cleaner and rubber gloves.

No more Eden family charity.

I raised my hand, my finger poised above the screen. One touch to answer phone call number 127 and life would be easier again.

All I had to do was sacrifice…me.

All I had to do was give up.

Don't give up.

Give up, Memphis.

My hand trembled and I touched the screen. But I was too late. It had already kicked to my voicemail.

The air rushed from my lungs and that's when the tears came in steady streams with sobs that I'd been holding back for too long.

The sound of knuckles tapping on my door cut through my hysterics. My face whipped to the window, and there he stood. His expression was unreadable. I hadn't heard him drive in or pull into the garage.

I turned away so he couldn't see me wipe away the tears. He'd caught me crying, but considering I cried most days, considering he was probably here just to drop off a meal because it would be bad if their charity case starved to death, who the hell cared?

Not me. Not anymore. I was numb.

I squared my shoulders and walked to the door. The second I flipped the lock, he marched inside, stomping off his boots. And then he looked down at me with a scowl, like my tears just pissed him off. "If you want to pay more rent, fine. Pay more rent."

"I do. And I want you to stop making me food."

"No."

"I'm not a charity case, Knox."

His hands fisted on his hips. "Is that what you think? That I cook for you because you can't cook for yourself?"

"Well...yes."

He scoffed, turning his head to the ceiling. His Adam's apple bobbed as he muttered something. Then he faced me again, taking a long step forward to crowd my space. "I cook for you because it's how I show someone I care. I cook for you because I love the look on your face after that first bite. I cook for you because I'd rather cook for you than anyone else."

"What?" My jaw dropped.

"I don't know what the fuck I'm doing with you, woman."

My mouth was still open.

Which suited Knox just fine.

Because he raised his hands, framed my face. Then sealed his lips over mine.

CHAPTER 10

KNOX

I was a man who remembered few kisses. Maybe that was a guy thing. But I could only recall with clarity three.

My first. It was the summer before my freshman year in high school with a girl—*what was her name?*—at the summer fair. Then there was the time I'd kissed one of Lyla's friends when she'd been over for a sleepover. Memorable not because of the actual kiss, but because Dad had busted us making out in the closet and the next day he'd made me stack hay bales for eight hours.

And then Gianna. I remembered the kiss I'd given her before leaving San Francisco.

The last kiss.

Beyond those, they all blended together. The women too. In the years since I'd moved home to Quincy, I kept sex casual. I hooked up with tourists—uncomplicated nights, because come morning, they'd be gone from Quincy, easily forgotten.

In years, not one had made a mark.

Until Memphis.

I rubbed a hand over my lips, still feeling her mouth from last night. Her sweet taste, mixed with salty tears, lingered on my tongue.

"Goddamn it." What the fuck had I been thinking? This was Memphis. There hadn't been an uncomplicated minute spent with her. But damn it, when she'd answered the door last night, tear-stained and chin raised and undeniably beautiful, I'd shut off the rational part of my brain and said *fuck it*.

Her mouth had been heaven. Warm and wet. Her lips a fucking dream. Soft, yet firm. At first, she'd been hesitant, shocked probably, but then she'd melted into me and proved that she knew how to use her tongue.

Thinking of that wicked mouth had kept me up most of the night.

Temptation had almost bested me. But instead of pushing inside and carrying her to bed, I'd pulled away and retreated to my house, where a cold shower hadn't done much to cool the desire in my veins.

I craved her, more than I'd craved anyone in a long, long time. And that scared the hell out of me.

If this ended badly, she'd move out and go where? The rental by the bar? Or worse, another town? I didn't want to be the guy who sent her running from Montana and back to that fucking family of hers in New York.

Yesterday's snow had covered the ground. The driveway was a pristine sheet of white except for the twin tracks that led from the garage and down the road. Memphis had already left to drop Drake at daycare and head to the hotel. By rights, I should be gone by now too. There was plenty of work to do.

But I stood at the glass in my bedroom and stared at my loft.

No, not mine. It was hers. That loft would always belong to Memphis, even after she left.

There were things to say. Memphis and I had a long conversation in our future, mostly about how she thought she was a charity case. I'd be clearing up that bullshit soon. We needed to talk about the kiss. What she wanted. What I wanted.

What the hell did I want?

Her. But it wasn't quite that simple. Not with Drake.

With the guest count low at the hotel, it would be a quiet day at Knuckles. On Wednesdays, Lyla brought over pastries from the coffee shop for the guest breakfast. Skip was there this morning to make a spread of scrambled eggs, ham and bacon. Prep work was inevitable, but when I finally tore myself away from the window and headed to my truck, it wasn't to drive into town.

I aimed my wheels for the ranch.

Maybe this was Griffin's place now. It would always be Mom and Dad's. But the ranch was mine too. It belonged to our hearts.

There was a line of hay in a snowy meadow and it was surrounded by grazing cattle. The Eden brand on their ribs, an *E* with a curve in the shape of a rocking chair's runner beneath, gave me a sense of pride at my family's accomplishments. Driving through the gated archway always made my shoulders relax.

Mom and Dad's house was the epicenter of the ranch.

Their log house was surrounded by a shop and the stables. The barn had a loft too, an inspiration for my own, and Uncle Briggs had just moved in.

Mateo had offered the space so Briggs could be closer to our parents in the hopes they could monitor his dementia. Meanwhile Matty had taken Briggs's cabin in the mountains.

That was how we were raised. We watched out for each other.

Two of the hired men walked out of the barn as I pulled up, both wearing Carhartt coats and Stetsons. They climbed into a truck with the Eden brand emblazoned on the door's side. I waved as they rolled out of the gravel lot and headed down the gravel road that wove through the meadows and trees to Griffin's place.

The snow on Mom's Cadillac was already melting under the bright morning sun. By midafternoon, it would all be gone. This storm had just been a teaser for what was to come.

I parked beside Dad's truck and headed up the steps to the wraparound porch. Before I could knock, the door opened.

"Morning, son." Dad smiled. His glasses were perched on his nose and he held a cup of coffee in his hand.

"Hey, Dad. You leaving?"

"Nope." He handed me the mug. "Saw you coming down the road."

"Thanks." I took the coffee in my left hand to shake his with my right.

"Come on in. Your mother is in the kitchen with, and I quote, 'more goddamn apples from the freezer.'"

I chuckled and followed him inside, where the scent of cinnamon and sugar infused their home. "Sounds like I'd better check on her."

"I'm hiding out in the office. Find me before you leave. I'd like to talk about the hotel. See if you've thought about taking it over."

"I haven't."

His smile faded. "I'd really like to know what you're thinking."

"I know." I rubbed my jaw. "Give me another few weeks. Get past Thanksgiving."

"Sure." He sighed. "I don't mean to pressure you. I just want to make a plan."

"Understandable."

He gave me a small smile, then retreated to his office.

The Eloise was part of this family, like the ranch. Letting it go would be like cutting a limb on our family tree.

If not for the lawsuit, if not for Briggs, Dad wouldn't be in such a hurry for an answer. But every time I saw him, he brought it up.

The hotel ran mostly on autopilot for my parents. They'd had decades of experience, especially Mom. Yes, they had to pitch in here and there. But their accounting firm handled most of the financials. And Eloise took her role as manager seriously, coordinating employees and schedules and guests and supplies.

Could I handle it? Yeah. Did I want to? That was an entirely different question.

I walked into the kitchen, finding my mother at the counter, her hands in a bowl of dough. "I hear you're into the apples."

Mom glanced up and gave me a devilish smirk. "I'm cutting down that apple tree."

"Grandma's apple tree?"

"Do you know how many five-gallon buckets I filled this

year? Six. I've spent forty years picking apples and coring apples and freezing apples. I'm so sick of these damn apples, I can't see straight. You know what kind of pie I want to make? Peach. Or cherry. Or chocolate."

"So you're saying that this apple pie is up for grabs?" I went to the counter and threw an arm around her shoulders, kissing her hair.

"No. You can't have it." Mom took her hands out of the bowl, taking the floury dough out and laying it on the counter. Then she reached for a wooden rolling pin, handing it over. "Roll that out for me."

"Pastries are Lyla's forte, not mine," I said, setting the pin aside so I could wash my hands in the sink. Then I went about rolling out the pie crust, doing my best to barely touch the dough so it would be as flaky as possible.

Mom came back with a glass pie pan, watching at my side as I worked. Once upon a time, she'd have offered suggestions and tips, but these days, she simply watched. "See? You're not so bad."

"Dad wants to talk about the hotel."

She hummed. "What are you thinking?"

"I don't know," I admitted. "It will break Eloise's heart."

"Your sister loves that hotel. But she also loves you. Just because you take it over doesn't mean she can't when she's ready. But she's not ready, Knox. We all know it. And if she were being honest with herself, Eloise would know it too."

"Are you sure about that?"

"Yes. Maybe." She blew out a long breath. "We sheltered her during the lawsuit. That was probably a mistake."

"No, I think you handled it right. It was hard enough on her as it was."

Eloise had hired a man in housekeeping last year. He'd

started out fine, working part-time. Then one day he'd skipped a shift. Eloise had let it go and covered for him. It had happened three more times before Mom got wind of it.

Dad had come in, met with the employee, and given him a warning. Yet it had happened again, so Dad had canned the guy's ass. One week later, we were sued for wrongful termination and sexual harassment.

The asshole said Eloise had propositioned him. She'd invited him out with some of the other staff for a drink at Willie's, trying too hard to be a friend instead of a boss. He'd gone with them, and at the end of the night, she'd hugged him.

My parents were in the right. Eloise should have fired him the first time, but because she'd allowed it, the man's smarmy lawyer thought he'd get rich suing the Eden family.

Lawsuits were never easy and though they'd come out victorious, it had caused plenty of unwanted stress.

"I'll think about the hotel," I told Mom. "But I'm not ready to decide. Not yet."

"Fair enough." She nodded and handed me a knife.

I laid the pie plate over the crust, tracing the curve of the dish, then fit the sheet to the bottom while she came over with a pan of apples coated in cinnamon and sugar.

We worked in silence, making the pie and getting it in the oven, a task we'd done a hundred times because Grandma's tree was a monster and Mom wasn't the only one who'd spent summers picking apples.

When it was in the oven, I washed my hands and put my coffee in the microwave to heat up.

"Do you need to get going?" Mom asked. "Or can you stick around to take this pie to Memphis?"

"Memphis? My Memphis?"

She arched her eyebrows. "*Your* Memphis?"

Shit. "You know what I mean."

"She's a beautiful woman, inside and out."

I blinked. "I didn't realize you'd spent much time with her."

"Oh, I just talked to her a few times at the hotel. But I like her."

I sighed. "I do too."

"You say that like it's a bad thing."

The microwave dinged and I took out my coffee, carrying it to the island, where I took one of the stools. "It's complicated."

That kiss last night had changed everything.

"Ever since Gi—"

Mom held up a hand, cutting me off. "Do not say her name in this house."

Mom hated Gianna. Not only for what she'd done to me, but because Mom and Dad had been hurt too.

"It's the kid," I confessed. "If it was just Memphis, exploring something would be one thing."

If it was just Memphis, I would have kissed her weeks ago and never stopped. But the baby...that baby changed everything.

Mom gave me a sad smile. "You're a good man."

"Am I?" Because I probably shouldn't have kissed her last night.

"Don't let what happened in the past cloud the future."

"I can't...," I closed my eyes, admitting my fears. "I can't lose another baby."

Mom took the stool beside mine and placed her hand over mine. "This is not the same situation, Knox."

"I know." But it could end just as badly.

I was already attached. To them both.

We sat in silence, sipping coffee and contemplating the past, while the pie baked. Halfway through the oven's timer, Dad joined us, and as though he could sense the mood, he didn't bring up the hotel.

"How's Briggs doing?" I asked, ready for a change of topic.

"Good." A bit of sadness always filled Dad's blue eyes when he spoke of his brother. "No episodes this week, thank God."

We spent the rest of the time talking about Briggs and his latest trip to the doctor. Then the pie was done and Mom took it from the oven, letting it cool while I had one last cup of coffee.

That pie, packed in a ceramic carrying container, rode shotgun with me to town and when I parked in the lot behind the inn, I took it straight to the break room, found a sticky note in a drawer and scrawled *Memphis* on top.

My intention was to head into the kitchen and get to work, but when I started down the hallway, my feet carried me to the elevator.

Rather than stop at the lobby, I took a gamble and headed to the second floor. Memphis wasn't there, but I found her on the third.

She was dusting a dresser with a yellow microfiber rag. Her hair was in a ponytail, the ends swishing against her spine. Her cheeks were flushed, her eyes narrowed in concentration. She was entirely too attractive to resist.

I rapped my knuckles on the door, then strode into the room, making sure to keep more than an arm's length between us so that I didn't kiss her again. Not until this conversation was over.

"If you want to pay more rent, then pay it."

She blinked, standing straight. "I do."

"Done." I nodded. "Like I said last night, I enjoy cooking for you. If you don't like extras from the restaurant, fine. I won't bring them over. At home, I usually have plenty of stuff on hand, but if I'm ever short, maybe you could hit the store."

The corner of her mouth turned up. "Just send me your list."

"You're not charity." I lost the battle with the distance and closed the space between us. "My mom made you a pie. It's not charity either. She makes pies for people she likes."

"I like her too."

"This job is not charity. You've earned it. You've kept it. *You*. Got it?"

She nodded.

"Out loud, Memphis."

"Got it," she whispered.

My hand lifted to tug at the end of her ponytail. "That kiss was not charity."

"I didn't think it was."

"Good." I took her hand and pulled her to the edge of the bed, taking a seat. "I'm not one for complicated these days."

"I get it." She slipped her hand from mine, dropping her gaze to her lap. "This doesn't have to be anything. You don't owe me an explanation. We can forget the kiss ever happened."

I couldn't forget it if I tried. "Is that what you want?"

"No."

"Neither do I."

Her entire body sagged. "I don't want to be your mistake."

Those words held so much pain. So much weight. She'd been someone else's mistake.

If I had to guess, I'd say it was Drake's father.

Memphis hadn't offered that story. Considering she hadn't told her own family and, to keep her secret, had given up a trust fund, I doubted she'd confide in me.

Not yet. Maybe if I made my own confession, she'd realize she wasn't the only one with a story.

"When I lived in San Francisco, I was dating a woman. Gianna. We were together for about a year. And during most of that year, she was pregnant."

Memphis sat straighter, her eyes widening. "You have a child?"

I gave her a sad smile. "No."

"Oh, God." Her hand came to her mouth.

"It's not what you think. Gianna has a child. A son. His name is Jadon."

"But…he's not yours?"

"Thought he was mine. We started dating and she got pregnant. Neither of us expected it, certainly wasn't planned, but we made the best of it. Gianna moved in. I went to the doctors' appointments. Tagged names in the baby-name book. Helped her decorate the nursery in our cramped apartment. Held her hand through labor."

"You were the dad."

"I was the dad. After we got home from the hospital, I spent long nights walking the baby back and forth across the apartment."

Just like I'd done for Drake.

"That was your look." Memphis's eyes softened. "When you'd come over at night, there were times you looked miserable. Just for a second. This is why."

"Yes." I hadn't realized she'd noticed. But I was learning that Memphis didn't miss much. "Jadon was two weeks old when it all fell apart. Gianna took him in for a doctor's appointment. I came home from work four days later and she told me that he wasn't mine."

Memphis gasped. "Knox."

Gianna had dropped a bomb on my life and everything had exploded. After a long day, I'd come home, dead on my feet, and found Gianna on the couch. Jadon had been asleep. I'd sat beside her, instantly knowing something was wrong. And then she'd looked at me with tears in her eyes. She'd apologized first.

Then she'd taken my son. She'd changed my life.

"She cheated. At the beginning of our relationship, she slept with a guy she knew from college. She suspected Jadon might not be mine but chose not to say anything. She told me she'd hoped I was the father. But then he was born and... she wanted the truth."

Memphis's hand closed over mine. "I'm sorry."

"Me too," I whispered. "I haven't talked about Gianna in a long time."

"I get that. It's painful to dredge up the past."

"Is that why you don't talk about yours?"

"Yes." It was only one word, but there was a plea for me not to ask. Not yet.

"I would have stayed in San Francisco," I told her. "Been there for Jadon. But Gianna and I were done, and she made the decision that if we weren't going to stay together, it was better to call it quits. She moved out. And I..."

"Came home."

"Yeah. I came home."

"How long ago was this?"

"Five years."

"Have you spoken to her?"

I shook my head. "There's nothing to say. And I needed to leave that behind."

Memphis studied the carpet for a long moment, my story heavy in the air. "Then where does that leave us?"

"I was hoping you had that answer."

Her chocolate eyes met mine. "I don't have a lot of answers these days."

"Getting attached to you is risky. Getting attached to him is..." I swallowed hard. "It's petrifying."

"If it hurts. If it's petrifying..." A crease formed between her eyebrows. "Why did you come to the loft? Why do you keep coming?"

I lifted a shoulder. "I can't seem to stop."

"Do you want to?"

I lifted my hand, tucking that stubborn lock of hair away once more. "No."

CHAPTER 11

MEMPHIS

Knox's story kept spinning in my head, like a book or movie I couldn't stop replaying.

He'd gone through a pregnancy. He'd watched the birth of his child. He'd been a father. Then in an instant, his baby had been gone, ripped from his life.

I ached for him. I raged for him. In the hours since I'd been home, my emotions had been riding a rollercoaster.

Knox and I had sat in the hotel room earlier, shrouded in silence until finally he'd brushed his lips to mine in a chaste kiss and left without another word.

Drake let out a string of babbles from his play mat. The oohs and aahs and guhs were coming more often these days.

I stretched out beside him, watching him kick his legs and work his arms. Above him, the mobile of safari animals smiled and swung as he hit one with a fist.

He smiled.

I smiled.

He cooed.

I cooed, mimicking his sound.

The idea of someone taking him away made my stomach churn. How Knox had endured it, how he'd walked away...

I pressed a hand to my heart and stared at my son.

We were still navigating through rough waters. Drake and I were close to drowning more often than not. Just last night I'd nearly cracked and answered my phone.

Then Knox had kissed me and as much as I wanted to say it had helped, that kiss had just sent me careening over a waterfall.

The imprint of his large hands lingered on my cheeks. The soft pressure of his lips. The sweep of his tongue.

A kiss to change a life. Or destroy one.

Beyond the windows, the sky was darkening, the Montana days growing shorter and shorter as winter approached. A flash of light had me shooting off the floor and tiptoeing to the glass. The hum of the garage opening below the loft rippled beneath my feet as Knox's truck eased into the driveway and into its stall beside the Volvo.

I held my breath as a door slammed shut, watching at the window to see which direction he'd head. When he started across the driveway for his own home, I sighed.

Was I relieved? Disappointed? Both?

Knox hesitated on his front porch, glancing over his shoulder and up to my window. He spotted me and lifted a hand.

I waved back.

Then he was gone, under his own roof, flipping on lights as he moved through his home.

I closed my eyes and pressed my forehead to the cold glass.

Knox was a good man. He was as reliable as the sunrise. As breathtaking as the Montana sunsets. He was the type of person I wanted Drake to become.

I stared at his house as he moved into his bedroom and disappeared into the bathroom, probably for a shower after being in the restaurant all day. Only a door separated me from a naked Knox. I pictured the water sluicing over his muscled arms. Dripping over those tattoos. Cascading down the rippled planes of his chest and stomach.

My imagination would have to suffice.

I tore myself away from the window and picked up Drake from the floor. He was up later tonight than normal, but Jill had told me that he'd had a longer nap at daycare, so we'd spent more time playing tonight.

"It's better this way," I told Drake as I ran his bath in the sink.

He smiled as he splashed in the sudsy water.

It hurt to lose Knox. It hurt to lose him before I'd even had him. But it was better this way. I had no idea what the future held. I struggled to plan for tomorrow, let alone the next five years.

And I would not be the woman who took another child from Knox.

· · ·

The beep of my phone's alarm jolted me out of a dreamless sleep. I fumbled to shut off the beeping so it wouldn't wake Drake.

Drake.

He hadn't woken up.

"Drake." I gasped, panic racing through my veins as I flew out of bed, running to the crib. My heart was in my throat as I reached for him. What was wrong? Why hadn't he woken up?

He stirred as I hefted him into my arms, his eyelids heavy as he blinked them open.

I scanned him head to toe, feeling across his pajamas. Two arms. Two legs. I pressed my hand to his chest, feeling his breath expand his ribs and letting his heart beat against my palm.

"Ohmygod." The air rushed from my lungs.

He'd slept through the night.

That was why he hadn't woken up. Not because he was sick or...

I refused to let myself think of the alternative.

He'd slept through the night.

My heart hammered in my chest as I clutched him close. Tears flooded my eyes as the adrenaline spike ebbed. It was fine. He was fine. He'd just slept all night.

Why did that make me cry? I should have been ecstatic, but instead, I spent the rest of the morning on the verge of tears, my hands shaking as I rushed to get ready for the day.

The sound of the garage opening and Knox's truck rumbling to life sounded while I hurried through a shower. I dropped my brush three times while blow-drying my hair. My stomach was too jittery to eat breakfast. Even the sight of Anne Eden's apple pie made me queasy, so I filled a glass of water only to choke on the first gulp. My fingers fumbled with the snaps on Drake's onesie as I worked to get him dressed.

Everything felt...off. Unsteady.

"He's fine." I whispered those words to myself as I made

my way to the car. Then I said them again five more times as
I drove into town.

The parking lot at the daycare was bustling with parents
coming in and out. I pulled into one of the only empty
spaces, then carted Drake inside, passing another one of the
mothers in the hallway to the nursery.

The space was narrow, so I shifted Drake's car seat so it
was in front of me, but in the move, the keys I'd had in my
other hand fell to the floor. I set him down, bending to pick
them up, but that caused the diaper bag over my shoulder
to fall.

"What is wrong with me?" *Get it together, Memphis.* I
drew in a deep breath, willing my heart out of my throat,
then squared my shoulders and got back onto my feet.

With my keys shoved into a jeans pocket, I was hooking
the diaper bag over a shoulder when Jill's voice carried down
the hallway.

"Her biggest priority is finding a new daddy for her
baby."

My entire body froze.

Was she talking about me? No way. It had to be someone
else. Unless someone had seen Knox and me at Knuckles,
sharing a booth, and assumed we were a couple. That was
a stretch. But this was a small town. Maybe gossip traveled
that fast.

My head was playing tricks on me today. I shook it off,
unstuck my feet.

Another woman's voice carried from the nursery. "Are
you surprised she's already dating? I think she was seeing
this new guy before the divorce was even final. I told you I
saw them at Big Sam's that one night."

Okay, definitely not me. Big Sam's Saloon was one of the

bars on Main, and a place I'd never been.

What was my problem this morning? Of course they hadn't been talking about me. It wasn't like I shared my personal life with Jill. Drake wasn't talking either. When had I become this anxious, unraveled person? Old Memphis, for all her faults, had always held her head high.

I didn't miss her, but I wouldn't be angry if some of her former confidence worked its way to the surface.

The moment Jill spotted me from the nursery, she handed the baby girl she'd been holding to the other woman—one of the ladies I'd seen in the office a few times—then came over and stole Drake's car seat.

"There's my favorite guy." She smiled at him as she unsnapped him from his seat. In no time, he was in her arms, kicking his legs with a smile of his own.

"Here's his bottles and more diapers." I hung the diaper bag on Drake's designated hook.

Jill didn't even spare me a glance.

I walked over, touching Drake's hand. "Have a good day, baby. I love you."

Jill spun him so that he was out of my reach.

My heart twisted but I backed away, easing out of the room. My strides were slow and sluggish. So much of me wanted to go in there, get my son and never set foot in this building again.

"Is that the one living with Knox Eden?"

That question stopped me cold.

"Yep." Jill popped the *p*, the disdain in her voice as bright as the yellow color on the walls.

"There's another single mom looking for a daddy. I guess if I were her, I'd go after the richest bachelor in town too."

I cringed. This was what people were saying about me?

That I was after Knox for his money? Humiliation crawled up my skin, red and itchy. My cheeks flamed.

It took all of my strength to keep walking. Because while these women were awful to me, Jill at least loved my son. And for today, I didn't have any other options.

I had to get to work for my shift.

For the first time in weeks, I didn't park beside Knox's truck, choosing a space much farther away. After punching my time card, I went straight for a cleaning cart, skipping my regular cup of coffee and quick hello to Eloise at the front counter. Did she think I was here to chase her brother?

I was waiting at the staff elevator when footsteps sounded in the hallway. Knox was walking my way, a notepad and pen in his hand, his white chef's coat sleeves pushed up his forearms.

He smiled.

A smile so handsome I wanted to cry.

The elevator opened. I looked away, pushed the cart inside and rode to the fourth floor with my eyes squeezed shut.

The phone in my back pocket rang as I unlocked the first guest room door. I pulled it out, hoping that it was daycare with some reason why I had to leave and get Drake. Today, I didn't want the hours at work. Today, I wanted to curl up with my son and forget the world.

But it wasn't a Montana number with the four-oh-six area code.

One hundred thirty-two.

I declined it on the second ring and stowed it away.

As I was bending to get the bottle of toilet cleaner, it rang again.

One hundred thirty-three.

I threw the bottle and rag to the floor, ripped the phone out and, once more, hit the red button. "Stop calling me."

It was still in my hand when it rang again.

My eyes flooded. My chin quivered.

Don't give up.

I declined it once more and picked up my supplies, then I went to the bathroom and scrubbed the toilet to a sparkling white shine. The mirror and counter gleamed after a polish. The floor was spotless and the air smelled like bleach.

I cleaned.

And the phone rang.

Over and over and over, until finally, as I was stripping the bed, it stopped. There were days like this. Days when I'd get twenty calls in an hour. Others only one in twenty-four.

I tensed, waiting for it to buzz again, but when it didn't, I breathed.

The stress of the day was building behind my temples, and I lifted my hands, rubbing at the ache.

"What's wrong?" I jumped at Knox's deep voice.

How many shocks could a heart take in one day? I felt like I was in a haunted house with a creepy clown jumping out at me after each corner.

"Nothing." I waved it off.

"Memphis." He strode my way, stopping close enough that the scent of his spicy soap hit my nose.

God, he smelled good. Today, there was a hint of lemon too. Maybe he'd been making lemon meringue pie. It was my favorite.

"Talk to me."

"I'm fine," I lied. "Just a headache."

"Close your eyes."

"Knox, I'm fine."

"You're a horrible liar."

I huffed a dry laugh. How many times had Oliver told me the same? Though he'd been the king of lies, so compared to him, everyone was merely an apprentice.

"You ran away from me earlier." He inched closer.

"I've been thinking," I said, squaring my shoulders and raising my chin. If I didn't have confidence, I'd have to fake it. "I think it's best if we stop this, whatever this is, before it goes any further."

His eyes narrowed and those blue eyes saw straight through the façade. *Damn.* "Why?"

"Drake."

"Look…" Knox ran a hand through his hair. "About what I said yesterday. I was just being honest. But I didn't tell you the truth so you'd push me away."

"If we tried this and it didn't work, you'd lose him."

"Yeah." He nodded. "I know what's on the line, Memphis. But I'm standing here anyway."

"I still don't think it's a good idea." Another lie that made him frown. "Drake has to be my focus."

"Did I ask you to take him out of focus?"

"Well…no." I couldn't imagine Knox asking me to forsake my child.

He raised his hands and I tensed, sure that if he kissed me again, I'd crumble. But he didn't cup my face and lean in like he had on Halloween. He rested the heel of his palms on my cheekbones so that his fingers could rub small circles on my temples.

It was heaven.

And hell.

"I can't do this," I whispered, my eyes falling closed so that I didn't cry.

"Why?"

"I don't want to let Drake down. I *can't* let him down. I'm all he has." I had no backup plan. Failure was not an option.

And I was scared too. That was the whole truth.

I was hanging on by threads most days. I gave Drake all my extra. If Knox made me fall in love with him and then we fell apart, *I* would fall apart. I wasn't sure I had the strength to mend another shattered heart.

Knox was quiet for a few moments, the circling of his talented fingers never stopping. "Yesterday, I told you about the hardest part of my life. I told you about my first-worst day. I told you about the woman who destroyed me. I'm not asking you to tell me about Drake's father. But I'm promising you that if you want to give me that trust, I won't betray it."

When I opened my eyes, his piercing gaze was waiting. He was so gorgeous it almost hurt to look at him. I wanted to tell him about Oliver. If there was anyone who would take care with my secrets, it was Knox.

But...

I stayed quiet.

"You want to stand on your own. I get that, honey." His fingers shifted away from my temples to thread into my ponytail. "Standing on your own doesn't mean you have to be alone. There's a difference."

"But Drake—"

"Don't use him as an excuse because you're scared. You wanting me doesn't mean Drake has to suffer."

He was so...right. So damn right.

Knox's hands fell away, returning to his sides. "Figure out what you want. You know where to find me."

And then he was gone, striding out of the room, leaving

behind only his words.

What did I want? Did it even matter? I couldn't afford dreams for myself.

And Knox...he was a dream.

The rest of my day was spent cleaning alone with Knox's words to keep me company. It wasn't a best day. But it wasn't a worst either. The weight of the day sat heavy on my shoulders as I trudged to my car and drove to the daycare center.

I walked into the nursery, desperately wanting to hold my son, but as I scanned the room, I saw no Jill. And no Drake.

"Um, hi. Where's Drake?" I asked the woman changing a baby. It was the same girl from this morning, young like Jill, with strawberry-blond hair.

"Oh, he's not here."

I blinked. "What?"

"Jill had to run a quick errand and she took him along."

"Excuse me?" What. The. Fuck.

"She just lives next door." The woman pointed to the wall. "She'll be back in a minute."

"Okay," I clipped and plucked his diaper bag from his hook. Then I waited, arms crossed over my chest, foot tapping on the floor as I counted the seconds ticking by on the wall clock.

Three minutes and forty-one seconds later, the back door opened and Jill came inside with Drake on her hip. Her smile faltered for a moment when she spotted me.

I crossed the room and took Drake out of her arms. "Hey, baby."

He started crying, like he did every day, and reached for Jill.

Like she had done to me this morning, I twisted and pulled him out of her reach when she tried to touch his hand.

"I'd prefer it if Drake wasn't taken out of this building." I walked him to his car seat and put him in, working the straps as fast as my fingers would move.

"Oh, okay," Jill said. "I didn't think it would be a problem. We were just next door."

I didn't trust myself to speak another word, so as Drake fussed, I clicked his buckle, looped the diaper bag over my shoulder and walked out the door.

The moment his seat was clicked into its base and I slid behind the wheel, my phone rang.

I checked the number and hit decline. One hundred fifty-five calls in the two months I'd lived in Quincy. Since I didn't have to worry about daycare calling and there wasn't anyone I wanted to talk to anyway, I shut the damn thing off.

Drake's crying stopped by the time we hit the highway.

And that's when mine started.

I was so tired. Mentally. Physically. But mostly, I was tired of being alone.

All my life, the women in my family had been at the mercy of the men who kept them. My mother. My grandmother. My sister. I'd broken that cycle by coming to Montana.

If I let Knox or anyone help, wasn't that like taking a huge step backward? What happened when I depended on him?

Except I couldn't keep going like this. I needed...help. Admitting that, even to myself, made me just cry harder.

The tears fell in a steady stream as I turned onto Juniper Hill, winding my way down the lane. The lights were on at Knox's house, casting a golden glow into the night. His truck was in the garage.

I parked and took out Drake, planning on going upstairs and making myself a dry and depressing peanut butter sandwich for dinner. But my feet carried me across the gravel to Knox's front door.

He opened it before I could knock. His gaze tracked a tear as it dripped down my cheek.

"I want to not feel so alone. I want my kid to smile when I pick him up from daycare. I want Drake to have a normal life, and I feel like this is so far away from one, I can't even see which direction to start walking. I want you to kiss me again. I want to never eat a peanut butter sandwich again. I want—"

Knox silenced me with his lips, banding one strong arm around my shoulders while the other lifted Drake's car seat from my hand. His tongue dragged across my lower lip as his soft mouth pressed into mine.

Before I was ready for it to end, he pulled his lips from mine, but his arm stayed tight, pulling me to his chest. "There's one want granted. What else do you want?"

I leaned into him and told him the terrifying truth. "You."

CHAPTER 12

KNOX

Memphis laughed as I strolled into the hotel room she was cleaning. "Aren't you supposed to be working?"

"I'm on a break."

"Uh-huh," she deadpanned. "You had a break fifteen minutes ago."

"Twenty." I handed her the latte I'd just picked up from Lyla's.

"What's this?"

"A latte."

She stared at the paper coffee cup like I'd brought her a brick of gold, not a drink my sister had refused to let me buy. Memphis sipped from the black plastic lid, and that look of sheer joy on her face...

For that look, for a laugh, I'd bring her a coffee every day.

"Thank you."

"It's just a coffee, honey."

Her eyes softened. "Not to me."

"Don't look at me like that."

"Like what?"

I stepped closer, fitting my hand to her jaw. "Like you need to be kissed."

A smile lit up her face as she stood on her toes. She was too short to reach my lips so I bent and sealed my mouth over hers, my tongue sweeping across her lower lip.

She gasped, her hand with the coffee stretching for the TV stand to set it down. But her arm wasn't long enough so I took it from her, setting it aside, then I swept her up and carried her to the freshly made bed and laid her on the plush white comforter.

Memphis clung to me as I gave her my weight, pressing her into the mattress and wishing like hell I'd thought to close the door.

This woman made me hungry. Ravenous. Her tongue tangled with mine and I let loose a low moan into her mouth. She tasted like sweet coffee and vanilla.

She was the best damn time I'd ever had and so far, all we'd done was kiss.

In the past week, I'd barely managed to keep my hands off her. I'd had to put at least one hotel floor between us to get any work done, but even then, I'd constantly found excuses to leave the kitchen and hunt her down. And I'd kissed her as often as she'd let me.

But as soon as I'd been on the cusp of tearing her clothes away, I'd stopped. And for a week, my showers had run as cold as the early November air.

Fuck, but I wanted her. If kissing her was any indication,

we'd be goddamn fire in bed. But she wasn't ready.

Memphis needed slow. Steady. Maybe I did too.

But I'd been real with her last week. I knew what I was stepping into. With her. With Drake. And it was time to let go of the past.

She whimpered as I nipped at her bottom lip. That sound shot straight to my aching cock so I tore my mouth away and let out a groan, dropping my forehead to hers as we breathed.

"Knox?" Eloise's voice carried down the hallway.

Memphis gasped, trying to shove me away, but I didn't budge. "Knox."

"What?"

"She's going to see us."

"So?" My sister was either going to see me on top of Memphis or she'd see me standing with a larger than normal bulge behind my jeans.

Memphis shoved harder so I stood, swiping her hand and tugging her to her feet. She pushed the hair out of her face as I wiped my mouth dry and adjusted my dick. Her cheeks were flushed. She scurried away to the bathroom as my sister reached the threshold.

"Oh, there you are. What are you doing?"

I nodded to the coffee cup. "For Memphis."

"Ah. That was nice." She gave me a smirk, like she knew exactly what I was doing in this room. Maybe she did.

Memphis came out of the bathroom with a can of glass cleaner and a rag. "Hey."

"Hey." Eloise smiled. "I just came to get Knox. There's someone here to see you."

"Who?"

Eloise shrugged. "I don't know. He didn't give me his name."

Maybe it was a happy customer. Or a pissed-off one. "'Kay. Where is he?"

"The lobby. I'll point him out."

I nodded and glanced at Memphis, giving her a wink. "See ya."

That wink made her cheeks flame brighter. "Bye."

I chuckled and walked with Eloise out of the room, following her down the hallway to the stairway door. Behind me, Memphis was beside her cleaning cart, her eyes glued to my ass.

When she realized I'd caught her staring, she simply shrugged and smiled.

I grinned and hit the stairs, following my sister to the lobby.

Eloise pointed to the man standing beside the roaring fireplace, taking her seat at the front desk while I went over to introduce myself.

The guy stood with his back to me, his frame covered in a tweed blazer and his neck wrapped in a thick plaid scarf.

"Good morning," I said, maneuvering around the couch to stand by his side. "Knox Eden."

"Morning." He pulled off his brown felt hat, revealing his dark, bald scalp. He clasped the hat by the brim as he turned, his hand extended. "Lester Novak."

Lester Novak.

Fuck. Me.

I shook his hand, taking in the mustache above his lip. That mustache was the logo he used in his magazine articles and on his website.

Lester Novak, a wildly popular food critic, was standing in my family's hotel. And he wanted to talk to me.

"It's nice to meet you," I said, my steady voice betraying

the racing of my heart.

"Same to you." He motioned toward the couch. "May I have a few minutes?"

"Of course."

Lester didn't ask if I knew who he was either because he expected a chef to know his name or he'd seen the recognition on my face. Probably both.

We settled on the leather couch, twisting to face each other.

In the hearth, the fire roared, chasing away the late-fall chill that blew in whenever the lobby's doors opened.

The scents of coffee and cedar and charred pine filled the room. Scents that would normally give me a sense of peace. But I was sitting across from Lester Novak and his dark eyes gave nothing away.

"I believe we have a mutual acquaintance," he said. "Cleo Hillcrest."

"We do. Cleo was a guest here a couple years ago. She, uh…well, she took over my kitchen one morning and made enough breakfast pastries to feed the entire county."

He chuckled. "That sounds like Cleo. Her bakery is a favorite stop of mine whenever I'm in Los Angeles."

"She's damn talented."

I'd wanted to strangle Cleo the day I'd found her in my kitchen. Matty had let her in to *do a little baking*. She'd used more flour and sugar in a morning than I did in a month. But one bite of a muffin and another of a cinnamon roll and I'd gotten over my irritation. Then I'd stood back and just let the woman bake. It was her gift.

In her latest email, she'd mentioned that she was trying to plan another visit to Quincy with her bodyguard turned husband. Cleo didn't know it yet, but Austin had already arranged to bring her to Quincy after Christmas.

If Lester Novak gave me a positive critique, I'd comp Cleo and Austin's entire holiday vacation at The Eloise.

Hell, I should anyway simply because she'd sent me Memphis.

"Cleo told me about this charming hotel in Montana," he said. "I had a break in my schedule and decided to make a quick stop. As per usual, Cleo has exquisite taste."

"I'm glad you're enjoying your visit."

"That I am." He grinned. "Knuckles. Interesting name for a restaurant. The atmosphere was...unexpected. It reminds me of something I'd find in a city, not a small, country town."

Was that a good thing? I couldn't tell from his tone. "I could have put cattle skulls on the walls and let people toss peanut shells on the floor, but I'll let the bars on Main do what people expect."

"Good." His grin widened. "I had dinner at Knuckles last night."

Shit. What had I cooked? It hadn't been all that busy, and I'd rushed through the last hour because I'd been anxious to get home before Memphis fell asleep.

There'd been a few burger orders. Lester might have been one, but given that his reviews of anything with red meat were rare, I was guessing not. Maybe he'd been the grilled trout tacos. Or the sunny-side-up pizza.

"And?" I asked.

"I don't eat a lot of burgers."

Damn. He'd had a burger. They were good, all my food was good. But they were just burgers. It was hard to get truly creative—which was why my father, a lifelong cattle rancher, thought burgers were beautiful.

The burgers were a local favorite but I could do so much better with so many other things.

"It was…" He stroked his mustache. Plain. Repetitive. Ordinary. "Fantastic."

Oh, thank fuck. "I'm glad you enjoyed it."

"The waitress mentioned that you source all of your beef from your family's local ranch."

"I do. My older brother runs the ranch. Every year he finishes a handful of his best steers for me."

"I particularly enjoyed the ketchup. That's not a condiment I've ever been able to compliment before."

I laughed. "I'll have to give credit for that recipe to my mother."

"There's a story there, isn't there?"

"There is." I grinned. "Growing up, there were six of us kids. We went through ketchup like crazy. One day we ran out. It was the middle of winter and Mom didn't feel like driving into town on bad roads, so she decided to make some of her own with some tomatoes she'd canned from the garden the previous summer. I don't think she's bought a bottle of Heinz since."

Lester laughed and pulled a notepad and pen from the pocket of his blazer. "Would you mind if I used that story in my review?"

"Not at all."

He went about making a few notes, all while my mind reeled.

Quincy, Montana, was not known for its food scene. The locals didn't give a shit about a critic's review. They didn't worry about presentation. They cared that the food was hot when it reached their table and the prices were fair. It was a bonus if I sourced items from local producers.

That was the fantastic part about living here. There was no posh. Food was to nourish hard-working bodies and if it tasted good, well…that was the goal.

A review from Lester wouldn't drive foodies through Knuckles' front doors. But it was an accomplishment for me. It was something I'd be proud of for years to come.

"I've just started writing a monthly piece for *Travel and Leisure* magazine." Lester tucked his pen and notepad away. "I'd like to feature Quincy, The Eloise and, in particular, Knuckles."

"I'd be honored." I didn't bother hiding my smile.

"I'll be staying tonight and am looking forward to another dinner."

"Friday nights I run a special. I haven't decided what it will be yet. Any requests?"

He rubbed his hands together. "Surprise me."

"You're on." Ideas raced through my mind. Dijon chicken. Pork medallions. Beef Wellington. I dismissed them all instantly, needing to hit the walk-in to see what I had on hand. Maybe a fish?

Quincy was all about comfort to me. It was home. Maybe I'd make Memphis's mac 'n' cheese and fry up a chicken with my favorite chipotle batter.

"For the article, the magazine will want to send out a photographer," Lester said. "Would you mind?"

"Not a problem. Just tell me the day."

"Excellent." Lester stood, holding out his hand once more.

I got to my feet and shook it. "Thank you. Truly."

"As I said, it was my pleasure. Until tonight."

"If you're exploring Quincy, I'd like to recommend Eden Coffee. My sister Lyla owns it. Though Cleo's got her beat when it comes to cinnamon rolls and muffins. Please don't tell Lyla I said that."

Lester laughed. "Not a word."

"But Lyla makes a tart cherry turnover that is incredible. She gets the cherries from Mom's trees and her pastry crust is magical. She made some this morning. If they're not sold out already, you won't want to miss it."

"You know, I was just thinking about getting a coffee." He tightened the knot on his scarf. "I'll have to hurry over."

With a nod goodbye, I watched him cross the lobby's floor and head out the doors. When he was out of sight from the large windows, I did a fist pump. "Yes."

"Who was that?" Eloise asked as I passed by the desk and headed for the stairwell.

I held up a finger. "Tell you in a sec."

The first person I wanted to tell was Memphis.

I took the stairs two at a time, rushing to find her on the second floor. She was finishing in the same room where we'd been earlier. The sound of her ringing phone chimed down the hallway.

She was sipping her coffee when I walked into the room, declining the call. Memphis declined a lot of calls.

"Hey," I said so as not to startle her.

Her eyes whipped my direction and the crease between her eyebrows, the one that always came with those calls she never accepted, disappeared. "That was ten minutes."

I walked right into her space, once more lifting the coffee from her hand. Then I framed her face and dropped my lips to hers for a quick kiss. "Guess what?"

She smiled. "What?"

I repeated my conversation with Lester in a blur and when I was done she beamed.

"Knox, this is…" Her hands flew in the air. "It's Lester Novak. *The* Lester Novak."

"I know." God, I loved that she knew how big of a deal this was. That she was more excited than me.

"When I worked for Ward Hotels, we always tried to get him to stop by the restaurant and do a review. But he is nearly impossible to get. And he's here." Her hands went in the air again. "In Quincy."

"And he didn't hate my food."

"Of course he wouldn't hate your food. Duh. You're the best chef I've ever met."

The compliment was given so casually, like she was stating the obvious. The sky was blue. Snow was white. I was the best chef in the world.

Funny how weeks ago an opinion like Lester's would have been the ruler by which I measured my success. Now, as long as Memphis enjoyed her meals, I didn't need a critic's review or five stars on Yelp.

"What are you going to make?" she asked.

"I don't know. I was thinking comfort food. He liked the burger. I think sticking to food that is Quincy tried-and-true will be best. But I'll probably make it up as I go. That's usually the best."

She nodded. "I agree."

"Want to stick around? Go get Drake and have dinner here?"

"Yes, but I probably shouldn't. I don't want to distract you."

"You are rather distracting." I tugged at the end of her ponytail. Then because I couldn't stop, I dropped my mouth to hers and got lost in the woman who was consuming my every waking thought.

She leaned into the kiss, rising up to get closer.

I was banding my arms around her, trapping her to my chest, when a throat cleared from the doorway.

Memphis tore herself away, her eyes widening. Behind us, Eloise stood beside the cleaning cart in the hallway.

"Should I pretend I didn't see that?" Eloise asked.

"Nope." I chuckled, snaking an arm around Memphis and pulling her back into my arms.

She stiffened. "Knox."

"It's too late now, honey. She's not blind."

"Oh my God." She brought her hands up to her cheeks, whispering, "I'm going to get fired."

"Eloise, Memphis is worried that she's going to get fired."

"Knox," Memphis hissed, poking me in the ribs.

I ignored her and twisted to my sister. "Are you going to fire her for kissing me?"

"Of course not."

"See?" I gave Memphis a smirk. "Small town, honey. No one cares."

"Knox, I just came up to make sure everything was okay," Eloise said. "And since it is...when you're done here, would you make me an early lunch? I forgot one today and I'm starving."

"Sure."

Eloise retreated down the hallway, and when we heard the stairwell door open and close, Memphis sagged.

"I wasn't sure if Eloise would care."

"Nah. But I'd better make her lunch before she gets hangry. And before I need another cold shower."

Memphis gave me a sheepish smile. "Are you okay with this pace?"

"There's no rush." I kissed the top of her hair. "I'm not

going anywhere. When you're ready, I'll be here. We'll take it slow. But no hiding it. I'm not keeping you a secret."

The caramel flecks in her eyes danced. "No hiding."

It might be awkward if I took over the hotel and became her boss's boss. But that was tomorrow's problem. Tonight, I just wanted to make dinner for Lester.

Then get home to Memphis.

CHAPTER 13

MEMPHIS

When you're ready, I'll be here.

Was I ready?

A week ago, no. Knox had picked up on my hesitancy and hadn't pushed too fast. But now? Maybe I'd needed the week to wrap my head around this. To let him kiss me often. To smile when he smiled. To open my mind to the idea of a *someone.*

Maybe I'd needed the week to remind myself that Knox wasn't Oliver. And to remind myself that I wasn't the same Memphis who'd been blinded by Oliver's charm.

Not fooled.

Blinded.

The person who'd stolen my sight had been me. I'd shut my eyes to his faults and seen only good looks, money and status.

But I'd had my eyes opened thanks to a baby boy. And when I looked at Knox, I saw the best man I'd ever known.

He had the looks. He had the charm. He had the money and, in Quincy, plenty of status as an Eden. But none of it seemed to matter to him. He cared about honesty and integrity. Family and hard work. He treated me like I was precious and desired.

Was I ready?

Headlights flashed through the window and I leapt off the couch, racing for the door.

One glance at Knox at the base of the stairs and I didn't need to ask myself any more questions.

My heart answered with a resounding thump. The landing was frozen and cold, but I stepped outside in my bare feet anyway, waiting as he jogged up the stairs. "Well? How'd it go?"

Knox answered by sweeping me into an embrace and carrying me inside, pushing the door closed behind us with his foot. Then his mouth was on mine, our lips melding in that slow, delicious tangle I'd become addicted to this week.

I was breathless by the time he finally set me on my feet. "So? Did Lester like dinner?"

"He told me it was a bold move to serve him mac 'n' cheese. I told him I had a woman at home who'd promised me it was the best in the world. He agreed."

"Yes." I flew at him, jumping into his arms because I knew he'd catch me. "I knew it. I knew he'd love whatever you made."

"I've got leftovers in the truck. Want some?"

"Later." I dropped my lips to his, losing myself in his taste and his tongue. My legs wound around his hips and when I felt his arousal press into my center, this time, I didn't back away. As one of his arms moved to hold my thigh, I arched into him, earning a low growl from deep in his chest.

He tore his mouth away. "Fuck, but you can kiss."

I smiled, pressed a kiss to the corner of his lips. "Kiss me again."

"I better walk out that door while I still can."

"Stay," I whispered.

His hold tightened, his eyes darkened with lust. "Memphis—"

"I'm ready." I ran my fingers through his thick hair. "I wasn't a week ago. But I am now."

"You sure?"

"Yes." I trusted Knox. With my body. With my heart.

He was leaning in, his lips almost brushing mine, when he froze.

"What?"

"Drake."

Oh, shit. What was wrong with me? I'd been seconds away from jumping Knox and my son was sleeping in his crib. "I'm a horrible mother."

Knox chuckled. "You're not a horrible mother. But let's take this to my place."

"I don't have a baby monitor." They were expensive, and since Drake and I lived in a single room, what was the point?

"Think he'll stay asleep if you load him up?"

"Maybe."

"Worth a shot. You get him." Knox set me down on my feet. "I'll get the crib."

I tiptoed across the loft, picking up Drake and wrapping him in a blanket.

In the time it took me to pull on a cardigan and step into a pair of shoes, Knox had the crib folded up and the diaper bag hung over his shoulder.

Maybe this was reckless. Not long ago, I'd had a nuclear explosion of a breakup. Yet as I followed Knox across the driveway to his house, my feet danced over the gravel. A smile pinched my cheeks.

Every step was full of anticipation. Every heartbeat thrummed beneath my skin.

Knox Eden, for tonight, was mine.

He led the way into the house, then straight down the hallway toward the guest bedrooms. He set up Drake's crib like a man who'd done it a hundred times, not once.

Like a father.

I pressed a kiss to my son's head. Drake let out a squeak as I laid him in his bed. Then I held my breath, both Knox and I hovering over the crib's rail. "Is this weird?"

"What?" Knox whispered.

"Shuffling a baby around in the night so we can... you know." So I could climb Knox like a naked tree.

"You think this killed the mood?"

"Did it?" *Please say no.* My body was strung tight and after a week of kissing, I ached for more.

Knox took one of my hands, bringing it to his hard, flat stomach. Then, with his palm covering my knuckles, he dragged it lower and lower over his jeans. His hardness made me gasp. "That answer your question?"

My mouth went dry. That was not a small bulge behind his zipper.

Drake scrunched up his nose and shifted, but then he relaxed and drifted off again. *Sleep. Please, baby. Sleep.*

Knox kept a grip on my hand and dragged me out of the room, leaving the door open so we could hear Drake if he cried. Then we were hurrying down the hallway. He didn't slow his long strides for me, he just pulled, the urgency in his movements matched by my own.

But I guess I wasn't walking fast enough because when we reached the living room, he turned and swept me up and over a shoulder, carting me the rest of the way to his bedroom in a fireman's hold.

"Oh my God." I giggled as his palm smacked my ass. Then I was flying through the air, a yelp caught in my throat, before I landed on his bed. "Your house has a lot of windows for a caveman."

He grinned, his handsome face muted in the dim moonlight that crept through the glass. Then he leaned forward, his arms planted beside me in the bed. "You are mine. Whether we do this tonight or not."

He was going to make me fall in love with him, wasn't he?

I put my palm against his bearded cheek, then leaned in, closing the distance, and took his mouth.

Knox's intensity met mine, desire curling between my legs. The ache I'd had for him came to new life as his hands slipped beneath the thin fabric of the camisole I'd pulled on with my pajama bottoms.

He moved me deeper into the bed and then he was everywhere, kissing down my neck while his hands roamed my ribs and the soft swell of my breasts. My cardigan was stripped from beneath me and tossed to the floor.

My hands threaded into his hair as I let the scent of his bedroom wrap around me. Soap and sage and Knox.

Every touch, every caress, made the throb in my core pulse stronger. "More."

Knox ignored me and continued his delicious torture, never touching me where I needed him to touch me, just getting close. And damn it, we were both fully clothed. I was about to crawl out of my skin if I didn't get to touch his.

My fingers abandoned his hair to pull and tug at his shirt, but every time I had the hem tugged up his spine, he twisted and I lost my grip. "You're killing me."

"Slow. Remember?"

"That's a horrible idea."

"Just making sure you're ready." He dipped lower, dragging his tongue across my collarbone. His hand slid down my belly, dipping below the elastic waistband of my pajama pants. Then those long fingers were beneath my panties, gliding through my wet folds.

"Knox." I arched into his touch, my eyes falling closed.

His lips traveled lower and lower. A hand came to free my breast. Then his hot mouth closed over a nipple and I nearly came undone.

It had been a long time since I'd felt worshiped. Sexy. My body came alive beneath his touch and the more he toyed, the more I trembled.

"Don't come," he ordered.

My eyes flew open. "What?"

He gave me a wicked grin. "Don't come. Not yet."

"Then you'd better stop."

His hand came out of my pants and he climbed off the bed. The moment he reached for the hem of his shirt, I propped up on an elbow and refused to blink as he dragged it over his head. I'd seen him shirtless through the window, but damn. There was nothing like a close-up view of those washboard abs. The definition at his hips was mouthwatering. He had the V that disappeared past the waistband of his jeans.

The tattoos on his biceps wrapped up and around his

shoulders. One dipped low to his pec. If he let me tonight, I'd gladly trace the lines with my fingertips and my tongue.

He kicked off his shoes while flipping the button on his jeans.

The hitched breath that escaped my lips made Knox freeze. "Too fast?"

I shook my head, eyes glued to his long, thick cock. "You're, um…wow."

He planted a knee in the bed, covering me with that muscular body. An arm reached for the nightstand drawer and when he brought the condom between us, he gave me one more chance to hit the brakes. "We can save this for another night."

"Why are you trying to talk me out of having sex with you?"

He kissed the tip of my nose. "Because tonight will be the best damn time I've had in years. I want that for you too. No regrets."

"No regrets."

He held my gaze, searching for a shred of doubt. He wouldn't find one.

I shoved at his shoulders, forcing him up. Then I stripped off my own top, tossing it to the floor. His eyes flared at the sight of my bare breasts. That appreciation was enough to banish any fears that my body had changed after childbirth and I'd lost my appeal.

Knox surged, his lips fusing to mine. Then we were a mess of frantic movements as we both worked to shove away my pants, leaving nothing between us but heat.

His weight settled into the cradle of my hips. His body was a tower of strength. His arms bracketing my face kept him from crushing me, but he stayed close enough that the dusting of hair on his chest rubbed against my sensitive nipples.

"You are...you are a dream," he breathed. "I gave up on those."

My breath hitched. "So did I."

His kiss was soft and gentle as he positioned himself at my entrance. Then he rocked us together, inch by inch.

I savored the stretch, the feel of him so hard inside me. My entire body ignited as he moved, in and out, in deliberate, measured strokes until I was clawing at his shoulders, urging him on, faster and faster.

This man, holy God he had stamina. Knox never tired. He never stopped, just fucked, exactly like a woman should be fucked. Long and with rapt attention.

The sound of our labored breaths echoed in the dark room. The magnificent tension built higher and higher with each of his thrusts until I felt like glass ready to shatter.

"Come." Knox dropped his mouth to my pulse and sucked. Hard. Then he pistoned his hips, hitting that spot inside that made me see stars.

I exploded around him, pulsing and squeezing, as the world disappeared. There was nothing but us and the fall over the edge.

Tremors racked my body and with a groan, he buried his face in my hair, his own limbs shaking, and gave in to his own orgasm.

His heart thundered as he collapsed on top of me. "Goddamn, Memphis."

"That was..." I wrapped my arms and legs around him, not wanting to lose the weight. But he shifted, rolling to his side and pulling me into his chest.

"That was fucking fire."

I smiled against his throat, content to sleep exactly like this, our bodies damp with sweat and tangled together. But my son had other ideas.

A tiny cry carried through the house. I rolled off the bed, scurrying for my clothes. Then I jogged to the kitchen, rushing to get a bottle and formula from the diaper bag.

I'd just filled it with water when a shirtless Knox came striding down the hallway, passing the kitchen for the guest bedroom. He emerged moments later with Drake in his arms.

"I can take him," I said.

"I've got him." He stole the bottle from my hand and walked to the couch, settling down with the baby.

I curled up on the other end, tucking my legs beneath me.

Those two were a sight. A dream.

Drake looked content in Knox's arms. Knox seemed happy too.

"This was a best day," I whispered. "Top five."

"Tell me about them. Your top five best days."

"You already know the first."

"Drake's birthday."

I nodded. "Early on in labor, when the contractions weren't coming one on top of another, this nurse brought me in a basket of knitted baby hats. A woman who volunteered in the nursery made them for all the new babies. I picked out this soft gray one, and as I held it, I had this feeling like I was exactly where I needed to be. Have you ever felt like that?"

"Yeah. The day I moved home from San Francisco and walked into the kitchen at The Eloise."

"It's a good feeling."

"That it is." He glanced down at my son. "What about the other days?"

"My third best day was the day I graduated from college. My girlfriends and I planned this amazing party. We got all dressed up and went clubbing and drank champagne and danced all night."

The memory of that night wasn't as bright as it had been. I hadn't spoken to any of those friends in months. We'd drifted apart some after college, each of us busy with fledgling careers. Then I'd gotten pregnant and my clubbing nights had disappeared and with them, my friends.

Friends who weren't really friends. I still liked their photos on Instagram. They sent the occasional text to check in. But our lives had gone in different directions.

"My fourth-best day was a trip I took to Hawaii for work," I said. "We'd just opened a hotel on Maui, and I'd gone out to work with the local marketing team to get some pictures and content for social media. I flew out early and spent an entire day on the beach, reading and napping and doing nothing but listening to the sound of the waves."

"When was that?"

"A couple years ago. It was my most peaceful day." Because not long after, I'd met Oliver. And he'd brought chaos to my life.

"I haven't been to the beach in ages." Knox took the empty bottle from Drake and set it on the end table. Then he shifted my son over his shoulder, patting his back. "Okay, what's the next best?"

"The day I moved into my townhouse in the city." Another best day tainted.

I'd hoped to buy the townhouse from my parents. The location had been fantastic, just a short walk to some of my favorite restaurants. There'd been a coffee shop three blocks away. Its only rival for a vanilla latte was Lyla's. The townhouse's interior I'd decorated exactly to my style, classy and chic and comfortable.

I gave Knox a sad smile. "I really loved that place."

"Is that why your dad took it away?"

"Probably."

My father had wanted his way. And like he had our entire lives, he kept his children in line by taking away the things we loved.

"Sorry, honey. Gotta say… I'm not cool with your dad."

"I'm not cool with him either."

When I'd first told Knox about my family, I hadn't wanted them to seem ugly. But as the days passed, as Knox interacted with Eloise or Anne popped into the hotel to check on her kids, I began to see my parents' true colors. Black and lifeless and empty.

Drake let out a burp so loud it filled the room. I blurted out a laugh, so did Knox, and then Drake cooed a sleepy yawn before passing out.

"So what was your fifth-best day?"

"I just told you. The townhouse day."

His eyebrows furrowed. "So today was your second-best day?"

"Yeah."

"You said top five. But it was number two?"

Without question.

He'd brought me my favorite coffee. He'd visited me all morning for kiss after kiss. Knox had made me feel special. Wanted. After he'd talked to Lester, he'd come to tell me first. And then tonight… Maybe I was giving away too much. Old Memphis would have played it differently. But I wasn't playing. Not anymore.

"It was a really good day," I said.

So why wasn't he smiling?

Silence stretched through the room like the darkness and the night beyond the windows. A chill crept along my skin as Knox stared straight ahead, sitting motionless and giving nothing away.

Had he not liked today? He'd probably had countless best days. This one probably paled in comparison to the memorable days in his life. Maybe he thought my ranking good and bad times was silly.

Not for me.

When you lived with sharks, you marked the days when a life raft came floating your way.

"What did I say wrong?"

"Nothing." Knox stood and carried Drake to the guest room.

I followed, hovering by the door as he laid the baby in his crib. My stomach knotted as Knox turned and acted as though he'd walk straight past me. But as his chest brushed my shoulder, he snagged my hand and towed me through the house.

He dropped my hand when we stepped into his bedroom and rubbed his palm over his jaw. "Today was your second-best day."

"Well...yeah. What's wrong with that?"

He shook his head. "It was just a normal day, honey."

"Maybe for you." I lifted a shoulder. "My normal days aren't like this."

"That's..." Knox paced at the foot of the bed, stepping over the shirt he hadn't put on. "That's not right. And fuck, it hurts. It hurts me for you."

"Why? What is wrong with today being a best day?"

"Because today was normal." He threw up a hand. "Just a normal, good day. You worked. I worked. We came home. That's it."

"But it was a best because of you."

"Memphis." He pressed a hand to his heart. "You honor me."

"It's just the truth."

He strode toward me, taking my face in his hands. "Then here's another truth. I'm going to take them. I'm going to take all of your bests. Every damn one until you can't keep track of the top five anymore because there are so many bests that you'll need a hundred to capture them all."

"Promise?" I whispered.

"I swear it."

CHAPTER 14

KNOX

I was three steps down the hallway when the sight in my favorite chair stopped me midstride.

Memphis had Drake on her knee, holding him up by the armpits. She leaned in and blew a kiss on his neck, making him giggle. When he laughed, she laughed. When her eyes twinkled, his did the same. He had her eyes, chocolate brown flecked with gold.

The pair of them were in their own little world in that chair.

Memphis had rolled out of bed when he'd started making noises this morning. I'd rushed through a shower but now I saw the error of my ways. I should have been right here, watching from the sidelines because goddamn it, that was a view.

Nothing beyond my windows would ever compare.

Memphis pulled in an exaggerated breath, then kissed him again, earning another laugh. A big laugh for such a small person.

Drake would have a happy life. She'd make sure of it.

And after last night, I would too.

There was no going backward now. Not after last night.

She'd given me her best days. I'd give her mine.

Both of them.

I unglued my feet and padded into the living room, going to the back of the chair.

"Hi." Memphis smiled as she looked up at me.

"Hi." I pulled her blond hair out of her face and leaned forward, bending at the waist to kiss her. Then I stole Drake from her lap. "Morning, boss."

He drooled and shoved a chubby fist in his mouth.

I kissed his cheek. "You're getting big."

Drake answered by popping that fist free and letting out a squeal that filled the house. The noise startled him, his eyes wide, and then he did it again, stretching it out louder and louder.

Memphis laughed. "This is his new party trick."

"I like it." I settled him against my ribs and carried him to the kitchen, opening the refrigerator door.

Memphis followed, taking a seat on a stool at the island.

"When does he start getting solid foods?" I pulled out a carton of eggs.

"When he's six months."

"Couple more to go. Then I'll hook you up, little man. We're not doing boring baby food in this house." I glanced over at Memphis. "Can babies have—what? What is that look for?"

She looked like she was about to cry. "You're really not

going anywhere, are you?"

"No." I abandoned the fridge and walked around the island, crowding her space. "This is new. We'll take a little time. Get used to each other. But I'm not the kind of man who gives up what's good. And we're good. We're fucking good, honey."

She nodded and smiled, wiping at her eyes. "We are good."

I kissed her forehead, then handed her Drake. "What do you want for breakfast?"

"Whatever you're making."

"How hungry are you?"

She shrugged. "I'm not starving."

"Think you can wait an hour? I can make a quiche."

"I'll wait."

I winked. "Good choice."

"Wait." She held up a hand as I pulled out a mixing bowl. "What about work?"

"I'm not working today."

"But...it's a Saturday."

And since the day she'd moved in, I'd worked every Saturday. "I texted Roxanne last night and asked if she could cover today."

"You did? When?"

"After you fell asleep." I wanted a day with them. A full day, no distractions. Just another normal day to show her how good normal could be. "Got any plans today?"

"Um...no. I was going to clean the loft. Do some laundry."

"How about we hang here instead?"

The smile that stretched across her pretty mouth made the flack I'd catch from Roxanne later worth it.

Never in my life had I canceled on work to be with a woman. Roxanne had already been teasing me for ditching out on prep work to hunt Memphis down in the hotel. So last night when I'd told her I'd give her an extra vacation day over Christmas if she worked for me, she'd sent a string of heart and eye-roll emojis and a single thumbs-up.

I went to the pantry for flour and salt to make the pie crust.

Memphis put Drake on a blanket on the floor in the living room to kick and squeal. Then she sat at the island and watched me work, her attention fixed on my every move.

"Watching you cook is better than TV."

I chuckled and put the quiche in the oven. Then I washed my hands and tossed the towel aside before I slid onto the stool beside hers, fitting her legs between my spread knees. I skimmed her thighs, looking forward to Drake's first nap, when I could strip her out of these pajama bottoms. "Kiss me."

She leaned in but stopped, a whisper away from my lips. "Say please."

"What if I don't?"

"Then I won't kiss you."

I grinned, dragging my mouth across hers. "Sure about that?"

"Say please."

"Please."

She launched herself at me, flying off her stool. Her arms wrapped around my shoulders and her tongue was in my mouth. Fuck breakfast, I didn't need a damn thing more than this woman.

Drake gave a wail, causing Memphis and me to freeze. Then we both laughed when he kept on babbling, testing the acoustics of my house.

"I'm going to run to the loft and grab a few more diapers." She glanced at the timer on the oven. "Maybe take a quick shower."

"Go for it. I'll watch Drake."

"Are you sure? I can just take him with me."

"Nah. He's happy." My hand glided over the curve of her ass. "Bring over anything you want for today. And tonight."

Now that she'd slept in my bed, there was no way she'd be spending another night in the loft.

"Thanks." She kissed my cheek, then hurried for the door, stepping into her shoes and pulling her cardigan tighter.

When she was at the staircase to the loft, I stretched out beside Drake on the floor, pinching his toes and tickling his tummy.

The pain of being near him, the ache I'd felt early on, had vanished. When I looked at him, I didn't see Jadon. I just saw Drake. My tiny boss.

"We need more toys." Every time I'd gone to Griff and Winn's place, Hudson had at least three new toys. Their living room had a basket overflowing with stuffies and plastic baubles. "Maybe you and Hudson can play together one day too. Build forts. Chase dogs. Be buddies." *Cousins*.

I rolled onto my back, staring at the white ceiling. My brain was getting way too far ahead of reality.

That had been my problem with Gianna too. I'd been so lost in planning the future, in the idea of my own family, rowdy and rambunctious, that I'd missed the signs that she'd been keeping a secret.

Not long after she'd found out she was pregnant, Gianna would stare at me and open her mouth, but nothing would come out. There'd been times when I'd found her staring at a wall, her arms wrapped around her belly and her knee bouncing wildly. Other times, when I'd talk about the future and maybe moving us all to Montana one day, her face would pale.

"What's the deal with your father?" I rolled to my side and looked at Drake. He had his feet in his hands and a glob of drool on his bottom lip. I wiped his mouth dry, then sighed. "Want to tell me about it since your mom doesn't seem like talking?"

Another trickle of drool escaped.

She'd tell me. Memphis would eventually explain, wouldn't she?

"What else should we have for breakfast? Fruit?" I jackknifed off the floor and swept Drake up, ruffling his hair. Then we retreated to the kitchen, where I shut down my own mental bullshit and concentrated on the meal.

There was no point in worrying. Memphis was not Gianna. She hadn't confided in me about her past or Drake's father and I had to believe that was for a reason. That she'd tell me when she was ready. We just hadn't gotten there yet.

Like I'd told Memphis this morning. We'd take a little time. Get used to each other.

I was raiding my fruit bowl, pulling out a couple of peaches, when the crunch of tires and the hum of an engine sounded outside.

"Of course they show on my day off," I muttered, sure it was either a parent or a sibling. But as I peered through the window that overlooked the sink, an unfamiliar black SUV rolled to a stop in the driveway.

"Someone got lost, didn't they?" I asked Drake, walking

to swipe up his blanket and wrap him up.

I was just pulling on a pair of boots when a man about the same age as my father stepped out from behind the SUV's wheel. He adjusted the tie at his neck and tugged at the sleeves of his suit jacket.

But he didn't come toward my door. He had his gaze on the loft.

Memphis stood in the middle of the staircase, her hand wrapped so tight around the railing that even from this distance I could see her white knuckles.

"What the hell?" I hustled to get my boots on.

By the time I opened the door, Memphis had come down the stairs to stand in front of the man, her shoulders stiff. Her expression was blank and as cold as the November morning. Her eyes narrowed. Her lips pursed.

The SUV's passenger door opened as I came down the sidewalk and a woman dressed in an ice-blue pantsuit stepped out. Her heels teetered on the gravel as she walked to stand at the man's side.

It was only when she looked over her shoulder—not at me, but at Drake—and pulled the sunglasses off her face did I recognize the resemblance. The brown eyes. The blond hair. The pretty nose and lovely chin.

Her mother.

My free hand balled into a fist.

"You're unwelcome here." Memphis's voice carried strong and clear.

Damn straight they were unwelcome.

"Unwelcome?" The man I assumed was her father scoffed. "Enough of this act for attention, Memphis. We are leaving. Today."

"Safe travels." Her voice was as flat as her gaze.

I walked past her parents, taking a stance behind Memphis. It wasn't easy, but I kept my mouth shut as her father looked me up and down with a sneer. When the mother stared at Drake like she was about to snatch him, I spun him away.

"I've been calling," her mother said, her eyes still locked on the baby.

"And I haven't answered." Memphis shifted, putting herself in front of Drake.

That was who'd been calling. For months and months. Persistent, wasn't she?

"Get in the car," her father barked.

"No." Memphis's lip curled. "You have no say in my life. Leave."

"You call this a life?" He curled his lip and glared at the loft. "You're living above a garage. You're cleaning rooms. You're living on minimum wage."

"That's—wait." Her spine, already stiff, became a rod of steel. "How do you know where I'm living and where I'm working?"

"Do you really think I'd let you just leave?"

Memphis scoffed. "You had me followed."

Her mother dropped her chin. Her father raised his.

Months ago, right after she'd moved here, I'd seen that flash of headlights on the road one night. I'd thought it was someone who'd been lost. But maybe it had been whoever they'd sent to follow Memphis.

"How long did you have me followed?" Memphis asked.

Her father didn't so much as blink at her question. It was clear he didn't deem her worthy of an explanation. "We're leaving. Get in the car."

It was Memphis's turn to blink.

"You signed a noncompete clause," her father declared.

"Your point?" She crossed her arms over her chest.

"You're working at a hotel."

"Is that what you're worried about, Dad? That I'll share company secrets? I'm a housekeeper. And Quincy, Montana, isn't exactly the market for a Ward Hotel development."

"I could take you to court."

Was this motherfucker really threatening to sue his own daughter?

"Sue me." Memphis shrugged. "Noncompetes are not enforceable in Montana. Yes, I checked. Nor have I violated the terms of my nondisclosure agreement by sharing confidential Ward Hotel information. But sue me. If you want to sever the very thin threads of our relationship, sue me. In the highly unlikely event a judge rules against me, then you can have the twenty dollars to my name. I'll scrub bathrooms and make beds until I earn another twenty. But threatening me, ordering me around, didn't work in New York. It sure as hell won't work here."

That was my girl. There was the fire. It took every ounce of restraint to keep quiet, but she didn't need me stepping in for her. I would if I had to, but determination was creeping into her eyes. Like she was getting the chance to say the things that had been building in her mind for months.

"You have thirty seconds to load up that child and get into the car."

"Or what?"

"Or you'll hear from our lawyers."

Memphis shook her head. "Why are you really here? Why have you been calling? What do you want from me?"

Her father stood taller. "You are my daughter. There are things to discuss. In private." The man's eyes flicked to mine. Maybe he realized right away that I wasn't the type to be intimidated, but his gaze didn't hold mine for long.

"I have nothing to discuss with you." Memphis crossed her arms over her chest.

He reached for her, wrapping an arm around her elbow.

And that's when I got really fucking pissed.

I grabbed that bastard's wrist and tore it free. "You're trespassing. Get the fuck off my property."

"You have no say in this." He shook his hand free, stretching for Memphis.

"Touch her again and they'll never find your body."

The mother gasped. The father paled, barely, but it was enough.

Without another word, I clasped Memphis's hand and stormed past them, walking so fast that she had to jog every few steps to keep up.

The oven timer was beeping when we walked inside. I handed over Drake, kicked the door closed and stalked to the oven, taking out the quiche. The crust's edges weren't burnt but they were too dark.

I braced my hands on the sink, staring through the window as her parents climbed into their vehicle and disappeared. "Memphis—"

When I turned, she was standing by the window closest to the door, her eyes glued on the road. A stream of tears streaked down her face and she held Drake so tight that he began to squirm.

"Memphis." I strode to the windows, reaching for Drake. But she didn't let him go. "Give me the baby, honey."

She shook her head. "I've got him."

"I'm just going to set him down so we can talk."

It took her a moment, but she finally let him go so I could lay out the blanket and set him down to play. Then I returned to the window and wrapped her up in my arms.

"Why won't they forget me?" she whispered. The pain in her voice was enough for me to hate them and I didn't even know their names.

"Because you're hard to forget."

"I hate that I'm crying." Her voice cracked.

"Why?"

"Because after all they've done to me, I shouldn't care. But I do." A sob escaped. "For a moment, when I saw them drive up, I thought...maybe they were here to apologize. Maybe they were here to give me a hug and say they missed me. And I was so happy to see them because for better or worse, they are my parents. But they don't care. Why don't they care about me?"

She fell forward and had I not been holding her, she would have crumpled to the floor. So I spun her in my arms and held her tight, letting her cry into my T-shirt. When she finally stopped, she stood straight and the look on her face was heartbreaking.

She looked more beaten down than she had on the day she'd arrived.

"They didn't even ask about Drake." Her chin quivered. "They've never even asked me his name."

"I'm sorry." I used my thumb to catch a tear. "I'm so sorry."

"They are ugly, aren't they?" Memphis stepped away and walked to Drake, dropping on her knees at his side. Then she held his hand, drawing comfort from his tiny fingers. "We don't need them, do we?"

No, they did not.

"I forgot his diapers." Her shoulders fell.

"I'll go get them."

"I can."

"No. You stay." I was too pissed to stay still and needed the task to calm down before Memphis and I had a conversation.

I marched to the loft, the scent of Memphis's soap in the air. There was an empty laundry basket on the counter so I swept it up and filled it to the brim. Diapers. Formula. Shampoo. Clothes. If I had to move her into my place one laundry basket at a time, so be it.

When I made it home, Memphis had moved to the living room. Drake was sucking down a bottle and she was curled into the corner of the couch, shrinking into the cushions.

Fuck those people.

"What are their names?" I asked, setting the basket down and taking the seat beside her. "Your parents. What are their names?"

"Why do you want to know?"

"So that when I curse them, either in my head or out loud, I can be precise."

She gave me a sad smile. "Beatrice and Victor."

Fuck Beatrice and Victor. "What am I missing, Memphis?" Because there had to be more to this story. Why had she declined her mother's calls? Why had her mother kept calling? Why had they come to Montana to try and drag her back to New York?

"I don't know," she whispered. "But if I had to guess... I'd say they found out about Drake's father."

"You ready to tell me about that?"

"No," she whispered. "Not yet."

"Soon, honey."

Dread crept into her expression.
A knot formed in my gut.
Another woman with secrets.
I guess I did have a type.

CHAPTER 15

MEMPHIS

Knox rapped his knuckles on the bathroom door, then walked to me at the counter, setting down a steaming mug of coffee. "Here, honey."

"Thanks." I put my brush down and gave him a smile through the mirror. My hair hung in damp strands down my back and the plush white towel I'd cinched around my chest was so big it hit me at the knees.

He dropped a kiss to my bare shoulder and gave me a look that said today wasn't going to be the relaxing, stress-free Sunday I'd hoped for. Our Saturday hadn't been a lot of fun either.

"I called the hotel. Talked to Mateo. He checked in a couple with the last name Ward last night."

My hands fisted. "They didn't leave."

"Nope."

"Well…shit."

"Pretty much," he muttered.

Of course they'd be at The Eloise, polluting what was mine. There were a few motels in the area but none were as nice.

What were my parents doing here? Why the phone calls? Why the private investigator? They'd turned their backs on me when I'd needed them most, yet now they showed. Now? Maybe I could believe there wasn't some ulterior motive if only Mom had visited. It had been her calling for months. But for Dad to make the trip to Montana, there was something else going on.

There'd been desperation in his voice yesterday. Urgency.

"I need to talk to them," I grumbled.

"Give me ten to shower. Then we'll go."

"Wait." I held up a hand before he could take off his shirt. "I'd better talk to them alone."

"No."

"Knox—"

"No, Memphis."

I stepped closer, fitting my hands to his ribs, feeling the tension in his body beneath the long-sleeved thermal he'd pulled on this morning after rolling out of bed. "I love that you're ready to follow me into battle. But I know my parents. I know my father. If you're there, he won't tell me the truth. He'll be on the defense."

Knox dragged in a breath, his nostrils flaring. Then his frame relaxed and he wrapped me in his arms. "I don't like this."

"Me neither."

"I'm not staying here. We'll go in together. Drake and I will hang at the restaurant."

I nodded, burying my face in his chest, drawing from his strength. "Okay."

He kissed my forehead, then we both flew into action, me blow-drying my hair while he showered.

He'd taken seven trips to the loft yesterday, each time under the ruse of getting something for Drake. He'd leave with my empty laundry basket and return with it overflowing.

My shampoo and conditioner were in the shower. My other toiletries were in a drawer beneath one of the double sinks. My clothes were hung in his closet. My panties, socks and bras were in the dresser. And nearly everything of Drake's was in the guest bedroom.

In a single day, he'd practically moved us in.

We were moving at the speed of light, and even though my brain screamed for me to slow him down, my heart refused to put up a fight. Instead, I'd just helped him organize.

If we fell apart—God, I hoped we didn't fall apart—I'd be moving into town. So what was the difference between moving out of his place or the loft?

While I changed Drake out of his pajamas and into an outfit, Knox reloaded the diaper bag. When I stepped outside, ready to head for the Volvo, Knox's truck was running, the cab warm, and the base for Drake's car seat was secured in the back.

The drive to town was silent. This was the first time I'd been a passenger in ages, and seeing Quincy from this angle was different. Or maybe today as we drove, I saw it for what it had become.

Home.

The town council was already gearing up for the holidays. Pine-bow garlands twined around each of the lampposts that lined Main Street. Quincy Farm and Feed had fenced off a quarter of their parking lot for Christmas trees. The movie theater featured the latest blockbuster along with *Dr. Seuss's The Grinch.*

I hadn't been to the theater yet but when Drake was older, we'd be weekend regulars. A chalkboard sign for free apple cider had been placed in the window of the Wooden Spoon. Another store I hadn't been in yet but maybe I'd swing in and get Knox a kitchen gadget. I knew the storefronts but not their interiors. I hadn't made exploring Quincy a priority, but that was about to change.

Since I'd left the city, I'd been telling myself not to give up. But did I need the daily reminders anymore? Maybe not.

I wasn't giving Quincy up.

Or Knox.

"Hey." He stretched an arm across the truck's cab and captured my hand. "Change your mind about me coming along?"

I squared my shoulders. "No. I'll handle them."

"There she is." He shot me a grin. "There's my girl."

Yes, I was his. And I could do this.

As we drew closer to The Eloise, I spotted the SUV my parents had been driving yesterday. My heart rate spiked as we eased into the alley behind the hotel. I swallowed my nerves and focused on getting Drake out of the truck.

"I'll carry him," I told Knox when he reached for the car seat's handle. I needed the weight to keep my hands from trembling.

We walked inside and headed straight toward the front desk, where Mateo was drinking a to-go cup of coffee from Lyla's shop.

"Hey." Knox jerked up his chin.

"Hey." Mateo hopped off his stool and rounded the

corner of the counter, coming to stand beside his brother.

With a dusting of stubble on his jaw, Mateo looked more like Knox than ever. He had the same broad frame, but he hadn't built up as much muscle yet.

Mateo and Knox shared a look, then he nudged my elbow with his. "How's it going, Memphis?"

"It's all right."

"Yeah," he muttered. "They're in room 307."

"Okay." I set the car seat on the floor and bent to touch my son's nose. "Be good, baby."

The smile he gave me was all the incentive I needed to stand up to my parents. They weren't going to take this life from us.

Knox pulled me into his side when I stood. "We'll be here."

"Thanks."

He brushed a kiss to my mouth, then gave me a sure nod as I headed for the elevators. My footsteps were steady, a contrast to my racing heart, as I walked down the hallway on the third floor. I took one fortifying breath outside the room, then raised my hand to knock.

My father answered the door wearing another Italian suit. If he was surprised to see me, he didn't let it show as he waved me inside. "Memphis."

"Dad."

This was one of the larger rooms, a corner room with enough space for a small table by the window. Mom was seated, her back as stiff and straight as my own. Except it wasn't determination fueling her forward. She'd sat stiffly her entire life, on constant edge because of my father.

Her eyes dragged over my hoodie and jeans. Her lip curled, barely, but I caught it. Mom had never liked jeans.

She lived her life in tailored slacks and silk blouses. Today's were both a matching ecru. Diamonds decorated her ears.

"Sit," Dad ordered, taking a chair of his own.

It grated on me to obey, but there'd be plenty of time to fight. I chose the seat across from his so I could hold his gaze for this conversation.

He looked exactly the same as he had months ago. Blond hair with white streaks at the temples. Hazel eyes that would have been colorful if not for their constant cold glare. Thank God we didn't look alike. My sister and brother both resembled Dad, but I'd taken my features from Mom.

Houston and Raleigh hadn't bothered calling, so I didn't waste time asking about their well-being. They certainly hadn't given a shit about mine.

"Why have you been calling me?" I asked Mom.

Her eyes flicked to Dad, guilt creeping into her expression. Maybe he didn't know that she'd been dialing my number nonstop.

"If you really wanted to know, maybe you should have answered the phone," Dad clipped. Okay, so maybe he did know about the calls.

"Why the private investigator?"

"You packed up your car and left." Mom looked at me like I'd offended her. Like I'd spit in her champagne.

"There was no reason for me to stay in New York." I leveled a glare at Dad. "I had no job. No home."

He leaned back in his seat, giving me that impassive stare he was so feared for at Ward headquarters. "That was your choice."

"Was it?" I arched an eyebrow.

"We wanted to make sure you were safe," Mom said, her voice dropping to nothing more than a whisper.

She had wanted to know I was safe. Having me followed must have been her idea. From the look on Dad's face, he couldn't have cared less.

"If you were really worried about my safety, you would have come to the hospital when I was in labor."

"I'm sorry I wasn't there." Mom looked to Dad with blame etched on her pretty face. "That man from yesterday. Who is he?"

"Knox Eden. His family owns this hotel."

"Oh, is—"

Dad frowned. One single glare and Mom ceased speaking as he waved her away. A flick of the wrist that her questions were nothing.

She shrank into her chair. While Dad hadn't changed in months, Mom seemed...tired.

The lines around her eyes were more prominent, not that there were many. She had a team of estheticians who pampered her weekly along with a world-class dermatologist and the highest-paid plastic surgeon in New York City to ensure she didn't look a day over forty.

Unlike Dad, Mom hadn't come from money. She'd married into wealth, and because of her prenup, there was little she'd do to risk the six-carat diamond on her ring finger. She'd fight time and age tooth and nail until the end of her days.

At one point, I'd pitied Mom. She loved her lifestyle and it had trapped her to my father's every whim. But that was before she'd left me alone. Before she'd cowered to his will and, as such, forsaken her child. There was no pity left.

She could call every day from now until the end of her life. It was too damn late.

She'd made her choice.

And I'd made mine.

"Why are you really here?" That question I aimed at my father. "I'll take the truth this time. Because there is no way you'd travel here to rescue your daughter."

"You're to come home. Once we arrive in New York, we will have a more thorough discussion."

"Unless you plan to put a bag over my head and drag me onto the airplane, I won't be leaving Quincy."

Dad's jaw clenched. "You've made your point, Memphis. You've had your little tantrum. Enough."

"You think this is a tantrum?" I huffed a dry laugh. "This isn't me acting out to get your attention. I don't need or want you in my life."

Imagining Drake saying that statement to me would have been like a dagger through my chest.

Mom flinched.

Dad didn't so much as blink.

"If you want a *thorough discussion*..." I threw his words at him. "We'll be having it here. This is your window of opportunity."

He pursed his lips.

"Fine." I made a move to stand but he held up a hand.

"I received a call from a woman."

I settled into my chair as the hairs on the back of my neck stood on end. "Who?"

"She didn't give me her name. But she claims that you have Oliver MacKay's child."

It took everything I had not to react. I felt the color drain from my face, yet I didn't move. I barely breathed.

"She's blackmailing us. Either we pay her to keep quiet or she'll be going to the press. You're to come home so I can ensure you keep your mouth shut while my lawyers eviscerate her."

My heart beat so hard it hurt. Who was this woman? How could she know about Oliver? Unless this was all a lie. Maybe Mom's private investigator had done more than simply follow me to Montana. Maybe I'd screwed up and left some trace along the way.

Dad was stubborn enough to intrude into his daughter's personal life.

"Here's what I don't understand." I held up a finger when Dad opened his mouth. "Why do you want to know so badly? Why?"

"Why won't you just tell me so we can deal with this mess? Is it Oliver MacKay?"

"It's not your business."

"Damn it, Memphis." He leaned forward, a growl in his voice. "You are acting like an insolent child."

"You are not entitled to control of my life."

"I am your father."

I shook my head. "You do not understand the meaning of that word."

"Memphis, this is so petty," Mom said. "Your father is trying to help. But we need all of the information."

"This woman. This blackmailer. Let her go to the press." It was the last thing I wanted but I suspected my father felt the same. So I'd call his bluff.

As long as I didn't admit or confirm that Drake was Oliver's child, there was nothing but speculation. Considering I was in Montana, this drama wouldn't touch me in the slightest.

But it would definitely put a damper on Dad's day.

"Oliver MacKay?" Dad seethed. "Really, Memphis? I thought you were smarter than that. Instead you've acted like a whore and now I'm cleaning up this mess."

Mom tensed in her chair but she certainly didn't come to my rescue.

A whore. Maybe. It stung, but it wasn't the first time he'd used his words like a whip. "If you're worried about your reputation and a scandal, then pay the woman and be done with it. Or don't pay her. I don't care. But I told you months ago, my son is mine and mine alone. You can either accept that or not. It doesn't matter. We don't need you."

"I'll use the money from your trust fund."

"Are you here looking for my permission? Trust me, I realized the day I left that the money would never be mine."

"Is it true? Is it Oliver?" Mom asked.

I clamped my mouth shut.

"Memphis." Dad enunciated both syllables of my name. That meant he was moving beyond angry to infuriated. "You realize that if this gets out, people will believe we're linked to that family."

"So?"

Dad's eyes narrowed. "We cannot afford a scandal with the mafia. I've spent my life rebuilding our good name."

His life's work had been spent correcting his own father's mistakes.

My grandfather had started Ward Hotels in New York. He'd been extremely profitable in a time when other hotels had not. Dad had never confirmed exactly why, but when I was twelve, the FBI had investigated the business.

The only reason I'd known about it was because an agent had come to our home one day. I'd been sick and hadn't gone to school. My nanny had made me stay in bed all day, but I'd wanted to watch TV. So while she'd thought I was napping, I'd snuck out of my room.

An FBI agent had been standing in our foyer asking Mom questions. I'd sat at the top of the stairs and listened to them all.

Whatever illegal undertakings my grandfather had done to get ahead, my father had unraveled them. Nothing had come from that investigation as far as I knew, and there were no illegal happenings at Ward, I'd bet my trust fund on it.

But our good name had become Dad's obsession. Just the idea that I'd tangled with Oliver MacKay, well...

I doubted he would have flown to Montana had Drake's father been any other man.

"None of this involves me. You have plenty of lawyers who can continue to protect your precious reputation. Sic your bloodsuckers on this woman, whoever she is. I don't care."

"You would turn your back on your family?"

"Be careful, Daddy. Your hypocrisy is showing." I stood from the chair, done with this conversation. "My family is here. My son is my family. You know, that little boy you couldn't even look at yesterday? His name is Drake, by the way."

Dad stood, pointing a finger at the table. "We're not done talking. Sit down."

"I didn't get the chance to say goodbye after you evicted me. So I'll remedy that today. Goodbye, Dad. Goodbye, Mom. Safe travels home."

Without another word, I stalked to the door, whipping it open and storming down the hallway. The elevator opened almost immediately after I pushed the down arrow and once I was safe inside, I closed my eyes and breathed.

If they stayed tonight, I'd be cleaning their room tomorrow. Humiliation crept through my veins, and I squeezed my eyes tighter.

This was just one more hurdle to cross. They'd leave and eventually people would forget that Victor and Beatrice Ward had a second daughter. They'd forget me too.

The ding of the elevator chimed before I was ready and the doors slid open. Mateo was at the front desk, his eyes on his phone. When he heard my footsteps on the floor, he glanced over, ready to speak, but the look on my face must have changed his mind.

He simply nodded and let me escape into Knuckles.

There wasn't much of a breakfast crowd. The hotel was quiet this weekend, but according to Eloise, every room was sold out for Thanksgiving in two weeks.

I hadn't thought about the holidays. I'd never spent one away from my family.

Family.

That word didn't hold much weight at the moment. It rang hollow in my mind.

But I had Drake. I'd always have Drake.

I stepped into the kitchen and, at the sight that greeted me, came to a full stop.

Knox stood at the sink, the water running over a potato, but he wasn't paying any attention to the spud. He was pretending to snack on Drake's cheek, earning a drooly smile.

The two of them together were so true and real that my eyes flooded. I'd left my composure on the third floor. The first tear streaked down my face as Knox glanced over his shoulder, finding me by the door.

He dropped the potato and smacked a fist on the sink to shut off the water, then he walked over and pulled me into his chest with his free arm. "I should have gone with you."

"No." I sniffled, reining in the tears. "It was best I went alone."

"Are they leaving?"

"I don't know. I hope so."

"Memphis, you gotta tell me what's going on."

"I know." I leaned away and looked up at my son. A beautiful baby boy with blond hair like mine.

And like his father's.

CHAPTER 16

KNOX

It was noon by the time we made it home from the hotel. I'd called and asked Roxanne to cover for me again. So while we'd waited for her to come in, I'd busted out some prep work as Memphis and Drake had waited in my office.

The drive home had felt too long, just like the hours before. All I wanted to do was find out what the hell had happened with Memphis's parents, but when we finally walked through the door at home, Drake started crying.

"He missed his morning nap." Memphis propped him on one hip while she mixed a bottle with the other. Then she took him to the chair, settling him on her lap.

"Are you hungry?" I asked her.

"Not really."

Yeah, I wasn't either. My stomach had been in a knot since she'd walked into the kitchen with tears in her eyes. So

I went to the couch and sat on its edge, propping my elbows on my knees. Waiting.

Drake finished his bottle in no time and then as Memphis held him, he quickly drifted off to sleep.

"Want me to take him and put him in the crib?" I asked.

"No, I'll just hold him." She looked down at her son and traced her fingers along his forehead, brushing the wisps of hair out of his face. "Some days it feels like he's all I have."

"Not anymore."

Memphis looked up and there were those tears again. Seeing them hurt every goddamn time. "I told you my dad was angry when I refused to tell him about Drake's father."

I nodded. "You did."

"He's not used to being denied. I don't know if I've ever actually heard anyone tell him no. So his ego is..."

"I get it." I'd worked for chefs like that early on in my career. They'd get spun up about something trivial and go ballistic, simply because their arrogance made it so.

"When I refused to tell Dad, he pressed and pressed. The more he demanded answers, the less I spoke. It's ironic because in the thick of it, he called me stubborn. I guess I learned it from him."

"He's an ass, Memphis."

"Pretty much." She sighed. "He could have just respected my wishes. I'd still be in New York if he had trusted me. If he had listened when I said I had my reasons for keeping the secret. Instead, we got into a huge fight and well...you know the rest."

The rest meaning she'd fled home, moving across the country alone with an infant. Because Victor Ward couldn't control his daughter.

Memphis glanced at Drake once more, her eyes softening.

"Drake's father isn't a good man."

I sat straight. "Did he hurt you?"

"Only my heart," she whispered.

And for that, I'd hate the bastard for the rest of my days.

"Drake's father is a man named Oliver MacKay." She met my gaze as her shoulders slumped. "No one but you has ever heard that sentence."

"No one?" Not even her mother? Or a friend?

"Just you." She swallowed hard. "And I know you won't, but I have to say it anyway. Please, never tell a soul. No one can know."

No one could know? "Why? You're scaring me, Memphis. If you're in danger—"

"I'm not. Oliver wants nothing to do with me just as much as I want nothing to do with him."

"Then why is this a secret?"

She dropped her chin. "Because his wife is the daughter of an Italian mafia boss."

If my brain could have exploded, it would have. What. The. Fuck?

The room went still. The light outside seemed to dim, like the sun was covered in a cloud. And Memphis sat perfectly still, her confession ringing in the air as she clutched her baby boy.

"I don't..." I dragged a hand over my beard, scrambling for something to say.

Fuck. The mob? I didn't know a damn thing about the mafia other than what I'd seen in movies and television. Hollywood embellished, but I was sure there was a thread of truth.

"Is that why you moved here?" I asked. "To escape the city?"

"No. I could have stayed, rented an apartment and found a job in New York, but the city had lost its appeal. Mostly because of my family. Putting thousands of miles between me and Oliver was just a bonus. I moved here because Montana sounded like a dream. I wanted Drake to have space to breathe. To roam and play. A home where the Ward name meant nothing and no one would attempt to control his life by holding a trust fund over his head."

"Makes sense." If I had her family, I probably would have split for the countryside too. Except I didn't know if I would have walked from that kind of money.

I'd thought it the first time she'd told me, but God, she was strong. Not many people would have walked away from millions. If Drake ever doubted her love for him, I'd be there to set him straight.

"Oliver..." She made a sour face. "When we met, I didn't know who he was. I hadn't heard his name before. It's not like he's ever in the news. And there are plenty of rich men in New York."

I tensed, my shoulders stiffening. This was never going to be easy to hear. I didn't like the idea of her with any other man, but especially the one who'd helped her make Drake.

Part of me would be jealous of that son of a bitch all my life.

"We met in a hotel in Miami," she said. "In the bar. I was there for work. So was he. We hit it off and spent the weekend together. Neither of us shared a lot of personal details. It wasn't that type of weekend."

My skin crawled but I sat quietly and listened, my teeth grinding together.

"It wasn't until the end of the weekend that we realized we were both from New York. He asked if he could see me again. I'd had fun, so of course I said yes. Oliver is older, in his early forties. He's charismatic. Handsome. Wealthy. Powerful. Being around him was…addicting. And I was a spoiled, stupid fool."

There was so much guilt in her voice. So much shame. It weighed on her slight shoulders and dimmed the light in her eyes.

"We started dating, if you could even call it dating. We spent most of our time at my townhouse. Some at his Upper East Side apartment. He was an entrepreneur. I worked constantly. But he was my escape. And I loved him. Or…I thought I loved him." Her forehead furrowed. "Can you love someone when they keep you in a bubble?"

"No, probably not." I'd thought I loved Gianna. Would have sworn it in blood. Except what we'd had wasn't love. Not even close.

"He didn't share many personal details. Neither did I. Communication was not the leading lady in our relationship. He asked me early on if we could keep our relationship to ourselves, just to see where it was going before it became public. That was fine by me because I was happy to keep him to myself. But after three months, I wanted more. I wanted to tell my friends. I wanted to show him off. So I asked him if he would accompany me to a party. It was this fancy, audacious function but I used to love fancy and audacious."

"Really?" That didn't seem like her at all.

"A lot has changed." She lifted a shoulder and nodded at Drake. "That version of me died the day he was born."

"Or maybe you found who you'd always been meant to be."

She gave me a sad smile. "Maybe."

"What happened at the party?"

"I don't know. We didn't go. I asked him to be my date and he told me that he couldn't go because his wife would be there. He said it like it was obvious. That I should have known I was just his mistress."

"You had no idea."

More guilt and more shame clouded her face. "No. Maybe I should have. But the old version of me liked the bubble."

"You trusted him."

"A mistake."

"Not yours, honey." That motherfucker had deceived her intentionally.

"I broke it off. Called him a lot of names and told him to forget mine. Then a few weeks later, I wasn't feeling well. I missed my period and..."

"You found out you were pregnant."

She touched Drake's cheek. "I was lax with my birth control. Irresponsibility was another flaw of the former me. I'd miss a day on my pill. I'd spend the night at his place and head straight into work, doubling up the next morning. Basically, I was a fucking idiot. But I don't regret it."

"You shouldn't." That little boy was a miracle.

From the sounds of it, he'd transformed Memphis's life. It was nearly impossible to look at her and imagine the woman she was describing. She was probably just being too hard on herself. But I didn't doubt that she'd changed.

"The whole truth came out after that. That apartment of his wasn't his home. It was just where he'd hidden his secret whore." Her chin quivered. "My dad called me a whore today."

"What the fuck?" God, I wished I had punched that asshole in the face yesterday. I shouldn't have let her go and talk to them alone.

Memphis shrugged, her eyes avoiding mine.

"Look at me." I waited until she lifted her chin. "Fuck him for saying that."

"Yeah," she mumbled. "Still...Google would have told me exactly who Oliver was. I looked him up the day he told me he was married. The internet was very informative. That was the second-worst day of my life. The day I realized just how gullible and shallow I was."

"This is not your fault. Trusting someone you care about is not wrong."

She met my gaze, her eyes softening. We'd both been fooled by the ones we'd loved. I'd trusted Gianna too.

The distance between us was too much, so I stood and skirted the coffee table, holding out a hand to help her to her feet. Then I took Drake from her arms, keeping hold as I pulled her to the guest bedroom.

Before long, we'd get a real crib. We'd haul this bed out of here and make it a nursery. Drake needed his own room.

I laid Drake in his crib, then pulled Memphis to the mattress, curling her into my chest. "What happened when you told him you were pregnant?"

"By that point, I'd learned who his wife was and the speculation about her family. It scared the hell out of me. I was afraid that she'd find out about the affair, about the baby, and decide to come after us. I wasn't going to tell Oliver at all, but he showed up at my house one day."

"Did he want you back?"

"No, he wanted my silence. He threw in a few threats about his wife and how she was often jealous. How she was connected to a dangerous family and it would be a shame to have trouble for my own family's business. It was all very practiced, a message he'd obviously delivered before. He offered me fifty thousand dollars to keep our affair quiet."

I leaned back, meeting her eyes. "But you didn't take it, did you?"

She shook her head. "I didn't want his money. All I wanted was his agreement. That my child was mine and mine alone. I'd stay quiet if he signed over all rights."

From the beginning, she'd fought for Drake. "That's my girl."

A smile tugged at her mouth. "I almost didn't tell him about the baby. I almost kept it quiet. But I didn't want to look over my shoulder my entire life, wondering if he'd find out. Wondering if he'd want Drake. It was my window to negotiate and I took it."

"So he's gone."

"He's gone," she whispered. "And unless I need that man's kidney or liver or any other organ to save Drake's life, I will never speak of him again. One day, I'm sure Drake will ask. But that's a worry for tomorrow. I don't want him anywhere near Oliver's life."

"Good." I blew out a deep breath and pulled her closer. It was better this way. And if Drake ever needed a kidney or a liver or any other organ, he could have mine, assuming they were a match.

"Not good." She pulled away, flopping onto her back to stare at the ceiling. "Someone knows."

"What?" I stiffened. "Who?"

"I don't know. But that's the reason my parents are here. A woman is blackmailing Dad. She said she'd go to the press and say I had Oliver's baby."

"Fuck."

"Pretty much." She rubbed at her temples. "I was afraid

to ask too many questions today. Mom and Dad suspect Oliver, but I wasn't going to confirm it. There's a whole convoluted history there. It's rumored that my grandfather had some mafia ties when he started Ward Hotels. If it's true, Dad severed those decades ago. But it has him spooked."

"Shit," I muttered. "What happens if this woman goes to the press?"

"I'll deny it. Oliver will deny it. But speculation will run rampant. And his wife will no doubt suspect we had an affair."

"That's her problem. What about Drake? What kind of agreement did you make?"

"I have a signed document stating he's waived all parental rights. But...it's not notarized. It's not filed. I'm banking on the fact that he'll never change his mind. If he does..."

"If he does, he'll have one fucking fight on his hands. He's not getting Drake."

"He's not getting Drake," she repeated.

"What about your parents? What are they going to do?"

"I have no idea." She groaned. "I'm sure this trip was not what Dad planned. He probably expected to come here, find me poor and miserable and grateful to be flown back to New York in their private jet. Instead, I told them to shove it."

When she stuck out her tongue, I chuckled. "You did the right thing, staying quiet."

"I hope so." She sighed. "My dad knows of Oliver and his connections. He also knows that any tie to them would damage his reputation. That's the only child he actually cares about. His precious reputation. Best case scenario, he pays the woman to stay quiet. He'll probably use the money from my trust fund."

"Worst case, this blows the fuck up."

"Yep." She put her palms to her eyes. "What a goddamn mess."

"Who do you think this woman is? Did your dad tell you?"

"He doesn't know." She sat up, scooting to the end of the bed to look at Drake. "Maybe it's an employee. Or another mistress."

The son of a bitch had probably been with other women while he'd been with Memphis. He'd had a treasure, a pure-gold treasure, and rather than cherish her, he'd used her for his own greed.

His loss. My gain.

"Do you think the woman who contacted your dad could be his wife?" I asked.

"Maybe." She shrugged. "Though why would his wife need to blackmail my family for money? She's got plenty. She could just divorce Oliver's ass and take his money too."

"Unless he's got a prenup." I climbed off the bed. Or, if the mafia was as ruthless as I suspected they were, she'd get her family involved and inherit his assets upon his untimely death.

"There's more. Something happened, right before I left," she said. "I was in the middle of packing, loading up the Volvo. I came out of my townhouse carrying a box and there was a woman waiting. An FBI agent."

My stomach dropped. "Is the FBI investigating Oliver?"

"I don't know. Probably. She showed me her badge and asked if I knew Oliver MacKay. I said, 'Who?' and excused myself to go check on Drake. I watched from the window as she walked away. The next day I was on the road."

I rubbed my jaw. "An FBI agent wouldn't blackmail your parents for money."

"No. It's got to be someone close to Oliver. Someone he pissed off. And someone who knows my family has money." Memphis wrapped her arms around her waist. "Why won't this go away? I just want it to end."

I sat beside her, pulling her into my arms. "It will end."

"How?"

"I don't know, honey."

"Maybe I should just go back to New York. Find out who this woman is. Pay her—"

"No. It's not an option, Memphis."

She looked up at me, those brown eyes full of apology. "I never meant to drag you into all of this."

"You didn't drag me anywhere. I came willingly. Out my front door, up a staircase and into your loft, remember?"

Memphis gave me a sad smile. "Knox, I can't put this on you."

"You've never been able to count on anyone, have you?"

She blinked, like the reality of her life had just hit her in the face.

"You were so alone that you left. Because you had no one. But you've got me now. And like I told you the other night, I'm not going anywhere." Maybe if I told her enough, she'd believe it.

"Promise?"

I dropped a kiss to her mouth. "I swear it."

CHAPTER 17

MEMPHIS

Eloise was checking in guests as I approached the front desk so I hovered back, waiting until they had their key cards and passed me for the elevators. She plopped into her seat and tucked a stray hair behind her ear as I walked over. "Phew. It's been nonstop today."

"You weren't kidding about the holiday rush."

Over the weekend, nearly every room in the hotel had been filled. The last of the guests had arrived today. We were fully booked for the entire week with visitors in town for Thanksgiving.

I'd been tidying occupied rooms all today, replacing towels and bedding and straightening up. The hallways had been vacuumed, the elevator cleaned. I'd just finished mopping the break room. Anything to keep busy. Frantic work and a maddening pace had been a godsend. It had allowed me to channel my nervous energy and keep my mind off of the unknowns.

My parents had checked out of The Eloise last week— not long after our discussion, according to Mateo. They'd probably left while we'd been in Knuckles. I hadn't heard from them since.

Months and months of my mother's constant calls. Now nothing but silence. Maybe she realized just how badly she'd hurt me. Maybe Dad had told her to stop calling. Maybe she'd given up.

I wished I missed my mother. I wished I could say that I'd missed the regular ringing of my phone. But it was a relief. I hadn't realized how much pain had come with each of her calls, the bitterness they'd brought to each day.

Someday, my heart wouldn't be so bruised. Someday, hopefully, these feelings toward her would soften. Someday, I might pick up the phone and call her for a change.

Just not today.

"Are you taking off?" Eloise asked, glancing at the clock.

"Unless you need me to do anything else." It was just after five. Drake had to be picked up before six, but I had time if she needed me to deliver slippers or champagne to a room.

"No, you've been working your tail off this week. Have I told you how much I appreciate you? Because I do."

"Thank you." My chest swelled with pride. When I'd worked for Ward Hotels, it had been rare to receive a compliment. From my boss. From my father. Dad set the tone for the office and friendliness was a distant priority over accomplishment.

But Quincy was a welcoming place. People smiled as

you passed them on the sidewalk and said hello. Neighbors watched out for neighbors. Strangers bought strangers a cup of coffee simply to be kind.

"See you tomorrow." I waved at Eloise, then hurried to the break room to clock out. With my coat on and my purse slung over a shoulder, I headed for Knuckles.

Knox and I hadn't seen each other since I'd left for work this morning. We'd both been swamped with the influx of guests, and today he'd started prep for the Thanksgiving feast he'd be serving on Thursday.

But even though we'd gone the whole day apart, there was comfort in knowing that he was always close by. If I needed him, he was there.

The restaurant's tables were set, a few already occupied. The kitchen was bustling when I pushed open the swinging door. Skip was at the prep table, mixing a bowl of corn pasta salad. Roxanne was standing beside Knox, reviewing a menu card. Everyone looked my way when I stepped inside.

"I just wanted to say hi." I waved to the room. "I'm heading out."

"One minute." Knox held up a finger. "Don't leave yet."

"Okay." I shifted out of the way so I wouldn't get bumped if a waitress came through the door.

"How's it going, Memphis?" Skip asked.

"Busy day. You?"

"Same." He tapped the handle of his wooden spoon on the side of the bowl, then took it to the dishwasher. Like Knox and Roxanne, he was wearing a white chef's coat and today he was in a pair of loose cotton pants with a cheetah print.

"New pants, Skip?" Normally he wore jeans. The wild, bold and baggy pants had always been Roxanne's forte.

"Pretty snazzy, huh." He did a little two-step shuffle, dancing my way. "Roxanne told me I couldn't pull off her style."

"Because he can't." She shimmied over in her pink camo pants. The bright color matched the streaks that ran through her blond hair.

Skip scoffed and struck a pose. "Can too."

The easy banter between the restaurant staff always made me smile. They teased each other. They teased Knox. But beneath the laughter and the jests, there was mutual respect.

Knox praised his staff regularly. He gave them advice and taught them new techniques. And in return, they adored him.

I adored him. More and more each day.

"All good, guys?" Knox asked, unbuttoning his coat.

"Yep." Skip gave him a mock salute.

Roxanne nodded. "All good. Get out of here."

"You're not working tonight?" I asked.

He answered by disappearing to his office, returning a moment later with his Carhartt coat and truck's keys. "There's a storm blowing in. I don't want you driving alone."

"Okay."

His protectiveness was second nature. He was a man who took charge. But unlike my dad's barked orders and inability to compromise, Knox did it with care, not control. Like the way he'd moved us into his house. He hadn't asked. He'd simply filled my laundry basket, one trip at a time, until all that remained in the loft were my empty suitcases. If I'd balked, he would have taken everything back.

"Hi." He stopped beside me and dropped a kiss to my forehead. "How was your day?"

"Hi. Good."

"You didn't come see me on a break."

"Because I didn't take a break."

He frowned and put his hand on my lower back, steering me out of the kitchen. A man at a table along the wall waved. Knox jerked up his chin but didn't stop walking. "Anything from your parents today?"

"Not a word."

"Damn."

"Pretty much," I muttered. We both wanted this over with.

After my confession last week, Knox and I had spent hours talking. Sharing about Oliver, spilling that secret, had lifted a weight from my shoulders. Knox had stepped in and a problem that had been mine was now ours.

I'd never been in a relationship of *ours* before. Not even with my parents.

Knox and I had decided that the only thing to do about my parents and this blackmailer was wait. Nothing good would come from me getting into the middle of the situation. If anything, it would only illuminate the truth.

This woman, whoever she was, had no proof that Oliver was Drake's biological father. Our affair had been secret— Oliver had made sure of that, even if I hadn't realized it at the time. She was likely acting on a hunch, so I'd keep my son and his DNA far, far away from the city.

If my father decided not to pay her off, then life would get complicated. But I was counting on Dad's first love: his image.

His reputation had always been his priority. It was the reason his hotels were labeled boutique hotels. He wanted the Ward name to be known for extravagance and exclusivity.

"We'll deal." Knox took my hand. "Whatever happens, we'll deal. Together."

Together. I stared up at his handsome profile and let that word roll through my mind.

Was this too good to be true? My heart couldn't take it if this fell to pieces. Because day by day, night by night, I was falling for Knox.

Maybe I already had.

Would he wake up tomorrow morning and realize he could have so much more than me? Would he resent the drama I'd brought to his life?

"What?" Knox nudged my arm.

"Nothing." I clutched his hand tighter, then let it go as we stepped outside.

A blast of snow hit me in the face. I gasped at the cold wind, burrowing deeper into my coat, then hurried to my car.

"Get in. I'll clear the window." He opened my door for me, and as I turned on the engine, he used his sleeve to wipe the windshield.

I cranked the heat while he cleared his truck, then I led the way across town to the daycare. Wind whipped snowflakes through the air. It was so thick I couldn't see farther than a block ahead. My knuckles were as white as the sky by the time I eased into the daycare's parking lot.

Knox parked beside me, waiting as I rushed inside to collect my son.

I was just down the hallway when Jill's voice caught my ear. "She's shacked up with him already."

My footsteps slowed, my hands fisting at my sides. *Not again.*

Nothing much had changed with daycare. Jill still

irritated the hell out of me, but she worshiped Drake. So even though I had to tear him from her arms every evening, I forced fake smiles with gritted teeth.

This was the first time in weeks that I'd overheard her gossip. Probably because she was usually alone in the nursery.

I quickened my steps, making it to the doorway. "Hi."

Both women's eyes went wide. Guilt crept into their expressions. Yep, they'd been talking about me. *Bitches*.

"Oh, hi." Jill had Drake on a hip, no surprise. She was always carrying him.

"Did he have a good day?" I asked, hurrying to collect his things.

"Yes, he was perfect." She kissed his cheek. "Weren't you? You're always perfect. But he didn't take an afternoon nap. So we just cuddled."

Meaning she hadn't laid him down so that he *could* take his afternoon nap. Meaning I'd have to put him to bed early and miss *my* time with him. My molars began their daily grind as I went to take him from her arms. "Hi, baby."

He saw my outstretched hands and instantly began to fuss.

I am so fucking sick of this. What the hell? Did she feed him sugar and tell him I was the devil all day? He'd be fine in ten minutes, but it was like she brainwashed my baby every day.

"It's okay." Jill bounced him. But she didn't hand him over. "Just one itty bitty sleep and then you'll be back. I'll see you in no time at all."

I forced a smile and took him out of her hands. After a quick kiss on his cheek, erasing the one she'd left, I put him straight into his car seat. Then the crying started.

He just hated his car seat. That was part of the reason for the daily theatrics, right? Maybe that drive from New York had turned him against this seat for life.

"Oh, Drakey," Jill crooned. "I know. I don't like it either."

I hate her. I hate her. I hate her.

The moment he was clicked into the harness, I left the nursery, not bothering with a goodbye.

Drake cried the entire walk to the door, and when we stepped outside into the snow, he just got angrier. Tears flooded my eyes as I hustled him into the Volvo. Then I was behind the wheel, reversing away.

One block away, I glanced in the rearview to see Knox's truck close behind. In the disaster that was daily daycare pickup, I'd forgotten he'd been following me home. But as the roads turned icy and the blizzard seemed to intensify on the highway, I was glad to have his headlights each time I looked in my mirrors.

The wind rattled the car's windows. The noise did little to improve Drake's mood and he continued to cry. When I finally reached the turnout to Juniper Hill, I breathed. *Almost home.*

Except it wasn't my home, was it? It was Knox's home.

I'd come all this way to start a new life. I'd moved across the country. And just over two months later, I was living under a roof I did not own. To steal Jill's words, I was *shacked up.*

What happened if Knox decided we were too much of a burden? That he wanted his single, easy life back?

Every doubt, every insecurity, plagued me on the drive home. Every day. My nerves shook like the trees in the wind as I drove down the gravel road. The house came into view and I hit the button for the garage, easing inside. I had Drake out and the handle of his seat over my arm as Knox parked in his own space.

"What's wrong with Drake?" he asked, stepping out of his truck.

"Nothing." I waved it off.

He knew it was a lie, but he stayed quiet, leading the way to his house and closing the door when we were all inside. "We're adding on to the house."

"Huh?"

"I don't like having to haul him through the snow to get inside." He bent and unbuckled Drake, lifting him out. Only when he was in Knox's arms did the crying stop.

Of course he stopped crying. He was with his second-favorite person.

I was a reluctant third.

"Memphis."

"Knox." I walked past him, taking the car seat and Drake's daycare bag to the guest bedroom.

My solitude was short lived. Knox's footsteps came into the room. "You walked out of that daycare on the verge of tears."

"Yeah, well..." I set the bag down and pulled out the dirty bottles. Heaven forbid Jill actually rinse them out for me. "That's normal."

"Why is that normal?"

"Because Jill, my daycare lady, loves Drake." I threw up my hands. "She loves him. She spoils him. And any other mother would just be happy that her baby is loved and spoiled, but it hurts me. It hurts me that he'd rather stay with her than come home with me. And it hurts me that we don't really have a home to come home to. This is *your* home. I

have no home. And my only family member is a little boy
who—"

"Loves you." Knox stepped forward and handed me
Drake, squashing the rest of my rambling outburst. Then he
wrapped his arms around us both. "He loves you. Because
you're a good mother."

I looked at my son, who'd stopped crying and was busy
fisting a handful of my hair. His brown eyes were so big and
expressive. His face so tiny and perfect. "He is my entire
world. I just wanted to be his."

"You are, honey."

I met Knox's blue gaze. "Am I?"

"Would I lie to you?"

No. The frustration seeped from my bones. "What
happened to me? I used to be so confident. Now I question
everything. I doubt myself constantly. And I *hate* it."

"Hey." He pulled me close and I burrowed into his
chest, dragging in his spicy scent. His arms and that smell
had been the only reasons I'd slept this week. He'd held me
every night, our limbs twined, our bodies naked, until I'd
shut down the fears and uncertainty to rest.

"Why do you want me?" I whispered. "I'm a mess."

"Come with me." He let me go and clasped my hand,
leading us to the kitchen. Then he dragged a stool out from
the island and patted the seat. "Hold Drake."

I took my son and propped him on a knee, bouncing him
gently.

On the weekends, it was easier to put him down. To let
him chill on his play mat. Weekdays, after he'd spent eight
or nine hours in Jill's arms, it was harder for me to let go. So
I held him and we both watched Knox round the island and
pull food from the fridge and pantry.

He opened a package of bacon and set it in a frying pan, the fat melting and popping as it splattered. He took out a container of flour, dumping a scoop directly onto the counter. Then he made a well, cracking three eggs into the white powder before sprinkling it all with salt.

He worked the flour and eggs into a dough, his fingers messy as he kneaded it from a sticky mess to this perfect, smooth ball. Then he went to work with a knife, chopping the crispy bacon and then parsley before grating cheese.

He kept on working until he had filled two bowls with pasta carbonara, and when he set mine in front of me, he simply kissed my temple and handed me a fork.

Drake began to squirm halfway through dinner so I excused myself and escaped to the bathroom to give him a long bath. Then I sat with him on the guest bed and fed him his bottle. He fell asleep almost instantly.

Knox was exactly where I'd left him, seated at the island, scrolling through his phone. Surrounded by a mess. When he heard me, the phone was put aside. "He asleep?"

"Yeah." I reached for my bowl but he took it from my hands, putting it exactly where it had been.

When he stood, his face was unreadable, his expression closed. "Did you like dinner?"

"It was amazing." Everything he made was amazing.

"Good. Now look around."

The kitchen was a disaster. He had grease splatters on his shirt, and flour dusted his jeans. The counters and stove would need a thorough scrubbing. The floors would need to be mopped and the dishwasher run.

"The craziest days in the kitchen end with food on every surface. Those are the days when I walk out the door so exhausted I can barely keep my eyes open on the drive home.

Passion comes from the mess, Memphis." He threaded his hands into my hair. "So does everything lasting."

My frame sagged. "You deserve—"

"You."

"I was going to say better."

"No. I deserve you. Because I want *you*. And damn it, I earned you. All the shit I went through. The hell you endured. Who fucking cares if it's messy?" He flicked a wrist around the room. "It's exactly the way it should be."

"But—"

"Goddamn it, Memphis. Stop arguing with me." In a flash he picked me up and set me on the island. A fork went sailing, clattering to the floor. Then he stepped in between my legs, holding my gaze, our noses touching. "Let me make this clear. You are mine. Drake is mine. For all of your todays and each of your tomorrows. Mine. Do you not want me?"

"Of course I want you."

"Then fucking kiss me."

I put my hands to his face but as he leaned in, I pushed him back. Because I had something to say too. "I'm scared."

"No shit."

I rolled my eyes. "I go a little crazy."

"So what?" He leaned in again, this time more insistent. "Go crazy. Be scared. You won't chase me away."

There was a dare in his voice. Like he knew I wanted to doubt him so he dared me to try. He dared me to push because he wouldn't walk away.

"You're mine too," I whispered.

"I know." He leaned in and this time I let him capture my lips. He stroked his tongue across my lower lip and when I opened for him, he delved inside, not hesitating for a moment as he swept me into his arms and carried me down the hallway to the bedroom.

The jeans and long-sleeved tee I'd worn were stripped off instantly, leaving me in nothing but a black bra and panties. I freed the button on his jeans as he reached behind his neck and yanked his shirt over his head.

My hands roamed over the strong muscles of his chest, falling to the rippled stomach and the cut lines around his hips. Beyond the windows, the snowstorm raged. Here, us, together, we were ablaze.

Knox banded an arm around my back as his tongue and lips devoured me, never breaking free as he kept me pinned against his warm skin. With his other hand, he delved beneath my panties, his long fingers finding my center.

He stroked through my wet folds, torturing me with his touch.

I gasped against his mouth as I began to tremble. He toyed with me, plunging a finger inside as he rubbed my clit. My hips rocked against his hand, matching his rhythm.

"Knox," I whimpered.

"Come on my fingers. Then you can have my cock." He dipped his lips to my neck, latched on and sucked as he pumped his fingers in and out, stroking my inner walls until I was panting.

I lifted a leg, hooking it around his hip, as my arms looped around his neck and I held on, riding his hand as he finger fucked me. Stars exploded behind my vision and I came on a cry, a burst of pleasure so pure I couldn't do anything but feel.

"Fuck, but that is hot." He nibbled on my earlobe as the aftershocks rang through my limbs. Then he unwrapped me from his body and laid me on the bed, stripping off my panties and bra.

He popped his finger into his mouth, humming at my taste, then he pushed my legs apart so I was spread wide. "Don't move."

I nodded, lifting my hands to my pebbled nipples and giving them a tug.

"Again." Knox stood at the end of the bed and watched.

I pulled at my nipples, loving the flare in his eyes. "Like this?"

"Again."

I smiled and kept toying with them as he stepped out of his jeans, his thick arousal bobbing free.

He wrapped his fist around the velvet shaft, stroking it over and over as he watched me play. A bead of come formed at his crown and I licked my lips. "You want your mouth on me, Memphis?"

"Yes," I breathed.

"Later. Tonight, I'm going to come on your pretty tits."

My breath hitched again.

"Touch your clit."

I let go of one breast, dropping it to the hardened nub between my legs. The second I touched myself, my back arched off the bed.

"Don't close your legs," Knox ordered.

I kept them wide as he settled between them, kneeling above me.

His hand on his shaft never stopped working as he pumped. The other hand swatted my fingers away from my center. "Touch your nipples."

I obeyed. Instantly. In the bedroom. In life. Whatever pleasure I brought him, he'd give it back ten times over.

His hand found my clit again, and he matched the rhythm

of his strokes on us both, working me up until I could barely breathe.

"That's it, honey. Come again."

I detonated, my eyes squeezing shut as the orgasm racked through my body.

Knox groaned and did exactly as promised. He came on my belly and my breasts. I watched as ecstasy washed over his handsome face. As his Adam's apple bobbed with his release. As he came undone. For me.

A shiver rolled over his shoulders as he opened his eyes. Then he gave me a sexy, devilish smirk. "*Now* you're a mess."

His mess.

In that mess, there was passion.

In that passion, we were perfect.

CHAPTER 18

MEMPHIS

Knuckles had never looked so magical. This restaurant was meant to be full of people, and not a single table sat empty. From the moment I'd stepped through the door, the noise had swallowed me whole. The clink of silverware. The rumble of conversation. The boom of unrestrained laughter.

The scent of spices and herbs lured me deeper into the space. Roasted turkey. Creamy potatoes. Tangy cranberries. Sage stuffing and sweet cornbread. My stomach growled.

Drake felt the excitement in the air and let out a little squeal, kicking his legs as we slipped past the hostess station.

Some of the people eating their Thanksgiving feast were guests I recognized from the hallways of the hotel. Others were locals, most faces I didn't know. But someday, like Knox, I hoped to walk through here and know most people by name.

I pushed through the swinging door to the kitchen, expecting chaos. Instead, I was greeted by more laughter as Roxanne, Skip and Knox stood around the gleaming prep table. The teenager who washed dishes was stacking clean plates.

"Am I in the right place?" I asked.

Knox chuckled and came over, lifting Drake from my arms. Then his mouth was on mine, his tongue sweeping across my lips.

I blinked, taken aback by the kiss, but then I lifted my hands to his face to hold on, laughing as he growled and let me go. "Whoa. Now there's a hello."

"Hello." His smile was breathtaking.

Drake latched a hand onto his beard and pulled.

"Hey, boss." Knox kissed his cheek, then pulled me into his side. "How was the morning?"

"Guessing not as hectic as yours."

Because daycare was closed for Thanksgiving, I'd spent the morning with Drake. Eloise, best boss in the world, had changed the shifts so I could have today and tomorrow off. I'd be working all weekend, but Knox had volunteered to watch Drake.

I'd spent an hour playing with my son, working on tummy time and rolling over. Then during Drake's morning nap, I'd cleaned Knox's house. He'd left just after four to get to the restaurant and prep for the holiday meal.

Knuckles had a single menu today and had been reservation only. Locals who hadn't wanted to cook and those visiting Quincy had blocked out the day months ago. Every seat had been taken.

"How did everything go?" I asked.

"Good. Easy." He chuckled as Roxanne and Skip both scoffed.

"This is the first time I've breathed since five," Roxanne said, stripping off an apron as she headed to the walk-in. She came out with three square silver bowls, each covered in clear plastic wrap. "I'm going home to eat myself into a food coma."

"Thanks for today," Knox said.

"You bet. See you guys tomorrow."

Knox waved as she disappeared down the hallway to slip out of the side exit. Then he let me go, handing Drake over, to unbutton his white coat.

"You don't need to stick around?" I asked, glancing to the door and all the people beyond.

"No, we're all done. Every table has food. There will be a ton of dishes to wash, but Skip's family dinner isn't until tonight so he's going to close up." He balled up his coat, taking it to a laundry bin, then retrieved his keys and jacket from his office. "Call me if you need anything."

Skip lifted a hand. "Happy Thanksgiving."

"Same to you." Knox stole Drake again, carrying him as we headed out of the kitchen. Not five steps into the dining room and a man stood from his table of eight, hand extended.

"This is quite the meal, Knox."

"Thanks, Joe. Appreciate you all coming down."

"We were just talking about how this will be our new tradition." Joe glanced my way and Knox put his hand around my shoulders.

"Joe, this is my girlfriend, Memphis. And this little man is Drake."

"Pleased to meet you," Joe said, shaking my hand.

"Hi." I nodded and smiled, hoping the shock didn't register on my face.

Girlfriend. I'd been a girlfriend before. Never had that status sounded so...lasting.

It took twenty minutes to get across the room because every table we passed, someone would stop Knox and compliment him on the meal. Then he'd introduce me as his girlfriend. Over and over. Each time, a shiver raced down my spine.

Until finally we made it to the doors and escaped outside to the snow.

"Let's just ride together. We'll get my truck tomorrow."

"Okay." I followed his footsteps through the snow to the Volvo in the parking lot.

The storm last week had brought in over twelve inches. It showed no signs of melting. But this early winter was fine by me.

The snow made Quincy even more charming. And in a way, it was like a cocoon, isolating us from the outside world. I still hadn't heard from my parents, and as the days ticked by, my anxiety ebbed.

Waiting wasn't easy, but I had plenty of distractions. A baby boy. And my Knox.

We piled into the car and Knox took the keys so he could drive. Then we set out for the Eden ranch.

My knees began to bounce as we pulled off the highway. I sat on my hands so they wouldn't fidget.

Knox's fingers drummed on the steering wheel, but unlike me, it wasn't nerves. Energy radiated off his broad shoulders, and the grin on his face was intoxicating.

"You're wired."

"Yeah." His blue eyes sparkled in the bright afternoon

sun. "It's the restaurant. Today was crazy busy. I'm still riding that wave."

"You really love it, don't you?"

"I really do."

A pang of envy hit. "I don't love cleaning rooms."

He took a hand from beneath my thigh, threading our fingers together. "What do you love?"

What did I love? "I have no idea. I was never really given the freedom to decide."

"You're nothing but free now, honey."

"Other than I need money to pay for rent and food. Speaking of which, you haven't deposited my last rent check."

"Haven't I?"

I frowned. "If you don't cash it, I'm moving into the loft."

He chuckled. "I'll cash it."

"Thank you." I glanced at Drake in the back and the mirror facing forward so I could see his face. His attention was rapt on the window and the world outside. "Mostly, I just want to spend time with him. More time."

"You've got an Ivy League education. I bet if you started looking, you could find something online. People are working from home more than ever. Hell, if you want, we can turn the loft into an office."

"Maybe." That was so tempting. "But not yet. Not until I have some cash reserves built up."

"I can cover you."

"Thanks, but no." My independence was too important.

"You're stubborn," he teased.

"Absolutely."

He brought my knuckles to his lips. "I like that you're stubborn. But I'd like it even more if you loved your job."

"I don't dislike my job."

"That's not the same."

"I know," I mumbled. "Eloise would not be happy with you if I told her you were trying to get me to quit."

"Eloise wouldn't be happy with me for a lot of things where the hotel is concerned." He blew out a long breath. "My parents have been asking me to take it over."

"What?" I sat up straighter. "When?"

"It's been a discussion for a while. I haven't really wanted to make a decision so I've put it on the back burner. But...I can't ignore it forever. Their vision is to have all of the family businesses stay in the family. Griffin has the ranch. Lyla has Eden Coffee. The hotel is the next question mark and they'd like me to take it."

Knox? Really? "Don't get mad at me for this, but...I've always seen it as Eloise's."

He gave me a soft smile. "I'll never be mad when you're honest. And it is hers."

"Then why wouldn't they want her to have it?"

"She's young. I love my sister's heart, but there have been times when she's led with that heart and made the wrong business decision. Mom and Dad just got out of a lawsuit with a former employee. It's been...stressful."

"Oh. I didn't realize." Eloise had told me a lot about her family and the hotel and Quincy in general, but not about a lawsuit. "Do you even want to run the hotel?"

"Not really," he admitted. "But I'd rather take over than have Mom and Dad sell it."

I grimaced. The hotel wouldn't be the hotel without the Edens. Without Eloise.

"If I did it, hopefully nothing much would change. I don't want to take Eloise's job. But rather than her answering to my parents, she'd answer to me. And I'd be fairly hands-off, just there to step in for the harder conversations."

Considering I rarely saw Harrison or Anne at the hotel, I doubted Eloise would mind going to Knox instead. Maybe she'd actually like having someone closer to bounce ideas off of. Still…why did this feel so wrong?

"Feels like a betrayal." He voiced the answer to my unasked question. "Did you know that Eloise was named after our great-great-grandmother, Eloise Eden? It was her hotel."

"She told me that on my third day."

"She's proud. She should be. She's worked hard." He waved it off. "Anyway… I wanted you to know. Get your thoughts. We don't have to talk about it today."

The nerves I'd been battling all morning spiked as we drove underneath a log archway. At its apex was the Eden ranch brand.

"Why am I nervous?" It wasn't like I hadn't met Knox's entire family. His siblings were often at the hotel. His parents were too. Talia was Drake's doctor.

But today was a family function at Harrison and Anne's home. And I was the girlfriend joining a holiday gathering for the first time.

"You've got nothing to worry about. Well, except Eloise mentioned baking cookies. Steer clear of those."

I giggled as he rolled down a gravel road bordered by barbed-wire fences. Beneath the evergreens that towered over the land, the ground was covered in a blanket of snow. It was peaceful. Serene.

"This is lovely," I said.

"It's a beautiful slice of the world."

I smiled. "It is. But I love your slice on Juniper Hill more."

"Me too." He winked and drove the rest of the way while I studied the countryside.

My heart raced when a log house with a wraparound porch came into view. The home stood proudly in a clearing through the trees. Beyond a wide, open lot was a shop building. Opposite it was an enormous barn and stables.

Every roof was dusted with snow. A plume of smoke came from the house's chimney. A string of vehicles was parked outside.

"Are we late?" I asked.

"No. We're not eating until later," he said, parking the car. "But I'm guessing everyone's been here most of the day, hanging out."

"Okay." My fingers shook as I unclipped my seat belt.

My family's holiday meals were usually short and quiet. We'd sit around the table, staring at our phones through the meal. After our last Thanksgiving, the staff had barely begun clearing the empty plates before we'd all scattered.

Dad and Houston would disappear to Dad's office to talk about work. Mom would drink too much champagne and go to bed early. Raleigh and I had never been close. Not as little girls, certainly not as teenagers. She loved shopping and traveling with her friends. She wouldn't do anything to risk her trust fund.

We'd all been our own islands.

Except I was tired of being on an island. Today, I wanted to belong.

Knox climbed out of the car and retrieved Drake. He had the diaper bag over a shoulder and I was still stuck in the passenger seat. He bent, staring at me from his open door. "Need a minute? I can tell them you're on the phone."

He'd make excuses while I got my shit together.

"No." I took one last fortifying breath and stepped outside.

The front door opened as we climbed the porch stairs. Harrison, tall and broad, like his sons, filled the threshold. The bright winter sun brought out the gray strands threaded through his dark hair. "Hope you two are hungry. Anne's cooking enough to feed a hundred people."

Knox laughed. "Sounds like Mom."

"She made me buy all new plastic storage containers at the store so she can send the extras home with you kids. Which means if I want leftovers, I'm going to have to drive to your house."

"I've got leftovers from the restaurant." Knox clapped Harrison on the shoulder as we reached the top stair. "So you can keep ours. I'll hide them in the garage fridge for you."

"Attaboy." Harrison laughed and pulled me into a hug. "Glad you're here, Memphis."

"Thank you for having us."

"Come on in." He shifted to tuck me against his side, making the squeeze through the door a tight fit. But he didn't let me go as he led me through the entryway to the kitchen. It smelled as fantastic as the restaurant. "Make yourself at home. I'm not much for house tours so just poke around until you find what you need."

Poke around. I hadn't *poked around* at my parents' house and it was the house I'd grown up in.

"Oh, good. You're finally here," Anne said as we walked into the kitchen, drying her hands on a towel before pulling me into a hug.

The moment she let me go, Lyla was there to take her place. Then Eloise joined us from the living room with her famous smile, the one that never failed to make me smile in return. Mateo wandered into the room with an older man I'd learned was Harrison's brother, Briggs. And finally Winslow and Griffin came from a hallway, having just put Hudson down for a nap.

"What are you working on?" Knox asked Anne, walking over to the stove and pulling a lid off a pot.

"Don't touch that." She swatted his hand. "I'm experimenting with the cranberry sauce."

"Want some help?"

"You've been cooking all day." She shooed him away until he stood beside me on the other side of the island. "Lyla and I are doing dinner."

"Can I help?" I asked. "I'm not much of a cook, but Knox has been teaching me a few things."

Our cooking lessons were infrequent and infused with foreplay. Whenever I'd stand at the counter, Knox would come up behind me to toy with my hair or drag his palms over my ass. But I'd learned how to make more than boxed macaroni and cheese.

Anne glanced past me to where Eloise was talking to Griffin. Then she nodded to the Ziploc bag of cookies on the counter. "If those accidentally found their way to the trash can in the garage while you went to grab yourself anything from the fridge out there, that would be fine."

"Are they really that bad?"

Anne and Lyla shared a look.

"Cookie disposal. On it."

"Thank you," Lyla mouthed, then went back to peeling potatoes.

The front door opened and shoes stomped on the floor. Then Talia breezed into the room in a pair of teal scrubs.

"Hello! Am I the last one to get here?"

"Yep." Knox moved to kiss her cheek but she ignored him and threw her arms around me for a hug.

The Edens had more than blue eyes and chocolate hair in common. They all knew how to give a hug that made me want to cry.

They hugged without hesitation. They didn't stiffen like my mother. They weren't worried about their makeup rubbing off like my sister. They weren't averse to general human contact like my father and brother.

The Edens hugged.

And with every one, I realized just how lonely my life had been.

"How's my little Drake?" Talia took him from Knox, kissing his cheek. She'd gushed and fawned over him at his checkup earlier this month. And when she'd declared him perfect, I'd immediately agreed. "Look how big you're getting."

"Don't be a baby hog." Harrison waltzed into the room and lifted Drake from Talia's arms. "Come on, buddy. Let's watch some football."

Drake let out a string of babble and drool, loving the attention.

"I'm not a baby hog." Talia reached for an olive from the snack tray on the counter. "Where's Hudson?"

"Asleep." Knox plucked up a pickle and popped it into his mouth as Griffin and Winn joined us.

"Hopefully with a nap he won't be a terror through dinner," Winn said. "He was exhausted."

"Because he wakes up before dawn," Griffin muttered, pulling out a stool. "My boy's a morning kid."

"Not mine." Knox pulled out the stool beside his brother.

"Mine's a night owl."

The entire room went still as my breath caught in my throat.

Mine. One short word, four simple letters, and if there'd been any doubt that I was in love with Knox Eden, it vanished.

I loved him because he loved Drake.

All eyes were on Knox. Anne stared at him with her hands clasped against her heart.

He simply shrugged and ate another pickle. "Lyla?"

"Yeah."

"Tell Mom that her cranberry sauce is about to boil over."

"It is no—oh, shit." Anne flew into action, ripping the pan off the stove.

A tiny cry carried from the hallway and it didn't belong to my son.

"So much for a nap," Griff said. "I'll get him."

But before he could go rescue Hudson, Talia flew down the hallway. "No, no, no. He's mine."

"She has baby fever," Lyla said. "Thank God it's not contagious."

The room laughed and settled into easy conversation. Griffin and Knox talked about the ranch and the upcoming calving season. Winn told us about the 9-1-1 call that had come in yesterday from a woman who'd mistaken a squirrel in her garage for a burglar. Then her grandpa, Pops, arrived with a small bouquet of flowers for every woman in the house, including me.

I had the bundle pressed to my nose when Mateo returned to the kitchen with Drake on an arm. "Do you need me to take him?"

"Nope. Talia thinks she's going to be the favorite aunt. But Uncle Mateo is about to steal her thunder." He tickled Drake. "Isn't that right, dude? You ever need anything— candy, toys, junk food—I'm your guy."

Knox chuckled. "This will be interesting to watch."

My throat closed. My lungs wouldn't fill with air. I held up a finger and slipped away, finding a powder room down the hallway. I eased the door closed, forcing oxygen into my lungs as I braced on the counter.

My eyes flooded as the door opened again and Knox was there, wrapping me in his arms.

"Your family is..." I looked at him through the mirror. "It's beautiful. It's so beautiful I couldn't breathe."

"Better now?"

I nodded, blinking away the tears. Happy tears. "This is the third."

"The third what?"

"The third-best day."

A magnificent smile stretched across his face. "Like I said, honey. I'll take them all."

I stood on my toes, stretching for his lips. "Promise?"

"I swear it."

CHAPTER 19

Knox

It was strange to stand in the kitchen at Knuckles and be nervous. Not even on opening night had I felt this rattled. My fingers kept skimming the prep table, so I shoved them into my jeans pockets before I smeared my prints everywhere.

I scanned every surface of the room, from the gleaming counters to the polished stoves to the shelves of white dishes that glinted beneath the room's lights.

The scent of bleach clung to the air. It hadn't bothered me while I'd been cleaning but now...this kitchen should smell like food. Like vanilla and flour and cinnamon.

"Cookies." I sprang into action, swiping a mixing bowl from its shelf. Then I began hauling out supplies from the pantry. I was just cracking a couple of eggs into my mixture of sugar and butter when the swinging door opened.

Memphis walked in with Drake on her hip. Her smile

dropped as she saw the mess on the prep table, then her eyes softened. "You're nervous."

"I'm nervous," I admitted, my shoulders falling. And now, instead of a clean kitchen, I had a half-started batch of cookie dough. "I'd better clean this up."

"No, don't." She walked over and stood on her toes, tugging at my coat so I'd bend and give her a kiss. "Make whatever it is you're making."

"Snickerdoodles."

"Perfect."

I dropped my forehead to hers. No one else in the world would tell me to keep cooking. They'd look at the clock on the wall, see it was after five and realize the photographer was due here any minute, then they'd help me sweep it all away.

But not Memphis. She knew what I needed. A task. The slight disarray that made this kitchen my sanctuary. And her. I needed her.

For the first time in months, the restaurant was closed. Mondays were typically slow and I'd wanted to give the staff a day off to rest before the crazed Christmas schedule hit. That, and I'd wanted the day to clean without guests getting in the way.

Two weeks ago, right after Thanksgiving, I'd gotten an email from Lester Novak's magazine asking when we could work in a photo shoot. I wasn't sure if they'd want photos of the restaurant and the kitchen, so I'd made sure both were available and pristine.

Memphis and I had driven in together this morning. She'd offered to go home and give me space, but I wanted her here for this tonight. I wanted them both here.

Drake kicked and smiled, leaning my way.

I took him from her arms. "Hey, boss. How was daycare?"

"Great." Memphis's lip curled. "He was an angel, according to *Jill*."

I chuckled. "Ignore her."

"I know." She sighed. "And I know this is just my insecurities showing. But I don't like her."

"You don't have to. We could take my mom up on her offer."

After Thanksgiving, my family had pulled Memphis into the fold. They loved her. They knew I loved her, even if I hadn't said the words.

Mom didn't like the idea of her grandchildren in daycare, so she watched Hudson most days while Winn was at the police station and Griffin was working on the ranch. She'd offered to take Drake too.

"That's a lot to put on her," Memphis said. "I don't want to take advantage."

"It's not taking advantage if she wants to do it." And Mom wanted to do it. She'd asked me five times in the past two weeks. It would be a longer drive for Memphis to take Drake out to the ranch each day, but we'd no longer be boxed in by pick-up and drop-off hours.

And secretly, I wanted her to do it. I wasn't going to push, it was Memphis's decision, but I wanted her to spend more time with my family. Because the more she was with them, the more she'd realize they were hers too.

"But two babies?" Memphis asked.

"She had six of her own. And Dad's around to help."

"I don't know." She scrunched up her nose. "I don't want to upset Winn and Griffin because I added Drake to the mix."

"Trust me. They don't care." They wanted Drake and

Hudson to be buddies too.

Memphis tapped her chin. "Do you think she'd let me pay her?"

I scoffed. "Definitely not."

"See? That feels like I'm taking advantage."

"Tell you what…if you catch Jill gossiping again or she does something to piss you off once more, we tell her to fuck off. Deal?"

"Deal."

I was guessing it would take approximately a week before Jill was history. Memphis had told me about walking into the center and hearing Jill's comments to her coworker. It hadn't surprised me. Small-town gossip in Quincy was as frequent as sunny days. And I'd been single for a long damn time. There hadn't been a woman I'd wanted to date and it was known that I only hooked up with tourists who knew it would end after a night.

Until Memphis.

She'd blown into town and there would be no other women.

"Any calls today?" I asked.

"No. Nothing." She worried her lip between her teeth.

It was driving her crazy that she hadn't heard anything from her parents since before Thanksgiving. The assholes hadn't bothered giving her an update, but I didn't want her reaching out to them either. Not until they showed with a goddamn apology.

At this point, I was taking no news as a sign that Victor had paid whatever to whoever had blackmailed him. If they all disappeared, I wouldn't be brokenhearted.

Memphis deserved a hell of a lot better for her family.

Luckily, I had the best one around.

"I was thinking about my sister today while I was driving to get Drake," she said. "We used to go shopping together before every Christmas. It was the one thing we always did and enjoyed."

"Spending money," I teased.

"Yes." She giggled. "She hasn't spoken to me in months. I didn't even realize how damaged our family was because we were all so good at keeping up appearances."

"I'm sorry." I pulled her into my side, kissing her hair.

"I'm not." She touched Drake's shoe. "He deserves better."

"You both do."

She smiled. "You'd better get going on these cookies."

"Shit." I laughed and gave her the baby. Then I worked with fury, mixing the dough and rolling it into balls while the oven preheated.

Memphis helped me clean up in a flash and as I stowed the dirty dishes in the dishwasher, the door opened and Mateo poked his head inside. "Your lady is here."

"Would you mind bringing her back?" My heart hammered as I spoke.

"Sure. Smells good in here. Did you make cookies?"

Memphis laughed.

"Yes. And you can eat them all." My stomach was in a knot. "It's just a few pictures but...damn. I wasn't this nervous when Lester was coming to eat. What is wrong with me?"

"This article is a huge deal." Memphis walked over, handing me Drake. Then she reached up to fix my hair. "When I worked in the city, I oversaw a lot of photo shoots. Everyone would get nervous. It's normal."

"Did you just make that up so I'd feel better?"

"Nope."

"Stay. Don't go anywhere, okay? I want you to be here."

"Then we'll stay."

The door opened as I brushed my lips against hers. I broke away and looked up, ready to greet the photographer. Except the woman walking in behind Mateo was no stranger.

"Gianna?"

Memphis tensed.

What the hell was Gianna doing in Quincy? In my kitchen?

"Hey, Knox." Gianna's gaze held mine for a moment, then strayed to Memphis and Drake. She swallowed hard and forced a smile. "Good to see you."

"You're Gianna?" Mateo had rolled a large case in for her. He set it on its wheels, then crossed his arms over his chest. He looked to me and I gave him a slight headshake before he decided to toss her into a snowbank for breaking my heart years ago.

Gianna stepped out of the way as Mateo frowned and strode from the kitchen. Then she looked up and tucked a lock of her sleek black hair behind an ear.

"I didn't realize you were the photographer," I said. The magazine had simply said they were sending their photographer. I hadn't asked for a name. Not in a million years would I have expected Gianna to step into my kitchen.

"I, um...I started with the magazine a couple of years ago." So she'd known exactly where she was headed. She'd chosen to come here. Why?

The oven's timer dinged and Memphis reached for Drake. "I'm going to give you a minute."

"You don't—"

"We'll be back." Before I could protest, she had Drake

in her arms and was out the door.

Shit. I rubbed my beard, then took the cookies from the oven, setting them aside before facing Gianna again. "Why'd you come here, Gi?"

"It's been a long time."

I nodded. "It has."

"I tried calling you a few times."

"Yeah." And I hadn't answered.

"When I saw your name for this assignment, I thought…" She glanced at the door where Memphis had disappeared. "You look good. Happy."

"I am happy."

"That's great. Really great." She burst into action, shrugging the camera case off her shoulder. She unzipped it and pulled out the camera she'd always carried with her everywhere. "I saw a few places in the dining area that might be great. And this space too. I'd like to get some different angles and shots. Maybe even have you make something."

"All right." I watched as she inspected the kitchen, avoiding eye contact.

Gianna. For years, I'd wondered what I'd say if I saw her again. If my reaction would be full of anger or resentment. But as I stared at her, I was just…relieved. Life had been rocky for a while, but I ended up exactly where I'd needed to be—home in Quincy, waiting for Memphis.

"Let's start in the dining space. Then we can move in here." She lifted the handle of the case, carting it through the doors.

I followed, glancing around, hoping to find Memphis. But the space was empty.

Gianna set her camera on a table and bent to open the large case, lifting out a tripod. The lights came next, followed by extension cords and umbrellas. She moved with purpose, staging her equipment around a square table. It was the exact table where Lester had sat his second night in the restaurant.

"How is Jadon?" I asked.

"He's good." Gianna tugged her phone from her jeans pocket and opened it before handing it over. "It's full of pictures. You can swipe through."

I got stuck on the first one and my heart squeezed.

This was the baby I'd loved before he'd been born. This was the son I'd had for only weeks. The boy who would grow up and look like his real father.

Jadon's hair was a shade lighter than Gianna's. His eyes were green. They sparkled as he gave a toothy grin to the camera. Gianna didn't have green eyes. She had brown eyes.

Maybe Gianna had seen it early on. Maybe that's why she'd finally admitted the truth. Because as I stared at his picture, I knew the truth would have eventually come out.

Jadon had never been mine.

But Drake...

He wouldn't resemble me either. He didn't have my blood. He'd never share my DNA. And I didn't give a damn. Drake was *mine* in a way Jadon never had been.

I set the phone down on the table. "He's cute as ever. Growing fast."

"Too fast." She glanced toward the main doors, curiosity written on her face, but she didn't ask about Memphis or Drake. "The restaurant is lovely. It's very...you."

"It's been an adventure. But it's nice to be home. Be close to family."

"That's great." Her smile didn't reach her eyes.

"Why'd you really come?"

She dropped her gaze, unable to look at me as she spoke. "I think about you. About us. About what we might have been if I hadn't messed it all up."

"Why did you? Why did you keep the truth from me for so long?" It was the question I hadn't asked before I'd left San Francisco. There'd been too much raw pain and I hadn't wanted her excuses. Her explanations.

Gianna's eyes were glassy when she finally faced me. "I was afraid you'd leave."

"I wouldn't have. Not if you had told me from the start."

"Then maybe because I didn't want to give up the fantasy. I wanted to pretend and the longer I pretended, the harder it was to admit the truth."

"So you came here to…what?"

"To apologize." She gave me a sad smile. "I am sorry. So, so sorry."

"You told me before I left."

"It still rings true." She lifted a shoulder. "And I just thought maybe we could talk. Eat dinner together. Drink our favorite red wine. Catch up. When your name came up, I volunteered for this assignment. I thought it might be… It doesn't matter what I thought."

No, it didn't. There would be no second chances. I didn't want one.

"I'll plug in the extension cord." I swiped up the end and dragged it to the nearest wall, fitting it in the outlet. When I returned to the staged area, Gianna had her camera in hand and clicked the button, the shutter snapping as she tested the light.

After a few adjustments, she had me sit at the table, relaxed and casual in the chair. Then she had me stand and balance a fork on my index finger. She took a few shots where

I stared at the camera. Some where I looked to the wall.

"I think that's enough for in here," she said. "Let's head to the kitchen next."

"Want some help moving equipment?" I asked.

"No, that's okay. I've got it."

"Then I'll be right back." I walked past her and out the doors to the lobby, searching the space for Memphis. But except for Mateo, it was empty.

"She ran to Lyla's for a coffee." Mateo pointed to the large windows that overlooked the street.

When I'd asked this morning, Memphis had told me to wear my normal jeans and a black thermal. One step outside, I wished I had grabbed a coat. The cold was like a blast sinking to my core.

Thankfully, I didn't have to walk far. Ten steps in the direction of Eden Coffee and Memphis came down the sidewalk. Drake was bundled in his parka, the red puffy coat nearly the same shade as the tip of his nose.

"What are you doing?" she asked. "Where's your coat?"

"Inside." I took her elbow and we retreated to the hotel. But instead of returning to Knuckles, I pulled her straight for the fireplace to warm up.

"Are you done?" She looked past my shoulder, probably for Gianna.

"Not yet. We've got some shots to do in the kitchen."

"Oh." She sighed. "So that's...her."

"It is."

"She's beautiful."

I nodded. "She isn't you."

"Knox." Her shoulders fell. "If you need time to talk, I can just go home. Stay in the loft tonight."

"Memphis." I hooked my finger beneath her chin, making

sure she was locked on me as I repeated my sentence. "She isn't you."

She fell into me, her forehead crashing into my sternum. "I didn't know if maybe you still wanted—"

"You." I kissed her hair. "Only you."

Memphis was honest about her doubts. With Drake. With me. She told me how much she missed her confidence, but it was there. It had always been there. A woman without a backbone of steel wouldn't have moved across the country. She wouldn't have hit the reset button on her life.

One of these days, she'd realize it too.

Until then, I'd cover the gap.

Drake whimpered and squirmed. He wasn't a fan of the puffy coat.

"And you, boss. I want you too." I slid the zipper down on the parka and set him free. Then I put my hand on the small of Memphis's back and steered her to Knuckles.

Gianna was taking her test shots when we walked into the kitchen. Her eyes traveled to me, then Drake, then our interlocked hands before she finally looked at Memphis. "Hi, I'm Gianna."

"Memphis." Spoken with a look as cold as the current temperature. My girl was not a fan and she wasn't going to fake it.

I fought a smile.

Gianna squirmed.

"We'll go hang in the office," Memphis said.

"No, stay." I rounded the prep table, standing in front of the lights that Gianna had staged. "Ready?"

"Yes. Shift to your left a bit." Gianna took twice as many shots in the kitchen as she had in the dining room. She didn't try to make small talk or drum up a conversation. The only words she said were orders for me to change positions.

Twenty minutes in, she checked the view screen on the camera. "I'm not crazy about these. The kitchen is too..."

"Clean," Memphis answered for her, taking a sip of her coffee.

"Yes." Gianna nodded. "It needs a mess."

I grinned at Memphis. "How about dinner? Mac 'n' cheese?"

"Have I ever said no to your mac 'n' cheese?"

I winked and got to work.

As I went about boiling water and hauling ingredients from the walk-in, Gianna blended into the background. Her camera's shutter clicked in a steady stream as I made my woman her favorite meal.

"I think I've got it," Gianna said as I dished Memphis a bowl.

"Want to stick around and eat?" I asked.

"No, I think I'll head out. The magazine is usually pretty good about sending you the final shot selections before they publish. But if you want any for yourself, my email is still the same."

"Great. Before you go, would you do me a favor?"

"Sure."

She had her faults, but photography wasn't one. Gianna had a talent behind the lens.

I walked to where Memphis was sitting, watching, and picked up Drake. Then I took her hand and pulled her to the prep table, putting my arm around her. "Would you take one of the three of us?"

Memphis's hands went straight for her hair, fixing it around her face. "I'm not very pretty for pictures."

"You're always pretty, honey."

Gianna studied us for a long moment, then lifted her camera. It clicked a few times, and as she checked the photos, an understanding came over her face.

She saw it. She saw the way I loved Memphis. "I'll get this one to you."

"Appreciate it."

Gianna tore down her setup in minutes, loading it into her case. Then she hauled it to the door, stopping before leaving the kitchen. "It was nice to meet you, Memphis."

"Have a safe trip home."

Gianna gave me a sad smile. "Goodbye, Knox."

"Bye, Gi."

She disappeared, returning to her world. While I sat down beside mine.

And ate dinner.

CHAPTER 20

KNOX

"Close your eyes." Memphis clasped my hand, pausing outside the hotel annex's doors. Then she led me through, pulling me in a few steps before we stopped. "Okay, open them."

In the past ten days, the ballroom had been transformed for an elegant winter wedding. Golden lights had been strung above the dance floor. Bouquets of red and green dotted tables dressed in white. Even the chairs had been covered. At their ties were sprigs of holly and red berries.

"Wow." I let Memphis pull me deeper into the room, passing tables set with gold-trimmed plates and crystal goblets.

"Isn't it a dream?" Memphis's smile stretched across her face. "It's been so fun to help set it all up."

The wedding tomorrow wouldn't be a large affair. It was

for a local couple and they'd limited the guest list to one hundred. Knuckles was catering the event. The hotel was sold out, not only from the out-of-town wedding guests but for those in Quincy for the holiday.

Christmas was in three days, and every member of the staff had been working nonstop, especially Memphis. She'd kept up with the housekeeping rush, and when the bride had asked for help getting this ballroom staged, Memphis had been the first to volunteer.

"The cake is going to go there. Then the bar is getting set up tomorrow in that corner." She pointed around the room. "And the DJ will be next to the dance floor. I'm going to pop in tomorrow morning and make sure all of the flowers have water."

"Are you working tomorrow?" It was a Saturday and she hadn't mentioned it. Though we'd been so busy this week that by the time I'd made it home each night, there hadn't been a lot of conversation. I'd save just enough energy to give her an orgasm or two before we'd both crash hard.

"No, but I was going to come into town and do some last-minute shopping. Maybe get your mom something small for Christmas."

"We already got her a present." A gift card to the local spa.

"That was from you. I want to get her something from me. Besides, it's not like I'm shopping for my own mother this year."

"Sorry."

She lifted a shoulder.

Weeks had passed with no word from her parents, not even a hint as to how they'd handled the blackmail situation. I checked the New York newspapers online each day. Memphis did too. There hadn't been a mention of any member of the Ward family or Oliver MacKay.

The calls from Beatrice had stopped, so I assumed that Victor had paid, and in turn, they'd disowned Memphis once more. They'd left her in Montana.

But she wasn't alone. Not any longer.

We reached the dance floor and I spun Memphis into my arms. "Dance with me."

"I miss dancing." She leaned her head against my chest as we swayed in the quiet room. "When I lived in New York, there was always an event or wedding or gala to attend. The dinner conversation was usually about business or who was buying a new yacht or where so-and-so was going in Europe. It was the same, every time. But I loved the dancing."

"And who would you dance with?"

She tilted to meet my gaze. "No one important."

"Good answer." I let her go, twirling her once, then pulled her close. "Did Eloise ever show you pictures of what this room used to look like?"

"No. Why?"

"Ask her for them sometime. Then you'll really appreciate the transformation." The building had been empty and dark and musty. Its renovation had been mostly cosmetic to clean away dust and brighten the walls.

"Okay." She smiled, taking in the room, her eyes dancing.

Memphis would get the same expression when she watched Drake play or studied me in the kitchen. But it was the first time I'd seen her light up for something here, in the hotel. "You love this, don't you?"

"I do. I've always loved weddings. Helping with this has made me think...the bride has done all of the planning herself. She's had to coordinate with the vendors and rental places. I asked her if she had a wedding planner but I guess there isn't one in town."

"There isn't. When Winn and Griffin got married, Winn organized their wedding herself too."

"What if…" She blew out a long breath. "What if I tried? I'd do it in my spare time. I don't know if there's a demand but I could organize any event. Corporate meetings or retirement parties or weddings."

"Yes." Whatever kept that look on her face.

"I see the way you love Knuckles. I want that too. If working means time away from Drake or you, I want to love it."

"Do it. I'll help with whatever I can."

She blushed. "Then maybe I will."

I spun her around again, then reluctantly let her go. "What's on your schedule the rest of the afternoon?"

"Not much. With the rooms full, I've just been tidying up as people come and go. There's a guest on the fourth floor who requested a late checkout, so hopefully that's empty by now. The next guest who was supposed to check in called about an hour ago. Their flight got canceled so it's actually an empty room."

Empty rooms were a rarity this time of year. "What if we booked it? Just you and me. We could see if Mom wanted to watch Drake tonight. I bet she'd stay at our place. Then tomorrow I can get up, head to the kitchen. You can check on the wedding before you head home."

She worried her lip between her teeth. "I've never left him alone at night."

"Gotta be a first. If we don't like it, we'll go home."

"Um…" She drew in a deep breath, then smiled. "Okay."

With her hand clasped in mine, I dragged her to the

front desk.

Eloise didn't bat an eyelash when I told her I wanted the room. It was too late in the day to fill the reservation, and it had been ages since I'd stayed as an actual guest, something we all did from time to time.

"I guess I'll go clean our room." Memphis laughed when Eloise handed her the key cards.

"Come see me when you're done," I said.

"Sure." She stood on her toes, fisting a handful of my shirt to drag me to her lips. Then we went our separate ways, her toward the elevators while I headed for Knuckles.

The dining room was empty for the lull between lunch and dinner. It would start to fill in the next hour as people began wandering in for a meal. But the kitchen was busy, all hands on deck, preparing for the wedding tomorrow.

Music blared from the radio in the corner. The scent of onions and garlic permeated the space. Skip and Roxanne argued over which drink was better—eggnog or Tom and Jerry's.

"Knox, which—"

"Eggnog," I answered before Roxanne could finish her question, then disappeared to my office to check a few emails.

The bride for tomorrow's wedding had been emailing me daily since we'd started planning the menu. As expected, the moment I opened my inbox, there was a note from her confirming we had enough champagne for the event. Something, if Memphis had been her wedding planner, she could have confirmed weeks ago.

It was a brilliant idea. Quincy, and The Eloise, could use a planner. Maybe we could hire Memphis to be the hotel's official event coordinator. It would mean a pay raise and if she wanted to expand into her own business, we could give her that flexibility too.

My computer dinged with another email and I tensed at Gianna's name. I clicked it open to find a simple message—*Merry Christmas*—and one photo.

It was the picture she'd taken of Memphis, Drake and me in the kitchen.

Memphis was the spotlight, her face so beautiful I struggled to tear my eyes away. She looked up at me while I smiled down at her. The only one actually looking at the camera was Drake.

I shoved away from my desk and weaved through the kitchen. "Be back."

Memphis was on the fourth floor when I found her in the empty room. She'd stripped the bed and was dusting when I walked inside.

"Hey."

"Hey." She smiled. "What's up?"

"Got this today." I dug my phone from my pocket and pulled up the email. Then I handed it over so she could see the photo.

Her eyes softened. "I love this."

"I love you."

Memphis gasped and the phone fell from her hand, landing with a thud on the carpet. "W-what?"

"Not exactly how I'd planned to say that," I muttered. But it was out there now, and well…it was the truth. "I love you."

Her eyes searched mine. "I love you too."

I slammed my mouth on hers, my tongue delving inside for a taste of her sweet.

She clung to me, her fingertips digging into my arms, her

heels rising off the floor as she lifted to her toes.

We kissed until we were breathless, then I tore my lips away and worked free the button on her jeans.

"Knox." Her eyes darted past me to the open door.

I held up a finger, then stalked over to kick free the stop and let it slam closed. When I came back, she arched her eyebrows. "I've wanted to fuck you in one of these rooms for months."

Her cheeks flushed. "I'm on the clock."

"Then tomorrow we'll clean it off the clock and call it square." I dropped to a knee, holding her gaze as I pulled her tennis shoes off her feet. Next came her jeans. I slid down the zipper and as I tugged them down, taking her panties along for the ride, she shimmied her hips and kicked them free from her legs.

"Climb up on the bed. Get that shirt off. Then hands and knees."

She nodded, obeying my every word. Off came her top, followed by her bra. Then she shot me a wicked grin as she planted a knee in the mattress and aimed that beautiful ass my way. Her pussy, pretty and pink, was wet and ready.

I freed my shaft from my jeans and hurried to pull on the condom I'd been keeping in my pocket. Then when I was sheathed, I dragged my cock through her folds as I stood behind her, earning a moan. "This is going to be hard and rough."

"Yes," she hissed, pressing back.

With one hand, I guided myself into her slick channel. With the other, I grabbed her ponytail, wrapping it around my fist. And then I thrust home.

"Oh, Knox." She arched into me, her bottom lip sawed between her teeth.

"Fuck, you feel good. So fucking good." Every time, it got better and better.

Maybe that was because I loved her, more every day.

Her inner walls fluttered around my cock as I pulled out and slammed inside. She moaned, a heady, sultry sound from her throat. It was the same moan she'd given me just last night when she'd dropped to her knees and let me fuck her mouth.

"Say it, Memphis. Say it again." I thrust forward once more, her breasts bouncing and swaying as my hips smacked her ass.

Memphis purred, "I love you."

I fucked her hard, thrust after thrust. I filled the room with the sound of skin slapping skin. Of her hitched breaths and whimpered moans. I worked her into a frenzy, her hands gripping the mattress, her toes curling over the side. I gripped her ass, squeezing hard, until she flew over the edge.

Memphis pulsed around me, squeezing and clenching through her orgasm. Being inside her was an addiction. I was at her mercy. There was only one box of condoms left at home, and when they were gone, I'd start going bare.

I'd claim her in every way. I'd send her to sleep every night dripping with my come.

Her climax retreated and she collapsed onto the mattress, leaning into her forearms. But I kept on pounding, working my hips faster and faster as I palmed her ass. The build intensified, the pressure at the base of my spine blinding, until finally I let go. When the white spots faded from my eyes, I fell onto her, holding her tight as the world came back into focus.

Memphis giggled as I pulled free. "I can't believe we just

did that."

"Round two, tonight." I chuckled, heading to the trash can to dispose of the condom and tuck myself away.

She pulled on her shirt and bra, then stepped into her panties. Her eyelids were heavy and she yawned as she sat on the mattress to tug on her jeans. "Now I want a nap."

My woman slept hard after sex. "I'll pop over to Lyla's and get you a latte."

"Double peppermint mocha, please."

"You got it." I kissed her forehead. "How much longer you got here?"

"Thirty minutes. I cleaned the bathroom already. I just need to dust, make the bed and vacuum."

"I'll call Mom and make sure she's good to babysit. If she can't, I'm sure Talia will. I'll meet you in the lobby in thirty with your coffee. Then we can go home and pack a bag." I headed for the door but before I could touch the handle, she called my name.

"Knox?"

"Yeah."

"I love you."

I pressed a hand to my heart. "I love you."

With a wink, I left her to finish working while I headed for the kitchen to check in and grab a coat. Snow covered Quincy, but the sidewalks were clear and the roads plowed. The sun was dipping toward the horizon, inching toward the mountain peaks. Streetlamps illuminated the faint light as I made my way to Lyla's.

A couple came out of the jewelry shop next door, both of them laughing. I froze as they passed by.

Memphis was mine. Drake was mine.

A Christmas proposal was cliché as hell, and I didn't

give two fucks.

When I walked through the door, the man behind the counter did a double take. His bald head was shiny beneath the store's florescent lights, every one designed to catch the jewels and make them sparkle. "Oh...hi, Knox."

"Hi." I lifted a hand and went straight for the center case.

"Can I help you find something?"

My heart thumped but my voice was steady. "An engagement ring. Please."

He blinked, then flew into action, laying out a navy velvet cloth. Then he placed ring after ring on the counter for me to inspect, rambling on about cut and clarity, while I lifted each and tried to imagine them on Memphis's finger.

It was the eleventh ring that was the winner. A square diamond surrounded by a halo of smaller stones.

"This one." I set it aside and dug my wallet from a pocket. Ten minutes later, I walked out of the jewelry store with the ring in my pocket and went to Lyla's for coffee.

I had two paper cups in hand when I pushed through the hotel's lobby doors.

Memphis was standing close to the couch beside the fireplace, her arms wrapped around her waist. The way she was biting her bottom lip and the worry line between her eyebrows made me walk faster.

"What's wrong?"

She nodded toward the office door just as it burst open and Eloise came storming out, attempting to shrug on her coat as she marched. The moment my sister spotted me, she snarled.

"Oh, fuck."

"Eloise." Mom rushed out of the office, followed by Dad. "Wait."

"They told her," I guessed. "About the hotel."

"Yep." Memphis nodded. "And she just quit."

CHAPTER 21

KNOX

"Eloise, wait." I handed Memphis our coffee cups and jogged to stop my sister before she could sprint out the door.

"You knew." Her nostrils flared. "How long have you guys been talking about this behind my back?"

"A little while."

"Fine." She tried to sidestep me, but I blocked her path. "If you want the hotel, it's yours."

"I don't." The reason I'd been avoiding this topic was because I'd always known what was in my heart. As my parents came rushing across the lobby, I looked over Eloise's shoulder and told them the same. "I don't want the hotel. It's never been mine."

"Because it's mine." Eloise gritted her teeth. "And none of you think I can handle it."

"We never said that." Mom came to her side, touching her elbow.

Eloise jerked her arm away. "You think I'm too soft."

"You have a big heart." Dad came to stand by my side. "That's not a bad thing. But this is a huge responsibility. We thought Knox might be able to take our place. Be there to give you some guidance."

Memphis inched closer, listening but staying back.

Eloise's eyes flooded with angry tears. "You should have told me, Knox."

"You're right. I'm sorry."

"This is because of the lawsuit, isn't it? I was trying to be a nice boss!" Eloise's voice carried through the room. "I had no idea he was going to sue us. And I never, ever harassed him. I'm sorry. I screwed up. How many times do I have to say sorry?"

I held up my hands, hoping to calm her down before a guest came wandering through. "How often does she need your input, Dad?"

"Lately, not much," he said. "Earlier this year…"

"Earlier this year I didn't have Memphis." A tear dripped down my sister's cheek.

Memphis's eyes swung to mine and went wide. She didn't understand how much she did here, did she? She had no clue how hard it was to find someone reliable and hardworking. She had no idea how much Eloise loved her.

There was no way Memphis would clean rooms for her entire life, but it had given Eloise a standard. A bar with which to measure everyone. I'd seen her hold the other housekeepers to a higher level. I'd seen her push them to do a better job.

And they were performing.

"I know I'm soft." Eloise's chin began to quiver. "I'm

trying. So hard. But you've already made the decision. I'm not good enough."

Dad's face paled. Mom closed her eyes.

"That's not it, Eloise." I stepped close and put my hand on her shoulder.

"It is. Maybe I should go. Start again in another town."

Mom's eyes flew open. "No."

"Just...hold up." A pair of guests walked through the lobby. I nodded as they passed us by, and then when the place was clear, I jerked my chin for everyone to follow me to the fireplace.

"You too," I told Memphis when she hung back.

"This is a family discussion," she whispered.

"And you're part of the family." I had the ring in my pocket to prove it. So I took her elbow and steered her to a couch, putting her on one side with Eloise on my other, waiting as Mom and Dad took the love seat.

I leaned forward on my elbows. "I don't want more than the restaurant."

Maybe I had earlier this year. Before Memphis. Before Drake. But if I added anything to my plate, it wasn't going to be here. It would be at home.

I wanted the flexibility to coach Drake's sports teams if he was into sports. Or take him to piano lessons or to the pool. I wanted more kids. I wanted nights at home on Juniper Hill with my wife.

Not longer hours in town.

"I'll take over the hotel," I said, reaching over to put my hand on Eloise's knee before she could bolt off the couch, *"until you're ready.* If Mom and Dad want to settle their estate, pass it down, then I'll take it until you're ready."

She scowled. "I'm—"

"Not ready." I gave her a soft smile. "You know you're not. Not yet. But you will be. There's no rush."

"No, there isn't a rush." Dad sighed. "If Knox doesn't want it, we can keep on with things as they are. This whole mess with Briggs, his dementia getting worse, it has me spooked. We just didn't want to leave anything unsettled in case something bad happens."

"We know you love this hotel," Mom told Eloise.

"Then don't take it from me," she pleaded and faced me. "Are you worried about me ruining it?"

"No," I admitted. She'd work herself to the bone before that happened.

"We'll leave it," Mom declared. "We'll give it time."

Eloise's shoulders fell. "Thank you."

Memphis dropped her chin, but not before I caught the ghost of a smile on her lips.

She'd been right. This was Eloise's hotel.

The bell at the front desk dinged and we all looked over to see a guest at the counter.

Eloise wiped at her eyes and rushed away.

Mom shook her head. "That went well."

"You were right." Dad sighed. "We shouldn't have brought it up today."

"Brought what up?" I asked.

"We had a conversation with Mateo this morning. He's moving."

"What?" I sat up straight. "Where? Since when?"

Mom dabbed the corner of her eye. "He's been looking for jobs in Alaska. He came over this morning to tell us he was hired as a pilot."

Shit. We were finally all in Quincy and now he was leaving.

"Mateo's a pilot?" Memphis asked.

I nodded. "He got his license in college."

"We came to tell Eloise," Dad said. "She said she knew. He told her about it but asked her not to say anything. I got frustrated and might have said something I shouldn't have said about her communication skills."

"It digressed from there," Mom muttered.

And in it all, they'd told her that they'd asked me to take over the hotel.

"Come on, Anne." Dad stood from his seat. "Let's go home before I get myself in more trouble."

Mom stood and followed him away from the fireplace, but he stopped before he could go too far, turning to look at Memphis.

"We're so glad you're here. I don't know if Eloise has told you that or not."

Memphis nodded. "She has. Almost daily."

Dad glanced over at my sister, who looked as happy and cheerful as she did any day. Like this argument had never happened. Later, when the guests were gone, she'd let down her façade. But right now, she would smile for the guests because this was her place.

"I think maybe I haven't been in here enough," he told Mom but his gaze was locked on Eloise.

"I think we've both missed a few things." She took his hand, then pulled him toward the door.

"Damn." I rubbed my hands over my face. "Didn't expect that today."

"For what it's worth, I think you made the right decision."

"I do too." I watched my sister hand the guests their room keys. "Are you done for today?"

"Pretty much. I'll see what Eloise needs. Do you still

want to stay here tonight?"

"Yes." Maybe I wouldn't wait until Christmas to give her this ring. Maybe I'd just do it tonight. "See if Eloise will let you go home early. I'll skip out too. We'll go to the house and pack for tonight. I haven't talked to Mom about babysitting yet, but I think after all this, I'll call Talia instead."

"Are you sure?" she asked. "We can postpone it."

"I'm sure." I stood and retrieved our coffees. "Roxanne is handling the restaurant tonight. I've got the wedding and dinner tomorrow. Let me just talk to my staff. Make sure everyone's good."

"Okay." She walked with me to the counter, waiting to talk to Eloise while I returned to Knuckles.

Fifteen minutes later, we were outside and heading to her car. I stole the keys from her hand and opened the passenger door to the Volvo.

We'd be about an hour and a half early to pick up Drake, but that would give Memphis more time with him before we came back to the hotel. More time for me too. The chaotic holiday schedule had kept me from them both.

It wasn't sustainable long-term. I wanted more nights at home than away, which meant I'd have to promote Skip and hire another line cook, but it would be worth it.

"How was Eloise?" I asked as I drove across town.

"Mad." Memphis shrugged. "I would be too. She feels like everyone doubts her. But she won't quit. She wants the hotel too much."

"Good."

"Will you do me a favor? I don't want to tell her about my wedding planner thing. Not yet. I don't want to quit the housekeeping crew. Especially now. What Eloise said... I won't let her down."

I took her hand. "I know you won't. And we can tell people whenever you want to tell them."

"But…"

"Oh, boy."

She smiled. "I know we were waiting for Jill to piss me off again before we yanked Drake. But if your mom is still up for watching him, I'd like to pull him out of daycare."

"Fine by me. Did Jill say something?"

"No. It's just…her." Memphis cringed. "I don't like her. I'm tired of him crying when I pick him up. Maybe that won't change with your mom, but that's different."

"Agreed." If Drake loved Mom, it would be because she was his grandma.

"I feel guilty. I just… I don't like it there. And he's *my* son. Not hers."

Actually, he was ours. But that was a correction I'd make once the ring in my pocket was on her finger. "I won't argue. When I picked him up on Monday and he cried, it pissed me off. I get it."

Memphis had been running late so I'd gone to get Drake before the daycare had closed. The moment I'd lifted him from Jill's arms, he'd cried.

Something about the whole situation sat wrong with me. It was like Jill didn't put him down all day. Like she intentionally spoiled him so that he'd want her. Maybe I didn't have a damn clue what I was feeling, but there was something slimy about her. Something that had rubbed me wrong.

Like Memphis, had she been mean to Drake, it would have been easier to pull him away. But that boy adored her.

"We'll ask Mom this weekend," I said. Because the daycare was closed all next week for the holidays, Mom had agreed to watch Drake. "See if we can make this Christmas babysitting permanent."

"I'm sure the daycare will make me give them a thirty-day notice."

"Probably, but as soon as Mom is good to watch him, we're switching."

"Deal." Memphis smiled. "God, I feel lighter already. This might be the last pickup."

"The last jailbreak." I pulled into the parking lot and left the engine running, then followed Memphis inside.

She walked down the hallway for the nursery, stopping inside the door to do a quick sweep of the room. "Hi. Um, where's Drake?"

"Hi." A woman who was not Jill glanced at the clock. "You're early to pick him up."

"So?" I stood behind Memphis and crossed my arms over my chest. "Where is he?"

"They, uh..." The woman swallowed hard. "She's not back yet."

"Back from where?" Memphis took a step closer. "What's going on?"

"I need to get my manager." The woman took a step, trying to pass us for the door, but I shifted and blocked her path.

"What the hell is going on?" My heart began to race. "Where's our kid?"

"Jill, um...she just left about thirty minutes ago. She took him to her place for a little bit to change some laundry or something. She promised to be back by five."

"She took him?" Memphis's jaw fell open. "She doesn't have my permission to take my child from this building."

"It's just—"

"Next door." Memphis held up a hand. "That's what you said last time."

Without another word, she swept up Drake's car seat and his diaper bag from his hook, then she marched to the center's office, where two older women were chatting.

I stood at Memphis's back and watched her read the riot act to the ladies and immediately pull Drake from their facility. Both claimed they had no idea Memphis hadn't given her approval.

"Jill said you didn't mind. That he could go with her."

"I did no such thing," Memphis barked. "We're done here. You will not see us again."

"We require a thirty-day—"

"Finish that sentence and I'll call my sister-in-law, the chief of police, and let her know that your staff is taking children off premises without parental permission." I leveled the women with a glare. "I believe they call that kidnapping."

Both blanched.

Memphis turned and walked out the doors, looking both ways. Her hands were shaking. "I don't know which house is hers."

"Hang tight." I stormed into the center and demanded Jill's address.

When I came out, Memphis was standing on the sidewalk, the car seat and diaper bag at her feet and her eyes full of worry.

"It's this one." I steered her to the home next door, a small, single-level home with blue siding and a green door. Every window was dark. The porch light was off.

There was nothing but silence as I rang the doorbell over and over. Then I pounded my fist on the door, but it didn't matter. No one was home.

"Are you sure it's this one?" Memphis asked.

"They said blue house next door." Every other home around the daycare was a shade of tan.

I pounded on the door again with no answer.

"What the fuck?" I backed away, scanning the street.

The color drained from Memphis's face. "Where's my son?"

CHAPTER 22

MEMPHIS

In just minutes the street had filled with police cruisers. Winn pulled in last, getting out of an unmarked SUV, and rushed over to where we stood. Her officers followed, crowding in close to form a blockade around us.

My entire body trembled as I stood tucked into Knox's side.

Winn took my hand, giving it a squeeze. "Tell me everything. From the beginning."

The idea of saying the words—*she took my son*—made my throat close. Like he knew I wouldn't be able to do it, Knox held me tighter and spoke for me.

He told her how we'd come to pick up Drake. How we'd gone to Jill's house only to find it empty. How we'd both raced for the center, panicked and frantic, and demanded information from the owner and other caregivers—there hadn't been much to share. No one in the building, not the women in the office or the girl in the nursery, had a clue where Jill would take Drake.

All we knew was that Jill had left with him, promising to return soon. And then she'd disappeared.

With every word Knox spoke, the tremors in my limbs amplified until I was sure that if not for his arm around my back, I would have buckled to the icy sidewalk.

Winn soaked in his statement like a sponge, listening without comment until he was finished. Then she began issuing orders to her officers. "Get Jill's information. Start with her car. Description. License plate. Make and model. Push an AMBER Alert immediately. Then run her plates and get it out around town. Dig into her phone after that. See if we can track her to a cell tower."

"You got it, Chief." One of the men took off running for the center's front doors.

"Search her house," Winn ordered two other officers.

They rushed off and only seconds later, I flinched at the boom of a door being kicked in.

"Has this ever happened before?" Winn asked.

I nodded, swallowing the lump in my throat. "Once. She took Drake with her to run home. But she was only gone for a few minutes. I told her she couldn't do that again."

"What's her relationship with Drake?" Winn asked.

"She loves him. She acts like she loves him." Maybe she loved him too much. My head was spinning. My legs began to crumble.

"Breathe." Knox held me tighter. "Breathe, Memphis."

I filled my lungs, the sting in my nose bringing a new set of tears. "Do you think she might have taken him? That she wants to keep him?"

"This is most likely just a miscommunication," Winn said. "Maybe she had to run to the store or something. You were here early today, right?"

I nodded. "Yes. I usually don't get here until after five."

"Okay." Winn squeezed my hand again and locked her gaze with Knox. The message passed wordlessly between them made my stomach knot tighter. There was dread there. Fear. And sympathy.

He was holding it together for me, but I wasn't the only one who stood shaking, numb from the cold and panic.

"Why don't you both wait in the car?" she suggested. "I need to ask more questions and make some calls."

"Come on, honey." Knox escorted me to the car, our steps slow because he must have known I didn't trust my feet. He helped me into the passenger seat, then rounded the hood for the driver's side. The moment the door was closed, he pulled out his phone and put it on speaker.

Harrison answered on the first ring. "Hi, Knox."

"Dad."

One word and Harrison heard the tremble in Knox's voice. "What's wrong?"

"We came to get Drake from daycare. He's gone. Jill, the woman who watches him, took him."

"Oh, God." Harrison sucked in a sharp breath. "Call Winn."

"Already did. They're pushing an AMBER Alert."

"I'll make some calls too." Without another word, Harrison ended the call.

Knox's fingers flew across the screen, pulling up another contact. Again, he left it on speaker.

"Thank you for calling The Eloise Inn. How can I help

you?" Eloise answered.

"Eloise. It's Knox." He repeated the same message and when Eloise gasped on the line, I had to squeeze my eyes shut to keep from crying.

"What can I do?" Eloise asked.

"Help us get the word out. The more people looking for them, the better."

"On it."

Knox sighed and stared at his phone, like he wanted to make more calls but couldn't find the strength to repeat the truth again.

"Is this a bad dream?" I whispered.

He set the phone on his thigh and looked to me, his own eyes full of unshed tears. "It has to be."

"What if we don't find him?"

"Don't go there." He took my hand, gripping it so fiercely that it hurt my knuckles. But I clung to the pain, clung to him, so that I stayed here, in this car, and didn't take a step down an unthinkable road. "We'll find him."

"We'll find him." There was no confidence in my voice. Only fear.

The two of us sat together in the cold car, watching as Winn and her team rushed back and forth between the daycare center and Jill's house. A crowd was gathering outside the daycare's doors.

The two women from the office had come outside, both bundled in coats. They made sure to keep their heads down and not glance our direction as we sat motionless, our short breaths curling into white wisps in the car. Neither of us thought to turn on the engine, to crank the heat. We were both too stunned.

I sat and stared through the windshield, a prayer running

through my mind on loop.

Find him. Find him. Please, let us find him.

"We left his stuff." Knox's words startled me as he burst out of the car, running to the sidewalk.

I'd grabbed Drake's car seat and diaper bag from the nursery. When had I set them down? Before or after we'd gone to Jill's? I couldn't remember now. Every minute seemed fuzzy, every second like a lifetime.

A fresh wave of dizziness hit, swirling around the what-ifs that I refused to let myself think, let alone voice.

Knox picked up Drake's things, carrying them to the backseat. Then he returned to the driver's seat and, this time, turned the key.

"I can't sit here," he murmured. The heat had barely begun to flow from the vents before he was out of the car once more, this time stalking toward Winn.

She stood in Jill's driveway, talking on the phone.

Knox walked right to her, waiting for her to end the call. The moment she put her phone away, the garage door at Jill's opened. It was empty. Where there should have been a car, there were only shadows.

Where would she have gone? Drake didn't have his car seat. What if she got into an accident? Had she gone into town? Maybe she'd ventured downtown for a coffee.

My hand found the door handle and I pushed it open, but before I could step outside, a blaring alarm sounded from my phone. The noise echoed through the air, not just from my phone, but from all the other people.

The AMBER Alert.

For my son.

That shrill sound slashed through my body, slicing to my heart. I clutched my chest, willing my heart to keep beating.

Find him. Please, find him.

Two cars pulled into the parking lot, both at almost the exact same time. Other parents were beginning to show to pick up their own children. Their faces were clouded in confusion and sudden worry before they each rushed inside.

Except inside, they'd find their children.

While I had not.

A rush of energy lit my nerve endings into a buzz. Sitting in this car, waiting, was no longer an option. I shoved outside, wrapping my arms around my waist, and hurried to join Knox.

He saw me and swallowed hard, then held out a hand.

I took it and faced Winn. "I can't sit here. I'm going crazy."

"We've got everyone in the department looking. The alert's out there. Let's hope we get a call."

"What if I just headed into town? Maybe I'll bump into her. Maybe she went to the store or Christmas shopping. She said she'd be back before I showed up. It's almost five."

"It would be better if you stayed here," Winn said. "In case we need information."

"You could call me." My eyes watered. "Please. Please don't make me sit here and watch. If this was Hudson…"

"Okay." She blew out a deep breath. "All right. Keep your phone close."

"I will." I moved to take a step, but before I could walk away, Knox's hand shot out and clasped around my elbow.

"Wait, honey."

"What?" I spun. "Are you coming too?"

"We need to tell Winn the whole story."

"What whole story?" she asked.

It took me a moment to read his face. Then realization hit me and my stomach did a cartwheel.

Oliver. My parents. The woman who'd tried to blackmail them for money.

"Do you think this is related?" I asked Knox.

"I don't know." His forehead furrowed. "But if it is, Winn needs the truth."

All this time, we'd waited for my parents to contact us. We'd endured their silence, hoping for the best possible outcome. Except what if that had been a mistake? What if Drake had been a target for months? What if we could have stopped this from happening?

"Memphis." Winn placed her hand on my shoulder, pulling me out of my head. "Talk to me."

"Last month, around Thanksgiving, my parents showed up in Quincy. Our relationship is...strained. They came because a woman was blackmailing them. She threatened to expose Drake's father's name. To tell people who his father is."

"Who is his father?" she asked.

I looked to Knox.

Knox was Drake's father. In all of the important parts of that label, Knox was Drake's dad.

They just didn't share the same DNA.

"His name is Oliver MacKay," I said, then told her the whole story.

Winn planted her hands on her hips. "Could they have taken Drake? Oliver or his wife or her family?"

"I don't know." Maybe they wanted him after all. Or maybe this was Oliver's wife's punishment for his infidelity.

"Chances are, Jill has him," Winn said. "You said she

loves him. The daycare owner confirmed that Drake's her favorite, by far. Given that, my hunch is that she's probably overstepped. She took him on a walk to a park or downtown or to visit a friend."

"But..." Knox voiced the doubts written on Winn's face.

"I need to know what happened with the woman in New York," she said.

"Okay." With shaking hands, I scrolled through my contacts and found my father's name. I tapped it and raised the phone to my ear, holding my breath as it rang. My heartbeat was so loud and hard that I felt my pulse blast through my veins.

"Memphis," he answered.

"What happened with the woman who was blackmailing you?"

"You made it clear that you didn't care about the outcome. You had your chance—"

"My son is missing." My voice cracked. "What happened? Please."

"What do you mean, missing?"

"Just tell me!" I screamed the words, the hold on my sanity beginning to break.

Before I could hear my father's response, Knox ripped the phone from my hand. "Talk. Now."

A tear sped down my cheek as I stared up at Knox. His jaw ticked and his nostrils flared at whatever my father said. Then he dropped the phone from his ear and ended the call.

"What?"

"He refused to pay. Told her to fuck off. Hasn't heard from her since."

"Oh, God." A hand flew to my mouth to hold in a sob.

How could I have been so foolish? In the past weeks, I'd let myself have hope. I'd let myself be blind. My father had never intended to help me. Not once.

I was about to crash to the sidewalk when a strong arm banded around my back, holding me up. "He called her bluff. And she called his."

"Does he have a name?" Winn asked.

Knox shook his head. "No. He didn't get one."

"This is my fault," I whispered. "I should have dealt with it myself."

"No. This isn't on you." Knox took my face in his hands, his thumbs wiping furiously to dry the tears. "We made this decision together."

"It was the wrong decision."

The anguish on his face only made my tears fall faster. "I know."

"What do we do? Where is he?"

"We'll find him." Knox pulled me to his chest, holding tight as he spoke to Winn. "What do we do?"

"I know you don't want to hear this, but I need you both to wait."

I growled into Knox's chest, the terror morphing to frustration and despair. "I can't sit in that car and do nothing. I can't watch mothers walk into the center and pick up their children. I can't."

"Walk to town if you want," Winn said. "But we've got a lot of people looking for Jill. I'll check in with the team and be back with an update shortly."

"Then let's go." He let me go and grabbed my hand, pulling me down the sidewalk as we set off toward Main.

My legs were stiff and wobbly over the first two blocks, but then they began to warm and my strides lengthened.

We walked in silence but the dull scream in my head grew louder with each step.

If my father had no idea who the woman was who'd tried to blackmail him, there was one person who would.

I stopped so abruptly that my hand slipped from Knox's firm grasp.

"What's wrong?"

"We have to know who this woman was. Even if it's not her, we have to know." The time for burying my head in the sand was over. I'd made the mistake thinking that in Montana I was unreachable. Maybe this had nothing to do with the blackmail but I wasn't going to take that chance.

"You're going to call Oliver," Knox guessed.

I nodded and dug out my phone, finding the number I'd hidden under a fake name.

"Yes," he answered, his voice as cold as the winter air.

"Who knows about us?"

"No one."

"Someone," I corrected. "Because someone is trying to blackmail my family for money to keep my son's paternity a secret. Who?"

"Shit," he hissed.

"Who is it, Oliver?"

"I don't know."

My fury spiked. "Don't you dare lie to me. This involves my son. I promised you I'd be quiet, I walked away, but you will tell me. Or my next phone call will be to your wife."

"Do that and I will take your child."

"You will never touch my son. I will use every dollar of my millions to ruin your life." Whatever it took to keep Drake safe. If that meant doing my father's bidding, so be it. "Who?"

The other end of the line went silent. So quiet I wasn't sure if he was still there. But then he breathed and I knew he'd chosen self-preservation over his secrets. "No one knew about us."

"Then why did the FBI stop by my house before I left the city? Someone has to know, Oliver. Who?"

There was a rustling noise in the background, then the closing of a door. "When did the FBI approach you? Why didn't you tell me?"

"We weren't exactly on speaking terms. And I told them nothing."

"What, exactly, did the FBI agent say?" There was an edge to his voice. Fear. Good. I was fucking terrified. He could be scared too.

"Nothing. The agent asked if I knew you. I told her I didn't." A half-truth. By that point, Oliver had been dead to me. "I didn't realize you were being investigated."

"I'm not."

Liar. "If the FBI knows, then someone else does."

"Maybe a friend of yours. Someone who'd know you had money and thought they could con you out of some."

"No. I told you before I left, I didn't tell anyone we were together." Because he'd asked me not to. And I was a goddamn idiot.

"It certainly wasn't me," he said.

My free hand balled into a fist. "Other than your wife, who would care that I had your child?"

"It is not my wife."

"Then who? Please?" I hated begging this man, but for Drake, I'd drop to my knees if that meant getting him home safe.

"It might be this woman I was seeing. We weren't together long. Six months. My time with her began shortly after my time with you. She was...demanding."

"You mean she knew you were married."

"Yes," he muttered.

"How would this woman know about me?"

"I don't know," he said. "Unless she had me followed. I wouldn't put it past her."

He'd come to my townhouse twice after our breakup. Once, the night he'd asked me to forget his name. The night he'd offered me money. The night I'd told him about the baby. Then, just days later, he'd come to sign his parental rights away.

If she'd been following him, maybe she'd kept following me too. Out of jealousy? Spite? Curiosity? When I'd had Drake, she must have guessed that Oliver was the father.

"A name. Give me her name."

"Averie Flannagan."

"Averie Flannagan," I repeated and Knox immediately took out his own phone, moving two steps away to call Winn.

"Goodbye, Oliver."

"Memphis." He stopped me before I could end the call. "This changes nothing."

"Nothing," I agreed and the line went dead.

Don't give up.

We'd find Drake. We had to find Drake.

"Winn's going to run her name," Knox said. "See what she can find."

"If she came to Montana, I doubt she would have stayed in Quincy. Maybe we should call some other hotels in the area."

"There aren't many. The closest is fifty miles away." He held up a finger and scrolled through his phone. Then he dialed a number and pressed it to his ear. "Yeah, hi. My name is Knox Eden. I'm the owner of The Eloise Inn in Quincy. I had a guest who bailed on a room charge this week. I've been calling around because I guess she's done it to a few hotels in the area. Any chance you've got an Averie Flannagan staying at your place?"

There was a pause, then Knox clasped my hand and began marching down the sidewalk, retreating the way we'd come.

"No problem. Do me a favor, I'm going to call the local sheriff. Don't let her know I called. Appreciate it." He shoved his phone in his pocket and began to run.

Any other day and I'd have a hard time keeping pace, but adrenaline and fear had me matching his pace, stride for stride, as we sprinted for the daycare center.

We ran right for my car, Knox hollering to Winn as he opened the door. "There's an Averie Flannagan staying at the Mountain Motel on the way to Missoula."

Winn snapped her fingers at an officer and took off for her own SUV. "Follow us. Stay close."

Knox whipped us out of the parking lot and when one of the cruisers tore away, with Winn right behind, he drove with white knuckles toward the highway.

The miles passed in a blur, but no matter how fast we drove, it wasn't fast enough. My knees bounced. My stomach churned.

"This is my fault. I should have called Oliver sooner. At Thanksgiving."

"No," Knox said. "This woman is crazy. If she really took Drake, she's crazy. You couldn't have stopped this."

"We could have paid her."

"And she would have asked for money until we had nothing left to give."

"What if she did something to him?" My voice was barely audible. "What if she hurt him?"

Knox didn't answer. Probably because those same questions were in his mind.

So we drove in silence, speeding along the road, until a small, U-shaped motel came into view along the highway, tucked into a grove of evergreens.

I gasped. Three sheriff cars were in the parking lot, each with their lights flashing.

"Winn must have called it in."

I refused to blink as we got closer and closer, until Knox slowed to ease off the highway.

An officer in a tan shirt and matching pants walked out of a room. Behind him, escorted by another cop in uniform, came a woman.

A blond woman about my height. Her hands were handcuffed behind her back.

"I know her." I shook my head, hardly believing my own eyes. "That's the FBI agent who came to talk to me."

"What?" Knox said. "Are you sure?"

"Yes." What the hell?

Knox parked beside a car with New York plates. The moment the tires were stopped, I was out my door. The sound that greeted me when my foot hit the pavement was the best sound I'd heard all day.

A cry. From a little boy.

My little boy.

I took off running. So did Knox.

"Hold up." An officer held up his hands to stop us but

we pushed past him anyway just as Winn came striding out of the hotel room with Drake in her arms.

"Thank God." I hauled him to my chest and burrowed my nose in his neck, peppering him with kisses. Then I felt over every inch of his body, making sure he was whole. "You're okay."

"He's okay." Knox wrapped his arms around us both, his cheek on Drake's hair. "We found him."

We found him.

"You're never leaving my sight again," I said, holding Drake tighter.

Knox and I clung to him, even as he wiggled and squirmed to be set free, only pulling away when a familiar voice carried from the hallway.

"I wouldn't have let anything happen to him." Jill, handcuffed and being pushed out of the room by an officer, had tears streaming down her face. The moment she spotted us, she froze. Her mouth opened and closed, like a fish out of water gasping for air. But before she could speak or make some bullshit excuse, I spun with my son and strode toward the Volvo.

Knox wasn't far behind.

Neither was Winn.

"Is there any reason we need to stay?" I asked her.

"No. Go home. We're taking them both into custody and I'll question them myself."

"Thank you."

She stepped closer, running a finger over Drake's cheek. "Drive safely. I'll see you soon."

Knox put his hand on her shoulder, then he took Drake and buckled him in his seat.

I slid into the backseat, waiting for Knox to get behind

the wheel.

He met my gaze in the rearview.

Then drove us home.

CHAPTER 23

MEMPHIS

Christmas Eve. It was Drake's first Christmas and there wasn't a shred of holiday spirit in the house. The events from two days ago were still too raw. Instead of trimming a tree or wrapping gifts, I'd spent my waking hours waiting for answers and hovering close to my son.

Drake cooed on the bed, picking up his feet with his hands, while I folded the last load of laundry.

Knox and I had both taken time off from the hotel. When his staff had learned what had happened with Drake, they'd all insisted he stick close to home. They'd handled the wedding and were making the Christmas Eve and Christmas Day feasts at Knuckles.

Mateo and Anne had volunteered to cover my shifts, cleaning rooms and bustling around the hotel until I was ready to come back.

I wouldn't stay away for long. I wouldn't put that burden on them. But for the moment, I wasn't comfortable being under a different roof than my son. And Knox seemed to feel the same. While I'd kept my mind occupied by cleaning the house and doing laundry, he'd been on his feet in the kitchen, prepping for the Christmas dinner we'd have at the ranch tomorrow.

Maybe I didn't have any Christmas cheer, but there wasn't a place I'd rather spend my holiday than with his family.

I'd lost all faith in my own.

My mother had tried to call once. I'd declined it, opting for a text to let her know that Drake was okay and home. She'd called four times since. If they continued, maybe next week I'd answer. Maybe not.

It was a strange feeling to lose your family. It would have been heartbreaking had Knox's not already claimed me as their own.

Anne had been over three times since Friday, Harrison and Griffin twice. Eloise had come on Friday night after we'd returned from that motel. Talia had been right behind her, insisting on doing a quick checkup to make sure Drake was fine. And then Lyla and Mateo had shown with dinner.

The only family member we hadn't seen was Winn.

And she was the one we'd been aching to see.

"Memphis," Knox called from the living room. "Winn's here."

"Finally," I breathed. The T-shirt I'd been folding plopped into the basket. I swept Drake into my arms and carried him down the hallway.

Knox opened the door for Winn, kissing her cheek as she came inside. "Hi."

"Hi." She smiled at us both. "Sorry to do this today. But I figured you guys were probably anxious to know what was happening and it would be better now than tomorrow with everyone around."

"Please." My heart was in my throat.

It was early still, just ten in the morning. Only yesterday Winn had told us they were still questioning Averie and Jill. But time had ticked by slowly and every hour spent waiting had felt like a week.

"Can we get you anything?" Knox asked, escorting her to the living room. "Water?"

"No, I'm good." She pressed a hand to her belly that was just barely beginning to show, then took a seat in the chair so Knox and I could sit side by side on the couch.

He lifted Drake from my arms and laid him on the play mat beside our feet. Then he leaned forward, elbows to knees, and gave Winn the nod to start.

"Averie and Jill both requested lawyers, which has slowed the process down. But Jill has finally started cooperating. And we've got some evidence to help fill in the gaps with Averie's side of the story."

"Was she an FBI agent, Averie?"

Winn shook her head. "No."

"But she showed me a badge." It had been in a black wallet that she'd flipped open when I'd seen her outside my townhouse.

"We did find a badge on her person. It was a fake. A good fake. There was no way you'd know."

"So she tricked me." My heart sank. "She was just trying to get information on Oliver. Why?"

"From what we were able to find on her phone, she's got a lot of video footage of Oliver. When I say a lot, it's the sort

I would expect to see from a stalker."

"When I talked to Oliver, he sounded like he'd already dismissed her," I said. "If he was being stalked, wouldn't he know?"

"Not necessarily. She also had videos of your father. I doubt he knew she was following him either."

"Why?" I shook my head. "I don't understand why any of this was happening."

"You and your family were a target." Winn gave me a sad smile. "I'm guessing that Averie was offered money from Oliver to stay quiet about their relationship."

I huffed. "He probably paid her the fifty grand I didn't take."

"Afterward, she must have learned about you and your family. Thought that if Oliver would pay her, you would too. And it would be an easy way to make money."

"You think she knows how much Memphis is worth?" Knox asked.

Winn nodded. "I do."

"I'm worth nothing," I said. "Not anymore."

Knox put his hand on my knee. "I doubt she saw it that way."

"She could have gone to his wife," I said.

"Nah." Knox sighed. "Too dangerous."

I was the easy route to millions. Except I didn't have millions. Not anymore. "Why would she want Drake?"

"This is where Jill comes into play," Winn said. "Again, without a confession, I can't be sure, but I suspect that after your father denied her money, she decided she needed more ammunition. Specifically, a paternity test. Something to hold over his head, maybe Oliver's too."

"Enter Jill," Knox mumbled.

"She's a piece of work." Winn rolled her eyes. "She doesn't think she did anything wrong. Averie reached out to her weeks ago. Fostered some sort of relationship. Told her that she was Drake's aunt. That her brother was his father. Averie's story was that you refused to admit Drake was her brother's son. And before they could get answers, you fled New York."

My jaw dropped. "What? And Jill believed her?"

"Apparently. They'd become *friends*. Jill thought she was helping Drake get reunited with his family."

"Oh, I hate her." My teeth ground together.

Knox seethed at my side. "That fucking bitch."

"Averie convinced Jill that she needed her help but they couldn't meet in Quincy. That you might recognize her. It was too much of a risk that you'd take Drake and disappear like you had in New York. So Jill agreed to take Drake and meet her at that motel. It turns out, we weren't all that far behind her. Thirty minutes, maybe. She thought she'd be back in town by five and you'd never be the wiser. Except it took longer at the motel because the money Averie promised Jill wasn't there."

"Wait." Knox held up a finger. "Money?"

"One hundred thousand dollars. Averie said it was a reward her 'brother' was paying to anyone who helped reunite him with his son."

"But Averie didn't have the money," I said.

Winn shook her head. "No and Jill refused to leave without it."

"And Jill believed all of this?" I asked.

"I don't know." Winn shrugged. "It's what she's claiming."

"Do you think it's the truth?" Knox asked.

"Unfortunately, yes. Jill's panicked. I don't think she's

got the guts to lie when she's staring at a kidnapping charge."

"Of course it's true. She thinks I'm a horrible mother," I said. "She was probably enamored with Averie and thinking Drake would be better off without me."

Knox put his arm around my shoulders. "You're not a horrible mother. She's fucking crazy, honey."

"Then what am I for leaving Drake with her?"

His eyes softened. "I left him there too. So did other parents. Don't put this on your shoulders. It's on hers. Hers alone."

"I should have trusted my instincts." And the guilt for ignoring them would plague me for years to come.

"Knox is right, Memphis," Winn said. "This is not your fault."

"Do you think Averie was really after his DNA? Or was she going to take Drake?"

"My hunch is DNA," Winn said. "I asked Jill if she was under the impression that Averie intended to take Drake away. She said all she wanted was his saliva and a hair sample. That she hardly spared him a glance."

"Because he wasn't the endgame." Knox huffed. "She was after the money."

Winn nodded. "It's a lot of speculation at this point, but most of the time, our speculation turns out to be close to the truth."

My mind was spinning again. Though it hadn't really stopped since Friday.

"What's next?" Knox asked.

"Because this is a case of child abduction, I've reached out to the FBI. They've got the resources we don't to examine Averie's life in New York. I want the investigation to be as thorough as possible in the hopes that she spends a long while in prison."

"Good." The air rushed from my lungs. "What about Oliver? Will they speak to him?"

"I expect they will. And, I expect, after everything you've told me, he will deny knowing you."

"Fine by me."

I had no intention of mentioning his name again, even if the FBI came knocking on my door. If Oliver's wife found out that he was an unfaithful bastard, that was his problem. It wasn't coming from my lips.

"They will take over and bring in federal prosecutors," Winn said. "I'll keep in touch with the lead agent on the case. Hopefully they'll keep us apprised as to what's going on. But mostly, we wait. You do your best to get on with your lives."

It didn't feel like enough. There wasn't enough closure.

But I suspected it would be all the closure we'd get.

"Thank you for coming out here today," I told Winn.

"I'm sorry I don't have more for you." She stood and we followed, walking her to the door. "See you tomorrow?"

"Yep." Knox nodded. "Merry Christmas Eve."

"Merry Christmas Eve." She pulled me into a hug. "You're a good mother, Memphis. Never doubt that."

"Thank you." I hugged her tighter, hoping that one day I'd believe those words. Maybe in time, when Jill and Averie Flannagan were just a dim nightmare from the past.

Winn waved and slipped outside. It had been snowing all day in fluffy, white flakes that dusted her dark hair. When her taillights were a blur down the lane, Knox closed the door.

"This feels…"

"Unfinished." He wrapped his arms around me. "I

doubt she'll confess, tell us everything, but damn it, I want answers."

That was exactly how I felt too. "How do we get past this? How do we get past the worst days?"

"By making more of the best." He kissed the top of my hair and let me go, shifting to dig something from his pocket. "I was going to wait until tomorrow. Give it to you when we opened gifts. But after everything that's happened, waiting feels like wasting time."

I shifted, trying to spy what he had in his fist. But he'd closed it in his palm.

It was only after he dropped to a knee that he loosened his hand, revealing a perfect diamond ring.

"Marry—"

"Yes." I dropped to my knees, not letting him finish, and smashed my lips to his.

He swept me up, not missing a beat as his tongue swept against mine, and carried me to the couch, trapping me beneath his broad frame. Then he kissed me like I needed him to kiss me. Like there were no unanswered questions. Like there was no evil in this world. Like all we needed was right here, in this house and in this town.

Knox kissed me and made today my fourth-best day.

Drake squawked the moment Knox's hand slid beneath the hem of my shirt.

He tore his mouth away and shot a scowl toward the play mat. "Son, we will work on your timing."

Son. "He is, you know? Your son."

"I know. We'll get married, then make him officially mine. Whatever it takes."

"Okay." It felt strange to smile after everything that had happened. But I did it anyway. I smiled so wide it pinched my cheeks. "I love you."

"I love you too." He kissed me again. "Until the end of my days, Memphis. You, me, Drake. We're good, honey. We're so fucking good. And we'll add in a bunch of babies to the mix to keep it interesting."

I laughed. "Oh, really?"

"I want a big, chaotic family to fill this house. I want to step on toys in the middle of the night. I want to break apart fights and bandage up skinned knees. I want the mess. I want the passion. I want to watch you grow our kids."

In his piercing blue eyes, I saw that future. It was full of best days. It was full of love for the man who'd stolen my heart. "Promise?"

Knox grinned. "I swear it."

EPILOGUE

KNOX

ONE YEAR LATER...

With my hand splayed on Memphis's rounded belly, I locked eyes with my sister. "You're sure?"

Talia scowled. "Every appointment you ask me if I'm sure."

"Well? Are you?"

"I wouldn't say that Memphis and the baby were fine if they weren't actually fine." She rolled her eyes and glanced down at my wife who was resting on the exam table. "He's exhausting."

"Try living with him. This morning I bent to pick up one of Drake's toys and he practically tackled me to grab it first."

"I thought it might be too heavy."

Memphis gave me a flat look. "If Drake, the one-year-old, can pick it up, it's not too heavy."

"Just being cautious." I crossed my arms over my chest.

Memphis was six months pregnant, and considering what had happened when she'd gone into labor with Drake, I wasn't taking any chances. They could complain with every breath that I was being overprotective. It wouldn't make me change. I'd been like this since the day she'd come out of the bathroom with a positive pregnancy test in her hand. If picking up every toy, fussing over Memphis's every move and pushing a little at these checkups was the only control I had during this pregnancy, so be it.

"How's her weight? Is she eating enough?" I asked Talia. "She didn't have much dinner last night."

"Because I wasn't very hungry. You're cooking for me six times a day. I can't keep up." Memphis planted a hand on the table, but before she could push herself up, I gripped her elbow. It earned me another eye roll from my sister. Still didn't care.

"Her weight is fine, Knox. Everything is fine. Would you chill? God, you're worse than Griffin, and I never thought I'd say those words."

I frowned. "Am I?"

Talia nodded. "Ten times worse."

"Hmm. Whatever."

Memphis simply shook her head and laughed. "I love you."

"I love you too." I bent to kiss her, lingering long enough for Talia to clear her throat. "Okay. We'd better get home and relieve Mom."

"I'll walk you guys out," Talia said. "You're my last appointment for today."

"Want to come over for dinner?" I asked.

"Sure. It's not like I have anything or anyone waiting for

me at home." She sighed. "Let me duck into the locker room and grab my things. I'll meet you at the front desk."

I took Memphis's hand and helped her off the table. Then once her coat was on, we wandered the hallways of the hospital. My phone vibrated in my pocket as we reached the waiting room on the first floor. A text from Mateo.

"Look at this." I twisted the screen to Memphis.

Mateo was flying planes as a bush pilot in Alaska, shuttling people and supplies to remote areas of the state. Today's photo was of rugged mountains draped in snow at sunset.

"It's going to be weird not having him home for Christmas," I said, sending him a quick text to fly safe.

"Your mom said the same thing earlier today."

We all missed him, but he'd needed to get away and do something of his own. He'd been gone for nearly a year, having left not long after the holidays. Mateo hadn't come out and said it, but I got the impression he'd felt like a shadow here. He needed space and time to find his passion. Maybe it was flying.

I only hoped that one day, his wings would lead him home.

The doors of the hospital's entrance slid open and a man strode inside.

I glanced over, then did a double take. "Holy shit. That's Foster Madden."

"Who?" Memphis asked, tracking Foster's path to the reception desk.

"Foster Madden. He's the reigning middleweight champion."

"Huh?"

"Remember that fight we watched this summer. The one

where the guy knocked his opponent out in the first round."

Memphis blinked.

"Honey, you're killing me."

She smirked and jabbed her elbow in my ribs. "Just kidding. I didn't recognize him, but yes, I remember that fight."

"That's him."

"I wonder why he's in Quincy."

I shrugged. "Have you seen him at the hotel?"

"No, but if he checked in today, I would have missed it."

We'd both taken the day off to do some Christmas shopping with Drake. Then we'd met Mom at home so she could babysit while we'd come to the hospital for Memphis's appointment.

"I like that name," she said. "Foster. What do you think?"

"Meh." From the moment we'd found out we were having a boy, she'd been tossing out name ideas constantly. And each of them, I'd nixed.

"I give up." She tossed her hands in the air. "You're impossible."

"Hey, uh...sorry to interrupt." Foster waved to get my attention, then hooked his thumb over his shoulder toward the desk. "Do you know if anyone's working here today?"

"The nurse might have left already." The clock showed it was five. "Are you looking for a room? We could point you in the right direction."

Behind him, a door opened and Talia came striding out with a smile. Her long dark ponytail draped over one shoulder and she'd pulled on a jacket over her baby-blue scrub top.

"I'm looking for a doctor who works here," Foster said.

"Talia Eden."

Why would Foster Madden be looking for Talia?

Talia's smile fell. Her footsteps halted. Faster than I'd ever seen her move, she darted behind the reception counter.

"Uh..." What the fuck?

Foster glanced over his shoulder, following my gaze, but she'd crouched so low that it was like she'd vanished.

"You might try the ER," Memphis blurted. "Maybe they can track her down for you. Just head out the doors and down the sidewalk to the other side of the building. You can't miss it."

"Appreciate it." Foster nodded, then as quickly as he'd come in, he was gone.

Memphis and I shared a look, waiting until he was out of sight.

"Coast's clear," I called.

Talia inched up, her eyes barely over the counter's ledge. "Is he gone?"

"Yeah." I nodded. "Want to tell me why you're hiding from Foster Madden?"

"Nope." She got to her feet, tiptoeing around the desk. Her eyes stayed glued to the glass windows, checking to make sure he was gone. "I should go."

"What about dinner?" Memphis asked.

"Rain check." And before we could say another word, she ran—not jogged, but sprinted—out the doors. She hit the sidewalk and did one quick check for Foster, then bolted to her car in the parking lot.

"Okay," I drawled. "What the hell was that about?"

"Does she know him?"

"No idea." Apparently enough to recognize his voice and from the back. "I'll call her later."

Not that I expected her to tell me anything. Talia was a lot like me. If she didn't want to talk about something, she wouldn't. Lyla and Eloise wore their emotions on their pretty faces for the world to see. Talia kept hers locked behind our family's signature blue eyes.

"I'm sure it's nothing." I kissed Memphis's temple, then helped her into the car. I did not want my wife stressed about my sister. "I got an email from Lester today."

"Really?" Memphis sat up straighter. "What did he say?"

"He's coming to Quincy in January. The magazine wants him to do a best of the best article or something."

"And he picked you. Of course he'd pick you." She did a fist pump. "This is amazing."

Lester's article from last year had brought more people than I'd expected to Quincy. The hotel was poised to have its biggest year in history and the restaurant had doubled my initial income projections.

That kind of money meant more staff. And more staff meant that Memphis and I had more freedom and flexibility.

She wasn't working as a housekeeper these days, but once or twice a week, she'd cover the front desk because she genuinely enjoyed the work and helping Eloise at the hotel. She loved being a part of the family business.

"I've been thinking about that wedding in May," Memphis said. "Maybe I should tell the bride no."

"Absolutely not."

She sighed. "We're going to have so much going on. Drake's only one. We'll have a newborn. Our schedule is so busy already. I don't know if it's smart to add a wedding planning job into the mix."

"Do you want to do it?"

"Well...yeah."

I reached over to take her hand. "Then we'll find a way."

If Memphis's dream was to plan weddings and events, I'd do whatever necessary to make that happen.

She'd planned two weddings in the past year—one of which was our own. We'd gotten married on the ranch, in a meadow filled with summer wildflowers. Then we'd had a reception at the hotel, cramming the space with friends and family who'd all danced beside us beneath a blanket of fairy lights.

Two days later, we'd gone to the courthouse, where I'd adopted Drake.

We were all Edens. And I, for one, had been happy to see the Ward name vanish.

Contact with Memphis's parents had been minimal this past year. She'd told them we were getting married, sans an actual invite. Her mother had sent flowers. Her sister had sent a card. Not a word from her father and brother, but Memphis hadn't cared. She'd already decided that if by some miracle she inherited her trust fund, she'd take the money and set it aside for the kids.

We were six months into this pregnancy and she had yet to inform Beatrice and Victor. Maybe she would eventually, probably after the baby was born, but as time passed, as we built our own life, she seemed more content with their distance.

I suspected that distance would become permanent.

She didn't need that family.

We were building our own.

And I'd be overprotective every step of the way.

It had been nearly a year since the incident with Jill and Averie Flannagan. There were days when I didn't think about it, but those were rare. The fears were a constant nuisance, and I only hoped that in time, they'd surface less and less.

Averie Flannagan would be spending most of the decade in a penitentiary. That bitch could rot in jail.

Jill was nearing the end of her prison sentence, and though she'd be released on parole soon, I doubted we'd see her face in Quincy ever again.

Just like we hadn't heard from Oliver again. The FBI had questioned Memphis and me once after Drake's kidnapping. During her statement, Memphis hadn't mentioned Oliver's name. She'd simply spoken to Averie's blackmail attempt and going into daycare to find Drake missing. If they'd contacted Oliver during their investigation, we didn't know and didn't care. With any luck, he'd be long forgotten.

I slowed at the turn to home, easing off the highway and down our quiet lane. "What about Harrison?"

"Your dad?" Memphis asked. "What about him?"

"No, the name. Harrison."

"Oh." She splayed a hand over her belly. "I think that would be lovely."

"Me too." I grinned. "Then the next one we can name Annie, for Mom."

She laughed. "You're already thinking of the next one and this one isn't even born yet."

"You can pick for the two after that."

Memphis shook her head, her chocolate-brown eyes sparkling. "You want five? This is news to me."

"I'm good for six."

"Five." She drew a line in the air. "That's my limit."

"Five." I pulled into the garage and, as soon as the truck was off, leaned over the console to finish the kiss I'd started at the hospital.

The loft had been mostly empty since Memphis had moved out. But every time I walked up those stairs, I'd think of the nights I'd spent pacing the floor.

The nights when I'd fallen in love with a little boy. And the woman of my dreams.

The best nights on Juniper Hill.

EXCLUSIVE BONUS CONTENT

KNOX

A kid streaked past the kitchen, naked as the day she was born. Her dark hair was wet, the tendrils dripping down her back.

"Annie, slow down."

"Okay, Daddy!" Annie didn't talk, she yelled. Every word was delivered at the highest volume she could muster. She was five and would be starting kindergarten in a couple of weeks.

Memphis was holding out hope that her teachers could convince her not to shout.

I wasn't holding my breath.

"Drake!" Harrison hollered from the room they shared. The boys had been bunking together for three years, not because we didn't have the space for them each to have their own room, but because they'd decided to have a *campout* one night and hadn't split up since.

"What?" Drake yelled back from his spot in the kitchen.

"Want to play Nintendo?"

"Not right now. I'm helping Dad cook dinner."

This was our Monday night tradition. The restaurant was closed and it was rare for the kids to have a school or extracurricular activity on Monday nights, so it had become family dinner night.

We spent a lot of time with my parents, brothers and sisters. My parents never missed a dance recital or sports game, no matter the age group. Mom and Dad still watched the little ones during the week. The kids' best friends were all cousins and sleepovers were a regular occurrence.

But Mondays were just us. Mondays were for pasta dinners and cookie desserts.

And in the last year, Drake had become my willing sous chef.

I put my hand on his shoulder, watching as he kneaded the pasta dough. "Little more."

"'Kay. Then can I roll it out?"

"Yep. I'll get the water going." I left him to his task and moved about the kitchen, filling a pot with water. Then I checked on the chicken baking in the oven.

I got a lot of joy out of cooking at Knuckles. I experimented and played with flavors. The menu was constantly changing. But my favorite cooking was this.

Simple food that the kids would eat. And cooking with my boy.

His love for cooking might not last. But maybe, if I was lucky, this was something we could always share. Mom always said how much Drake reminded her of me at that age.

He looked like Memphis, but otherwise, he was mine.

My son.

A quack came from down the hallway, preceding Briggs as he marched, barefoot, into the living room. *Quack. Quack. Quack.* He quacked for every step he took.

Dad had given him a duck caller this summer on one of their ranch outings—one of the days when Mom had her hands full at the house and Dad would snag a kid or two to take with him as he drove around, inspecting cattle and horses.

Briggs slept with the duck call. He took a bath with the duck call. He walked with the duck call.

That fucking duck call was about to go missing.

Quack.

"Take a break from the quacking, bud."

"But, Daddy." My three-year-old's entire frame crumpled and he collapsed to his knees. "Mommy didn't let me quack *all day*. She said until dinner."

"Fine." I held up a hand. "But then we're putting it away so the ducks can get some sleep tonight."

Quack. Quack.

Two quacks for yes. One quack for no.

We'd named Briggs after my uncle, a man who'd been a role model to me as a kid. His dementia had gotten worse in the last few years and it was rare he recognized any of us when we visited him at the nursing home. But whenever we hauled the crew in to say hello, we'd introduce the kids and he'd get a huge smile on his face when he learned Briggs's name.

Well, what do you know? That's my name too.

My phone rang on the counter and I swiped it up, sandwiching it between my shoulder and ear as I took Drake a rolling pin. "Hey, Griff."

"Hey. I need a favor."

"What favor?"

"Winn just got home. She stopped at the school and was talking to one of the gals at the front desk. Found out that William is moving."

"What? When? I just talked to him two days ago."

William had a son in Hudson and Drake's fifth-grade class. He'd been coaching their flag-football team since kindergarten.

"I guess it came up pretty fast. He got a promotion and is heading to Missoula."

"Damn."

"Yup. And guess what my beautiful, thoughtful, infuriating wife did?"

"Signed you up to coach."

"Yeah. So I signed you up as the assistant coach. Thanks for the favor. Practice starts Thursday at five."

"Griff—" He'd already hung up.

"Who was that?" Memphis emerged from the hallway with Addison on her hip. Our youngest daughter was wrapped in a hooded unicorn towel.

"Griffin. He volunteered me to be his assistant football coach."

The rolling pin clattered to the countertop and Drake's eyes whipped my way. The smile, the hope on his face made my heart squeeze. "You and Uncle Griff are gonna coach us?"

"That okay with you?"

He nodded wildly and picked up his rolling pin.

With five kids and a restaurant to manage, we didn't have a lot of free time. But there was no way I'd back out, not if it meant that smile stayed on Drake's face.

Memphis walked into the kitchen and stood on her toes, pressing a kiss to my bearded cheek before whispering, "We'll figure it out."

"Yeah." I tucked a lock of hair behind her ear, taking a moment to appreciate my beautiful wife.

Ten years together and I loved her more each day.

"Da-dee." Addison put her palm on my nose and pushed me away. "Bye-bye."

I chuckled as Memphis swept her away to get her dressed. "Bye-bye, baby."

She was almost two and growing too fast. Her hair was Memphis's blond but she'd inherited my blue eyes.

"Okay, boss." I moved back to Drake to inspect the pasta. "Looks good. Go ahead and start cutting it into strips. Then they can go straight into the water. We'll pull out the chicken and let it rest while we make the sauce."

He did exactly as instructed, working carefully with the knife. The chicken was on a cutting board, the oven was off, and Drake had just added the pasta to the boiling water when the slap of bare feet came barreling into the kitchen.

"Da-dee." Addison launched herself at me. The towel was gone and she was as naked as her older sister. "Hi."

"Hi." I swept her up and tossed her in the air. "Where are your jammies?"

"No jammeez."

"You have to have jammies before dinner."

"No. Jammeez." She squeezed my face, pulling at my lips.

If it were up to me, I'd let her sit in her chair naked simply to avoid a tantrum. Memphis was the Addison whisperer, not me.

"Memphis, you've got a runaway."

It took her a moment, then she appeared, coming out of Annie's room.

Annie giggled and darted across the hallway, probably to terrorize Harrison. At least she was dressed. I'd give them three minutes before one or both were crying over the video game.

We'd added on to the house about five years ago, connecting the garage to the main structure and adding a couple of bedrooms for our brood. The loft had become the popular hangout spot for the older kids to squirrel away and watch a movie while the little ones went to bed early.

Drake, Harrison and Annie were sleeping up there tonight. And as soon as they were settled, Memphis and I were locking the bedroom door to have some fun.

Memphis came rushing into the kitchen and stole Addison. "Little lady, you must get dressed."

"No jammeez."

"How about the unicorns?"

"Yep. Yep. Yep."

"Okay, go find them." Memphis set her down and away she ran.

Then my wife smiled at me and followed.

"Dad? Is this done?" Drake asked, standing next to the pot.

"Yeah. I'll drain it. You go summon the crew."

Off he ran, yelling, "Dinner!"

Years ago, when I'd proposed to Memphis, I'd told her I wanted a big, boisterous family to fill this house. I often stepped on toys in the middle of the night. Not a day went by when I didn't break up an argument. Knees had been skinned. Shins had been bruised. The noise was deafening.

All because of the woman who'd pulled into my driveway,

tear-stained and exhausted with a screaming baby boy in her arms. A woman who'd changed my life.

She walked down the hallway, herding our kids to the dining room table. She caught me staring and her forehead furrowed. "What?"

"The house is a mess."

Her eyes softened. "Our mess."

Knox

"**B**oss. You are *killing* me." I bent and picked up the bow tie he'd just pulled off his neck.

Again.

I opened the clip, reaching for his collar. "You have to wear this today."

"Ahh!" he squealed and swatted at my hand, then took off running. His tennis shoes pounded on the floor as he toddled down the hallway at Mom and Dad's.

"Shit." This goddamn bow tie was going to be the death of me. "Drake. Get back here."

He glanced over his shoulder, nearly toppling into the wall, then gave me a drooly grin as he pumped his legs faster.

In the past few months, he'd changed so much. He'd gone from crawling to walking. Then, what felt like five seconds later, he was running and chasing around the house.

Everything was Drake-proofed. Outlets were capped. Cleaning supplies and laundry detergent had been relocated to higher shelves. I couldn't open a single lower cupboard in my kitchen without a magnetic key.

But his feet moved faster than his legs and the crashes were constant.

He slowed as he made it to the kitchen and let out a string of babble, pointing with a chubby finger.

"Oh my God." Mom's gasp greeted me as I walked into the kitchen. "What happened to his head?"

I swept Drake into my arms. "He tripped and connected with the corner of the coffee table."

Mom groaned. "Today?"

I sighed. "Today."

My wedding day.

"Hopefully the photographer can Photoshop out that welt," she said. "Did you put an ice pack on it?"

"Yeah. For as long as he'd let me." Which had been a whole two minutes.

"It's not that bad."

Oh, it was bad. Really fucking bad. Drake had a massive goose egg on his forehead with a big, red welt.

"I went to grab a new diaper." I pinched the bridge of my nose. "I was gone for thirty seconds, at most. Came running when I heard him scream."

"Knox, this isn't your fault. He crashes all the time. That's what toddlers do."

"I know." I pushed Drake's blond hair off his forehead. It wasn't quite long enough to hide the bump. "I just don't want anything to wreck today for Memphis."

Mom gave me a soft smile. "This is not going to wreck the day."

"I hope not." I glanced at the paper on the counter. "What are you doing?"

"Nothing." She splayed both hands over the page.

"Mom."

"Nothing," she repeated. "Go away."

"Is that for me?"

Griffin had mentioned that Mom had written him a letter on his wedding day. Earlier, he'd passed on to me the advice she'd given him.

Don't be late.

I wouldn't be late. But I would be arriving with a bumped and bruised ring bearer.

A ring bearer who refused to wear his bow tie.

"Okay, bud." I held up the bow tie. "Let's try this again."

Drake leaned away, squirming with fury. He kicked and wiggled, threw his body ramrod straight before turning into a limp noodle. Every time I thought I had it close, he'd spin, and the clip would snap on air, not his shirt.

"I give up." I set him on the floor and tossed the tie onto the counter. "I surrender. I've got to get the last of the setup done. Memphis bought that bow tie so he'd match my suit, and she's been so excited to see him wear it. But I can't get him to keep it on. He hates it."

Now, not only would he have that welt on his face, he also wouldn't be in the tie.

"I'll take care of it," Mom said. "You go. We'll be right behind you."

In a bit, she and Dad would take him up to the meadow where we'd be getting married. I didn't need him running around and getting hurt again or making a mess of his white shirt and gray pants.

"Thanks." I picked up Drake to kiss his cheek, then

handed him over to Mom. "See you soon."

"Bye."

The moment I walked toward the hall, Drake started to wail.

It tugged at my heartstrings. Every damn time. It was an effort to keep going to the door.

He loved Mom and Dad's place, and he spent plenty of time with them on the ranch. In two minutes, he'd be laughing again. But he always cried when Memphis or I left him behind.

I walked faster, slipping out of the house. Then I climbed in my truck and drove to the field where we'd be getting married.

The altar was already set up. Griffin had met me up here this morning to do the bulk of the work. But I wanted to make sure it was perfect.

Memphis had planned everything for today. She was treating our day as her trial run in wedding planning. Last night at the rehearsal, she'd delivered printed itineraries to each member of the wedding party.

Mine was two pages long and included everything necessary for me and Drake—including a bullet point for the bow tie.

The ceremony would be small with only my family members in attendance. The wildflowers were in bloom, and there wasn't a cloud in the sky. We couldn't have asked for a nicer day to exchange vows. After a few photos, we'd head to the hotel for the reception.

Memphis had spent countless hours decorating for the party. This morning, she'd left at six to make sure the floral centerpieces were watered. Then she'd tackled her own list— five pages long—before going into town to meet my sisters at the spa for hair and makeup.

In less than an hour, she'd be my wife.

I felt like I'd been waiting a lifetime.

After lighting the candles that we'd put in tall glass hurricanes around the altar, I retrieved my suit coat from the truck and pulled it on, adjusting my sleeves just as the sound of vehicles filled the air.

Mom and Dad's vehicle came to a stop beside mine.

Behind it was Winn's SUV with Memphis in the passenger seat.

The moment she stepped out, the air rushed from my lungs.

My wife. She was about to become my wife.

I was still frozen in place when she walked over, her cheeks flushed and her smile wide. Her dress was lovely, but it paled in comparison to the light in her eyes. "You're beautiful, honey."

"And you look handsome." She stood on her toes for a kiss. "Ready?"

"More than ever."

● ● ●

"Congratulations." Mom kissed my cheek once the ceremony was over, then dabbed at the corners of her eyes.

"Thanks, Mom. And thanks for helping with Drake." I leaned in closer, lowering my voice. "What did you do?"

The welt was almost entirely hidden. And that bow tie was beneath his chin.

So far, Memphis hadn't noticed. But since Drake had been ahead of her down the aisle and had quickly run off to play with his cousins, she hadn't gotten a close look at his forehead.

Mom shrugged. "Just a little concealer over the bump."

"And the tie?"

"Knox," the photographer called before Mom could answer. "We're ready for you."

I held up a finger. "Be right there."

"Here." Mom slipped an envelope into my pocket. "For later."

So I did get a letter. That was what she'd been doing in the kitchen.

Curiosity won out. I pulled it from my pocket, not waiting for later.

"Don't read it now," Mom hissed. "That's embarrassing."

"Too bad." I smirked and opened the envelope. "Don't run off."

She grumbled something under her breath as I started reading.

Dear Knox,

By the time you read this, you'll be married. I had planned to write you a long, poetic letter, but when I sat down to start, your father informed me that his suit coat was ripped so I spent an hour sewing instead. It's probably for the best. I've realized I'm not much for long letters. And I'm not all that poetic.

You'll make an incredible husband. You're already an amazing father.

I love you. I'm proud of you. And I'm happy for you.

xoxo
Mom

PS: You were right. Drake hates that bow tie. I superglued and stapled it to his shirt. You'll probably need to cut it off later. Sorry.

I chuckled. "Superglue *and* staples?"
Mom laughed too. "He really hates that bow tie."

ACKNOWLEDGMENTS

Thank you for reading *Juniper Hill*! This series is so special to me, and I love the Eden family. I hope you enjoyed Memphis and Knox's story too.

Special thanks to my editing and proofreading team: Elizabeth Nover, Julie Deaton, Karen Lawson, Judy Zweifel and Kaitlyn Moodie. Thank you to Sarah Hansen for the beautiful cover.

And lastly, thank you to my incredible family, who supports me with each and every book.

Don't miss the rest of the Edens!

*Don't miss the exciting new books
Entangled has to offer.*

Follow us!

f @EntangledPublishing

◎ @Entangled_Publishing

♪ @EntangledPub

AMARA
an imprint of Entangled Publishing LLC